Becoming Courageous Abeba: A Story of Love, Loss, War and Hope

By

Abeba Habtu, Hannah Habtu, and Sahra Habtu
With Michael Monroe

BECOME COURAGEOUS ABEBA: A STORY OF LOVE, LOSS, WAR AND HOPE

Prologue

Germany 2011

Berlin's crisp fall air beat on the hospital window. I paid it no attention. The poisonous spider had made my hip its home and it was shooting its venom down my leg and up my side. Its angry bite grabbed all of my attention.

Years earlier, I'd had surgery in Sudan. It didn't really help. The pain returned after being thrown in prison in my home country of Eritrea. Now, after escaping prison and leaving Eritrea at the risk of death, I was in completely new surroundings.

The pain made breathing difficult and my body sweat. The physical pain was matched with the emotional pain of a heavy heart from leaving my boys behind. But I had no choice. It was leave or waste away or even go back to that hellish prison.

I was unable to speak the German language. The doctors did tests and looked at me with concern.

My son, Muse, waited in the hallway. He was fiery when a boy, always ready to fight, but he'd turned into a good young man. When they wheeled me into the room he was seated in a plastic chair, a plaid shirt and khaki pants were draped over his lean body. He had given me a reassuring half smile. I was so glad to be with him.

An elderly doctor with thinning gray hair and a white lab coat opened the door and approached me cautiously. He wore a mask and did not get too close. He said something that I did not understand and held up a picture of my chest X-Ray. There was a spot on my lung. He spoke more, but I felt lost. I tried to breathe calmly.

He moved his hand over his chest. "TB," he said. I still did not understand.

He motioned for me to stay where I was and backed out of the room quickly.

I sat on the thin paper sheet on the edge of the bed. My hip pulsed with each beat of my heart. I looked around the room. The white walls were bathed in light and a couple of pictures with words I did not know hung on the walls. The floor tiles were white with specks of black. The light reflected off of them in a way that made me think of the African sun that scorched Eritrea on summer days.

Thoughts of my older sister, Hiwet, tumbled into my head. The childhood memories flooded my brain and my chest ached with sorrow. Heat built in my head until tears spilled from my eyes. One minute Hiwet and her beautiful smile that made those around her want to smile too, was with us. The next minute she was out of our lives. Like so many other Eritreans after the war with Ethiopia had begun and the Derg took control, she had decided to make the dangerous trek toward Sudan. I pictured her with her feet burning in the sand. No shade from the relentless sun, a rumbling belly with only a little oatmeal for food, and sips of water to fend off the harsh dryness. I heard the planes flying over her head and the whistling of their falling bombs.

For so long I had wondered what it was like for her to cross the desert. Now I knew.

The hospital door swung open and my childhood memory from nearly 40 years earlier vanished. It was replaced with three figures dressed in white from head to toe. They wore thick gloves. Their heads were covered in masks. They approached me with purpose. I leaned back and the throbbing in my hip sped up to match each beat of my old heart.

I tried to ask questions, but the words came out in my native language. I scooted backwards. The paper I had been sitting on crinkled under my legs. The spider in my hip shot its poison all the way into my foot.

One thought rushed through my head, *after all I have been through it is here that I am dying.*

I heard Muse before I saw him. "It is okay, Mother," he said.

He stood in the doorway, a man from the hospital held onto his arm. I started to speak, but he continued. "They think you have a contagious disease. They have to take you to a new hospital."

The clawing fear eased a bit. These people in white were here to help, but the thought of dying remained.

It seemed I was once again stuck in a moment where I'd have to be strong despite my fear. I'd been through so many of these moments. How many more would I be able to survive?

*

I dreamed that I was with my older sister, Hiwet. We were deep in the desert. The gritty sand beat against my skin. It even found its way into my mouth and crunched between my teeth. We were still one hundred kilometers from Sudan. It would be our salvation from this war between our home country and Ethiopia, rescue from the horrible oppression and danger. The Ethiopians had forced a curfew upon us. We couldn't go out after six in the evening. If we did, we could be shot on the spot. We'd become prisoners in our own land.

It seemed like morning time as there was a glow at our backs to the east. We heard the whine of the engine high in the sky before we saw the plane. Everyone crouched and froze. There was no cover on the barren sand. I craned my head upward and saw objects falling from the sky. They were just over us. We could not move.

The bombs got closer. Everyone curled into a ball and prayed.

I saw the bomb hit the sand. It erupted in fire and I watched it overcome my big sister. It then rushed toward me.

I shot up in the bed, eyes wide open, and stifled a scream as the spider pierced my hip. My sheet was soaked with sticky sweat. It took a moment for me to determine my surroundings. I had not been in the desert with my sister. I was in a room in a different hospital. It had nothing but a bed and a small television mounted on the wall. I sank back onto the bed and tried to calm myself. I had been given a shot of medicine earlier, but the spider pain in my hip remained and sweat still trickled off my forehead. The television was on, but I couldn't understand the German words.

Something had to be terribly wrong to feel as weak as I did. Maybe it was this TB of which the doctor talked of, or maybe it was something worse? It was an effort to lift my arms. My legs felt anchored to the bed.

Hiwet was a beautiful and strong girl, so full of life. I looked up to her. She was one of the strongest women I ever knew. For so long I thought of her daily after she left our home for a better life, and it was a long time before we learned of her fate. She was the first to leave my family. She wouldn't be the last.

When considering all the losses my family suffered, the struggles and hurt we've felt, the separation and the desperate attempts at reunification, one might say my life has been tragic. Yet, as I sat in pain in the hospital I raised my tired hands toward the sky, palms facing in, fingers spread, and I gave thanks.

*

I never knew exactly what time it was. I just lay in the hospital bed with my weakness and hurt as companions. The aliens, as I had come to think of the doctors in their all white suits covered from head to toe, came and went from time to time. They would check everything and give me medication, and then they would slip out of the room.

They were still unsure of what was wrong with me so I had to remain an outcast. Maybe it was me who was like the alien, trapped and feared, waiting to be understood. The doctors barely spoke to me because I could not understand them anyway. I felt so alone.

As I thought of my aloneness, the door opened once again. Three aliens in white suits approached me. I was indifferent toward them until I noticed that these aliens were not doctors at all. They were my children, Muse, Hannah, and Sahra. My lips parted in a smile and I raised my hands, my way of giving quick thanks for the unexpected surprise.

Hannah and Sahra stood next to the bed and both reached out and grabbed my hand with their white gloves. I could see their smiles through the clear masks that covered their beautiful faces. They were born just a year apart and had lived in Germany for many years. It was easy to remember the day when my husband, Zeray, sent Hannah and Muse to Germany when they were just kids. It was another time when I'd lost part of my family. And years later I lost Sahra too when she was sent to Germany to be with her brother and sister.

Muse stood at the foot of the bed, hands clasped in front of his body. He looked calm, yet concerned. Now in his early thirties he had learned to suppress his heated youth, but I knew that it bubbled under the surface.

"How are you feeling?" Hannah asked.

"I am fine."

"Are they treating you well?" This time it was Sahra.

"Yes, very well."

"They are running more tests," Muse said. "They are unsure if it is Tuberculosis, but they have to wait until they receive the results. Once they know for sure we will get you out of this room."

"Thank you," I replied. "I'm fine here. By the grace of God I will get better. He has led me through so much."

Hannah squeezed my hand. "You are very strong, Momma. You will get better."

I nodded my head in reply. We talked a while longer about things unrelated to my current sickness. It was so good to have my children with me, and so good to see them all doing well. It was Hannah and Sahra who worked to help me get over here after I escaped the prison. It was all of my children with me now who were working so hard to get my sons, Selemon and Michael and John out of Sudan. Selemon had escaped Eritrea not long before Michael, John and me, but now they were all stuck.

Escape would be horribly difficult; much like it was to get them out of Eritrea. Both my youngest boys were born in Eritrea and over eight years old. This meant they were not allowed to leave until they were 44 years old. They had to leave their lives behind as I scooped them up after school one day. They were both so brave, but now they were far away from me in Sudan. Fortunately, they had their big brother to look after them.

I prayed constantly that one day I would be with all my children: Muse, Hannah, Sahra, Solemon, Michael, and John. I even dreamed that Fili would be found, or at least I would know what happened to him. It had been almost 15 years since my oldest boy was lost in Ethiopia.

My children and I talked until I grew so tired. I fought to keep my eyes open, but they insisted that they leave so I could rest. When they had gone, the corners of my eyes became moist with tears. I held them there, not allowing them to slide down my cheeks. They were the product of a mixture of joy and sadness.

I had fought for so long for my family. I had done everything I could to keep us together and safe. Sometimes I had failed, sometimes I succeeded. Now Muse and Hannah and Sahra were fighting alongside me. Or because of my sickness they were now fighting for me.

Hope would remain until my heart beat for its very last time on this Earth. No matter what I had been through and no matter what may still lay ahead, I was sure of this. I would always hope.

The white walls of the hospital room were now my prison, but they could not contain my thoughts. It's truly a miracle that I am still here, and as I stared at the ceiling my thoughts fell into my tumultuous life.

It is unlikely that most have even heard of my home country of Eritrea. In 2001, 15 members of the Peoples Front for Democracy and Justice, the president's inner circle, wrote a letter to our

President Isaias Afewerki condemning much of his actions as illegal and unconstitutional. Not long after this, 11 members of what has become known as the G-15 were arrested along with ten journalists. The licenses of the eight independent newspapers were revoked and our country became dark to the rest of the world. Nobody knows for sure what has become of the G-15 members and journalists, but what is known is that Eritrea is ranked last when it comes to freedom of expression, just below North Korea.

I was born about the same time the war between Eritrea and Ethiopia began in 1961. I was just a baby when Ethiopian Emperor Haile Selassie dissolved the Eritrean parliament and took over the country. The Eritrean Liberation Front fought this annexation and fired upon the occupying Ethiopian Army. The war for independence was on, and it would rage for 30 years and intermingle with another war as well.

The fighting ended in 1991, but things have not improved. In fact, now they are much worse. My country is sometimes called the "North Korea of Africa." This may be accurate. I do not know because I've never had the pleasure of visiting North Korea.

I have lived through it all, and the world has remained unaware. We are a dark spot that in essence has been lost to the rest of humanity.

It comes with great risk, and I am fearful of what may happen, but I will try to shed some light by telling my story.

Chapter One

Eritrea 1968

My mother and sisters and I scrubbed the walls and floors with soapy water. I dipped my towel into the almost dry bucket.

"Abeba," my mother said, "go to the well and refill the bucket."

I was just a young kid and the duty of getting water from the well was new and exciting.

"Yes Momma," I said.

I grabbed the bucket's wooden handle and lugged it out the front door. I walked toward the well, it was not far, and looked around our land. My brother was feeding the sheep and horses. Further in the distance I saw my father. He was kneeling down between rows of green spinach. As a farmer, he spent his days in the fields and he was good at his job. We always had food to eat despite having no money. He was also a good dad when he wasn't drinking. He kept to himself and worked tirelessly. His hands were rough with calluses and his shoulders were broad and strong.

I made my way to the well, the bucket hitting against my leg with each step. Unlike much of Eritrea, our small village was an oasis of green thanks to the well and surrounding water. There was a great distance between our house and our neighbors. We were friendly with them, but we often kept to ourselves simply because the other houses were a long ways away. In the distance I could make out the tin-roof tops of two of our closest neighbors. The metal shimmered in the sun and seemed out of focus.

My family was strong. We loved each other and we worked well together, so it was easy to spend time working as a close group to coax the food from the Earth and make sure the farm ran efficiently.

As I lowered the bucket into the well, something caught my attention. I squinted toward the dusty road that connected the tiny houses in our village. A group of Ethiopian soldiers walked along the road. Their machine guns were slung over their shoulders and the dust kicked up behind them. Even though they were far away, I ducked my head and quickly got back to filling the bucket.

I prayed that they would not turn toward our house. So far we had been left alone despite the occupation and the escalating war. It had only been two months earlier when we heard the terrible news of the villages in the Hazemo Plains. The men in the villages had been rounded up by the soldiers. Their throats were slit and their wives and children were forced to watch. This horrible killing was not the first attack on villages. Earlier in the year many villages had been burned and the soldiers had used machine guns to kill almost one hundred thousand livestock.

I could not understand such meanness and I did not like thinking about it. Normally, I did not worry about it happening to us even though I understood that it could, but seeing the soldiers made it much too real.

I pulled the now heavy bucket back out of the well. I hazarded a glance toward the troops. They were moving on, away from our house. It seemed they were disinterested in slitting throats or shooting our livestock at that moment. Nevertheless, I lifted the bucket with both hands, and with the water sloshing up its sides I waddled back toward the house. I did not want to see the soldiers and I did not want them to see me.

Chapter Two

There was no electricity in Eritrea. When the sun went down the land was pitched into a darkness that we fought with not much more than candlelight. Still, we often spent our nights not far from a bar where my father would drink. We'd walk there in a little glow of candlelight that gave us nothing more than a few feet of vision.

The men would go to the bar, especially on the weekends, to drink away their worries about Eritrea's future. The mothers and children would spend time talking with each other in a small open area with a few old tables a block or so away.

This is how I spent many nights as a child. My sisters and brother and I would talk with our friends and we'd laugh and play. We did not notice it at the time, but as the years went by and the war continued, our parents grew wearier and spent less time laughing and more time looking over their shoulders.

Some nights we'd leave when our father left. Often though, we left well before him and still some nights we would not even go with him at all. It was always scary when my father drank. He'd come home smelling of booze and smoke and he'd be angry about little things we had done earlier in the day.

When he screwed up his face in a way that looked like he had just tasted something sour and started a sentence with, "I remember today when..." He was about to put a beating on at least one of us kids.

One night, Dad was at the bar drinking with his friends. My momma, my three sisters, and my brother and I sat in our tiny house and talked or played games by candlelight. Momma kept checking to see if Dad was almost home. He always came in at about the same time and in the same sour mood.

She rushed over to us. "Get up," she said, "out the back door to the kitchen now."

We had a small room out back where we cooked some of the food. It wasn't really a kitchen like most people would think, just a small room with a table and some utensils. We all looked at our mom like she was going crazy.

The routine was simple. Our normally indifferent dad who worked all day to put food on our table would come home drunk and angry, remember what one of us did, and give us the hand. It wasn't fun, but it was the way it was.

This time was different though. Our mom was shooing us out the back door as fast as she could. "To the kitchen, to the kitchen," she kept repeating in an urgent voice.

We all followed her instructions and my little sister, Letina, just got out the back door as the front door swung open and banged into the wall. We shuffled across the yard to the small room. Hiwet waited until we were all inside and then pulled the door shut. We huddled in the dark and waited.

"Where is my son?" our father yelled.

Then a minute later he yelled something about the horses, something else about the bucket at the well, and again, "Where is my boy and where is Abeba?"

I scrunched down a little more in the darkness of the room when I heard my muffled name being yelled by my father. I did not know what I had done, but it would come with severe consequences.

Our mother was replying to his demands, but we could not hear her through the walls. Something slammed against something else in the house. Then it was quiet. Then another burst of screaming. Then more quiet.

After fifteen or twenty minutes our mother stuck her head in the door. "It's alright. Come in."

We went back into the house and our father was sound asleep and snoring. Our momma had hidden us so we wouldn't have to take his heavy hand. She took the brunt of his anger and this became the regular routine whenever my father returned from a night of drinking.

My father was a good man in many ways. He worked hard for the family and even though he didn't show us much affection we could all tell he cared for us through his actions. Except when he was drunk of course, then his actions were mean.

Now, I understand it. It was not okay, but I understand. It is the way it was at that time in Eritrea. My father was no different than most other men. He was stressed from the war and worried about the future. Drunkenness and a raised hand was his relief. My mother, being such a strong woman and so wise, understood this. And she took the pain away from us. This is one of the reasons I have great respect for her. She helped show me how to give to others even at my own expense.

She helped show me how to survive.

Chapter Three

I was 12 years old. It was a windy day and a thin layer of dust drifted along with the breeze. I was tired after a day of school and now I was doing my chores. My father and brother were taking care of the horses. My mother was inside the house with my sisters. I hauled a bushel of tomatoes from the field toward the back of the house. They were not heavy at the start, but with each step my arms began to ache. Finally, I sat the bushel down and stretched my arms. As I did so I noticed a man approaching our house. He was too far away to really see him. He was just a tall, slender figure leaning into the dusty wind and walking with a purpose.

I did not recognize this man and there was no telling what he may want. I picked up my tomatoes and quickly walked around the house to the kitchen in the backyard where we usually hid at night. I pushed through the door and put the tomatoes in their spot.

As I walked back out to get the next load of food I saw my father walking toward the house to meet the man. I was curious, but I knew better than to follow him. Instead, I went toward the building where we had placed our recently picked food.

Once I got around the house I craned my neck to catch a glimpse of the man and my father. They shook hands and the man started talking. I could not hear.

Moments later, I returned with a smaller bushel of spinach. My mother and older sister, Hiwet, had joined them. I wanted to go over to them badly, but I finished my chores instead.

Just before dinner I learned why the man was there. He did not know my family, nor did he know Hiwet, but he had asked my father if he could marry her. Even though he had never met the man before, he agreed. I could not believe it. My sister, who was just 17 years old, would get married. I looked across the small room at her in a way that asked if it was really true.

She said nothing. She didn't need to. The look on her face told me that it was real. We went about our normal evening and the sun sank into Sudan to our west. My father drank at the bar and we hid in the kitchen upon his return.

It would be the last time I would hide with Hiwet. The very next day I was in the house helping Momma when there was a knock at the door. It was the man from yesterday. It was the first time I got a good look at him. He was neither attractive nor ugly. He was dark-skinned and tall with a wide nose and straight white teeth. He showed them when he smiled and greeted Momma.

"Hello," he said to me.

"Hello," I replied, but I felt shy.

I did not really understand why. He was here to take my big sister away from us. We did not even know him. This was often the case when it came to marriage. For some reason it had not registered with me that this would happen to Hiwet even though she was at an age when parents want their daughters to go.

After a drink and a little bit of talking, it was time for the man and Hiwet to leave. She gave me a hug. "Goodbye Abeba," she said.

"Bye Hiwet," I replied. "I love you."

She nodded, and tears formed in my eyes. I blinked them back as she walked out the door with a man we had never seen until the day before.

I went outside and watched my sister leave, and then I watched my father walk back to the fields as if nothing had happened.

Chapter Four

We settled back into life quickly. It was different without Hiwet, but we adjusted and continued on. The Eritrean separatists and their war for independence from Ethiopia also continued on, but we were mostly removed from it. We almost never saw troops and had not heard of any killings in villages for quite some time.

The Ethiopian Emperor, Haile Selassie, seemed to have his hands full in many areas besides dealing with Eritrea. Unrest had become normal amongst Ethiopians and Marxism had taken root. Much of the goodwill Emperor Selassie had enjoyed was going away. The Ethiopian people were becoming hungry for a change, and they were also becoming literally hungry.

Just to our south in Wollo and parts of Tigray, Ethiopia the people fell into a famine. Their crops were failing and thousands and thousands of people went hungry. It was terrible and it made me appreciate how good my father was at growing our food. He had to work so hard to put food on our table.

The famine became so bad that Ethiopians were dying by the thousands. This caused great harm to Selassie's popularity and began to give rise to serious opposition. On top of the famine, pockets of his own military, the very same one the Eritreans were fighting, fell victim to mutiny. And oil prices became so high it made the famine that much worse. It is estimated that up to 80,000 Ethiopians died, and the famine reached into Eritrea as well.

I was just 13 years old during this horrible period. We were poor and lived in a tiny house and feared the consequences of our country's battle for independence, but we had food.

One day, about a year after my big sister had been taken away, I saw her walking toward our house. I dropped the broom I had been using and ran to her. We hugged and I noticed that her lip was swollen.

"Why are you here, Hiwet?"

"I am divorced. He was a terrible man and he hit me often."

She reached up and lightly touched her lip when she said he hit her. A man hitting his woman was normal and accepted at this time. If a woman went to the police she would get no sympathy. Yet my sister took it upon herself to get away from the bad situation. I believe she was able to be strong because of what she had learned from our mother.

"You have left him and now you are home?"

"Yes, I am home, Abeba. I am home."

I was glad to have my strong sister back. I had heard during the last year that she had struggled with her husband, but I did not even understand the fact that she could leave him behind.

I believe she was glad to be back, but she was restless as well. She was now 18 years old and she had been away from our home. I asked her many questions. She told me much about the world that I did not know before.

Once again, our family adjusted and went on despite everything that was happening in our area of Africa.

I would never have guessed that I'd lose her so soon and I'd never see her again.

Chapter Five

It was Friday, September 13th in 1974. We were at our normal tables outside of the bar and the mood was tense.

"You are sure of this?" my mother was saying to a lady who seemed to get information before others. "Emperor Selassie is no longer in power?"

"I'm sure. The Derg took over."

We had started hearing of this Derg just a couple months earlier. It was the formation of a bunch of low-level Ethiopian military members and they quickly gained a great deal of power. They began arresting military officers and government officials.

"It happened just yesterday," my mom's friend said. "Selassie gave up without a fight. He is in prison now."

Nobody knew what to expect because of this development, but everybody was worried. Under Emperor Selassie things had not exactly been good, but they could have easily been much worse.

As the sun gave way to a sky full of twinkling stars, we began our walk back to our house. It was obvious that our lives would change, and we wouldn't have to wait long to find out how. With the Derg in control our land was flooded with Ethiopian troops. They treated the Eritreans as if we were dogs.

Soon, a curfew was implemented and we could not be outside after six in the evening. If we were caught outside of our homes we would be killed on the spot. Of course, being in our home did not give us protection. The soldiers would bust into a house and rape the women and kill everyone.

Every day I glanced toward the road numerous times. The soldiers would come for us. It was just a matter of time. My momma even mapped out hiding places in hopes that we would escape the hell that they would bring.

One morning as I walked to school with my sister we heard the cracks of gunfire. We hurried into a thicket of bushes and hunched down. There were more shots fired in the distance and then two planes flew overhead. We waited a while before finally finishing our walk to school.

This was the beginning of gunfire and planes. They just became part of our lives. Then there was a string of horrific attacks close to our village. In Asmara, our capital city, the Ethiopian soldiers strangled almost 50 students with piano wire and threw their bodies in alleys and doorways. Then a large number of villagers were killed while hiding in churches and homes and schools. Our lives had been ripped away from us.

Our house was so small that my siblings and I all slept in one room. There was barely enough space in it for us to all lay down comfortably. Our parents slept in the other tiny room. One night, I was roused from sleep by a faint rustling sound. I opened my eyes halfway, still in that state of being awake and dreaming. I felt, more than saw, a figure leaning over me.

Then there was a hand on my head. It was a soft hand and I opened my eyes a little more. It was Hiwet. She gave me a kiss on my cheek. "You are strong and courageous, Abeba," she whispered.

I fell back asleep, only to be awoken to a much more chaotic scene as the sun began to rise in the east above the Red Sea. My mother and father were looking for Hiwet. I remembered what had happened in the middle of the night. I had been unsure if it was real or if I was dreaming. Now I was fully awake and a sinking realization took hold of me. Hiwet was gone again.

Many Eritreans were trying to flee to Sudan. My sister decided she had to leave too. She told nobody in our family. She just left in search of a better life.

For years I hoped and prayed that she had made it to Sudan.

Chapter Six

I left my home as little as possible. Still, sometimes I came across the Ethiopian soldiers and it made my skin crawl like it was covered in beetles. One hot day when the Eritrean sky was so bright and blue that it hurt my eyes to look toward it, I was walking home from school. It was not far, but it was dangerous. I tried hard to avoid people and always looked out for soldiers.

I rounded a building and began to set out on a long stretch of dirt road. I noticed a group of men to my right. They looked at me differently than I had remembered men looking at me. Their eyes lingered on me or traveled up and down my body. I did not like it and picked up the pace.

People said I was becoming very beautiful. How my eyes were big and pretty and my skin was flawless. I liked these compliments even though they made me blush, but they did not completely register until I saw the men look at me that way.

Only one hundred meters later I saw four soldiers on a road that intersected with the one I was on. I was sure they saw me as well. I thought I should continue to walk, but it was not long before when my friend had been raped by two soldiers. She was younger than me and she was not the only girl I knew who had been attacked. I imagined the men's hands on me as they grabbed me and hit me. I began to feel sick because of it.

I looked to my right and decided to head for a field that was full of mounds of harvested wheat. The mounds were about five feet high and just as wide. I slipped behind the first one I came to and waited. Then I quickly moved to a mound a little further from the road. After doing this two more times I circled around a mound and peeked out from behind it.

The soldiers were almost even with me. They did not look my way. I waited for a moment and then moved forward, away from them. After passing two more mounds I doubled back to the road. My heartbeat began to slow and I took a few long breathes to calm myself. The soldiers were now well behind me. Even though it was hot and the dirt felt as if it was smoldering, I jogged the rest of the way home.

It would turn out to be one of the last times I made the trip home from school. The Derg were firmly entrenched in our lives and a man named Mengistu Haile Mariam was not one of the most well-known members of the Derg, but he was very influential and soon rose to power. There were even rumors that he smothered Emperor Selassie with a pillow case in 1975. Mengistu denied these rumors, but it is widely understood that he did order the deaths of 61 ex-officials. He also shut down our schools.

I was almost 16 years old and I didn't want to stay on our farm. I wanted to work badly. Finally, my father agreed and I found a job at a small shop in our village where I sewed sweaters. The dim room was poorly designed with a dirt floor and uneven wooden walls. There were just two openings for windows and the flies swarmed through them constantly. It was not the best job, but it was something. My fingers ached and my back hurt from bending over and sewing for hours on top of hours each day.

My boss, a stout older man with yellowish eyes and a bald and shiny head, did not like to give us breaks and we worked hard to earn a tiny bit of money. One afternoon, a man entered the shop. He had a cigarette between his lips and his once white teeth were slightly stained. He wore a plain shirt and tan pants.

"Zeray, my friend," my boss said, and the two men shook hands.

As they talked, I noticed Zeray kept looking at me. He finished the first cigarette and another was in his mouth. A ring of smoke hung around his head. I hate smoking and I hated the way he kept looking at me, much like the men had done on the walk home from school, except now it was for a long period of time.

I did not hear what he was saying to my boss, but by their actions I figured that they were talking about me. I tried to ignore them and continued to sew.

After that day he came into the shop once or twice a week. I did not know how old he was, but it was obvious that he was much older than me, and every time I saw him he smoked his cigarette and let his eyes wander over me in a way that made me feel unclean.

Probably a handful of times he came into the shop over the course of a couple weeks. Then one day I left after work and saw he was almost directly across the street from me. I started to walk and of course I looked out for soldiers. I did my best to walk quickly and remain unseen. As I turned a corner not far from my house, I glanced over my shoulder. Way back, maybe 50 meters behind me and close to a clump of trees, I saw this man, Zeray.

He is following me, I thought, but I tried to get the idea out of my head and simply walked faster. I had one more turn and then I would be on the long stretch to my home. Again, I glanced behind me and again I saw Zeray. The smoke from his cigarette trailed behind him as he kept pace with my steps.

As I approached my house, I checked one more time. He had stopped. He just stood in the dusty road puffing on his cigarette. This time when he saw me look his way he raised his hand and gave me a half-hearted wave. I did not return the gesture. Instead, I ducked my head and hurried to my house, glad to be home.

I did not comprehend that he now knew where I lived.

Chapter Seven

It had been two weeks since Zeray had followed me home. Each day I went to work and sewed until my fingers and hands throbbed. I was wary of seeing him again, but he did not appear for the first week. I'd begun to forget about him until the beginning of the second week. The door opened and I saw his silhouette against the sunlight. Then I smelled the smoke. It made me want to gag.

He talked with my boss for a while and once again let his eyes drape over me like a wet sheet. There was something else I noticed about his eyes. It was as if now he knew something that I did not, and this something was giving him great pleasure.

He left, and once again I shook it off. He did not come to the shop for the rest of the week, and even though I looked I did not see him following me home on any night.

Now, at the end of the second week since he had followed me, I had just finished helping my mother in the kitchen out back. We had cut vegetables and boiled meat on an open fire. The food was almost ready to eat and I walked around the house to get a bucket of water from the well. I saw four men in the distance. One of them was Zeray.

My heart quickened and I wondered why he was here. I hurriedly walked into the house. My father had just returned from the fields and he was pulling off his boots. "There are men here," I said. "One of them is the man I told you about from work, the one who followed me home a couple weeks ago."

My father gave me a sideways look and then pulled his boots back on. "Go take your mother's place in the kitchen. Send her to me."

I left without another word.

As I finished preparing for dinner my imagination ran wild. I tried to think of every possible reason he could be at my house, and I kept returning to one terrible thought.

He left after a short time, and my mother helped me bring food to the house. We ate in near silence even though my desire to know why Zeray had come was driving me crazy. Once the food was finished, my father leaned back in his chair.

I leaned forward in anticipation.

"The man you spoke of, Zeray, he came here with the elders to ask for your hand in marriage."

My throat went dry and the palms of my hands became damp. I could not think of much of a reply. "What did you say?" I finally croaked out.

My father glanced at my mother and then looked directly at me. "I told him he had my blessing."

I felt as if I had been punched in the chest. This chain-smoking older man who was not remotely what I would look for in a man would become my husband? My brain tried to chew on what I had just heard, but it would not accept the words. It was as if it spit them out and my ears felt flooded.

"I cannot marry him."

"You can and you will," my father said. "It's time for you to leave. Besides, do you want to get raped by the Ethiopian soldiers? You know how they look at you. We are lucky you have not been raped already. Zeray is half Ethiopian."

I did not care what country he was from. We knew nothing of this man and my parents did not spend the time to get to know him. My gut was screaming at me that this was not right. I was only 16 years old. He was at least ten years older than me. "What if he has kids? I don't want to raise anybody else's kids."

My father shook his head and leaned forward. "We already said yes. You will marry him."

"If you do not like him you can always get a divorce," my mother said in an attempt to make me feel better.

It did not help.

In a matter of moments my life had been ripped to pieces. I was scared. More scared than I had ever been.

Chapter Eight

With no input from me it was determined that the wedding would be in a month. It would be held in our backyard right next to our kitchen where I had helped make so many meals and hid from my drunken father. I felt like hiding right now, or better yet running away toward the west and the promise of better times in Sudan. Maybe I could even find Hiwet. She had left a couple years earlier and we had not heard from her.

As I lay in bed one night listening to the soft breathing of my siblings, I really considered running. I could just get up, pack some food and water, and start walking. It was a long way but I was capable of dodging the Ethiopian soldiers and I could survive. I willed myself to get up and go, sneak out of the house like Hiwet did and leave Zeray behind. But instead of leaving I finally drifted to sleep and had terrible nightmares.

A few days later I was at the shop. My days working there were numbered. The door opened and I saw Zeray. He talked with my boss for a moment and then walked toward me.

It looked as if the smoke was seeping from his pores. He smiled at me. "Hello, Abeba."

It was the first words he had ever spoken to me. "Hello," I said in a barely audible voice.

"We will be married soon," he said.

"I know."

"I cannot wait." He reached out to touch my shoulder. His hand rested there for a moment and I did not look up.

"I have to work, Zeray," I said.

"Of course, I will see you soon my wife." He walked away, but the smoky smell remained.

This was the last time I saw him before the wedding. Each day I worked and wondered about what my life would soon be like, and each night I struggled to fall asleep. I was terrified of the future and yet I could not stop thinking about it.

The night before the wedding I lay in my bed staring at the ceiling. A terrible thought struck me. This would be my last night in our little house, my last night with my family. Tears bubbled up in my eyes and silently streamed down my cheeks. My eyes lost their focus and it seemed as if the darkness blurred.

I had no idea where I would be sleeping tomorrow. I also had no idea what to expect or what would be expected. I would not be sleeping alone. Zeray would be next to me and I would be his possession. Fresh tears filled my eyes and traced down my cheeks. My small pillow became wet. I did not care. The darkness blurred even more, and then I was asleep.

The next day it felt as if my eyes remained blurry. I was dressed in a traditional Eritrean wedding dress, white with gold. It was not expensive, but very beautiful. I suppose I looked pretty in it. My hair was flattened to my head and my body was adorned with much jewelry. My mom and sisters fussed over me. I did not really like it.

Soon I walked out my back door to my wedding. It was only family, just 15 or so people in all. Music played and I walked toward Zeray. He stood near a makeshift altar. Oddly, I was surprised that he was not smoking. He did not smile, just stared at me.

I found myself standing across from him. The pastor talked. The words barely found my ears. It was all so unreal. I was standing across from this man I did not really know or like. I was talking to him and saying my vows. I was giving myself to him even though it was the last thing I wanted to do.

Maybe it was something of a defense mechanism, but the day was in a fog in my brain. I went through it. I got through it. I walked away from the altar with my arm wrapped around Zeray's.

I had woken up a kid and now I was a wife. I felt numb.

Chapter Nine

Germany 2011

I had been sitting in the hospital in Berlin for what felt like months. In actuality it had not been that long, just a little over a week. The doctor came in my room. When I saw him I tried to sit up, but my back and hip would not let me. I wondered if I was dreaming because he was not in the white suit and mask that covered his entire body and made him look like an astronaut. Instead he was just a normal doctor in his lab coat.

I learned that I did not have this tuberculosis as they had thought. They were confused because I had so many different things wrong with me. My repaired hip had broken for no reason. My back hurt horribly. My lungs had problems and breathing was a struggle. I was a mess and they still searched to learn why.

Later that afternoon, Hannah and Sahra came to my room. It was so nice to see their smiling faces without the mask covering them. "My girls, how are you?"

"We're good, Momma," Hannah said. "How are you feeling today?"

I did not want them to worry. "I am fine, just tired."

Sahra lifted a bag and shook it. "We have some new clothes for you."

I was happy to get new clothes, and I was happier to see my girls. They were a bright spot in my otherwise horrid day of lying in my bed like a lump of quivering pain. It was as if the aches did not come from within my body. Instead they sucked in from around the room like a tornado, and drummed on my skin until they found their way into the deepest parts of my bones.

This is how it was always, even with the drip of morphine. My daughters and I talked for a while longer. They helped me keep my mind off the hurt, but soon they had to go. We said our goodbyes and the aches started throbbing in my bones.

I was miserable because of whatever was hurting me, but the idea of not knowing what was wrong was just as bad. The doctors decided to do more tests. A plump nurse with curly black hair and a slight double chin entered the room. Not far behind her was a cleaning lady who just happened to be from Eritrea. She was a thin lady who was quick to smile. She walked with a slight stoop despite being a few years my junior. I was sure it was from many hard years in Africa, just like the ones I had suffered through. She was a Godsend for me when my daughters were not there to translate.

"They would like for you to drink this," she said.

The nurse held out a bottle of liquid and said something in German.

"Sorry, it does not taste good," my Eritrean friend translated.

If it helped them learn what was wrong with me I would gladly drink it even if it tasted like urine. It turned out that it tasted like bleach. It was hard to get down, but I did.

I had to drink more of it later, and then I was told that I would go for more tests. I was wheeled down to a room with a machine that looked as if it could double as a futuristic cannon. The doctors moved me onto a bed and I understood that I would be going inside the cannon. It was a tight fit and the machine made horrible noises as it took pictures of my entire body.

In the midst of the clicks and whirrs I tried to relax and I thought of my family. I was so happy for Muse, Hannah, and Sahra. They had turned out fine here in Germany. I also longed to get Selemon and Michael and John over here with all of us even though I knew very well it may never happen. And I thought of my childhood too, when I was young and innocent, and a time long ago when I was married and my innocence was lost.

It was a day after being in the machine when the doctors and my Eritrean friend came into my room. It had been almost two weeks since I was admitted to the hospital. I was so hungry to learn what was wrong with me, but as I looked at the concerned faces of the people who stood around my bed I had a sudden urge to bury my face in the blankets. Maybe I wasn't so eager to learn of my fate.

One of the doctors spoke, and then he nodded to my friend. She swallowed hard. "The doctors know what is wrong." She paused for a moment and glanced at the doctor as if asking for support. He nodded solemnly. "They have found that you have thyroid cancer. It has grown throughout your body, both of your lungs, your left hip, and your spinal column. That is why everything hurts."

The air drained from my ailing lungs and I felt like I would blackout. I had been up close to death and skirted it before. This time I was sure I would not be so lucky.

"They will need to remove your thyroid very soon," my friend was saying, but I barely heard the words. I was already praying to God, asking Him for strength and courage once again.

Chapter Ten

Eritrea

My feet and back ached because of the walk to Asmara. I was also in pain elsewhere. After the wedding I said goodbye to my parents and siblings and walked away from the only life I had known. I found myself in a dirty little shack with Zeray. I did not know what to expect, but he drank beer and insisted that I had some as well. It made my head feel funny.

"Will we live here?" I asked.

"Of course not. We are going to Asmara where I can work. I already have a place for us to live. This is just a stop for the night."

His eyes had a wanting look in them, like a hungry lion. He put his cigarette down and his hands were on me. I could taste his smoky breath. My mind revved with fear. Each way he touched me was entirely new and I could not say no. I was now his wife. I was his.

He sat me down on a stained mattress on the floor and we did things that I had only heard briefly about. I did not like them, and now as we got closer to our capital city of Asmara I hurt because of them. After leaving his shack we took an old bus to a village some six or seven kilometers outside of Asmara. We then had to walk with our packs on our back and the sun pelting us. He talked some. I talked less. I still kept a watchful eye out for the soldiers despite already having a run in with them earlier in the day.

The war had experienced an uptick in action and we saw planes fly over from time to time. A few hours earlier, as we walked to board the bus, we saw a group of Ethiopian soldiers. I wanted to run up an incline and hide behind a wall that was some 50 meters away.

"Don't be ridiculous," Zeray said.

He puffed out his chest as the soldiers approached. Their guns were slung over their shoulders and my breathing was fast. I glanced at Zeray. He offered a smile to the group of soldiers; there were maybe twelve in all. None of them returned smiles.

One stepped forward, hand resting on his gun.

"Who are you?"

"I am Zeray Habtu."

"And this," the soldier nodded toward me.

"She is my wife, Abeba Habtu."

"Let me see your papers."

Zeray reached into his back pocket and fished around for a moment. He brought up white and yellow papers. They were folded and slightly warn. The soldier took them and squinted against the glare as he scanned the writing.

After a few seconds he handed the papers back to Zeray and then looked me up and down. "You are lucky."

Zeray said nothing.

"Go," the soldier said and then walked past us. The others followed.

After a few kilometers there were more and more people on the road to Asmara. We crested a small hill and the outskirts of the city were laid out before us. First there were little wooden huts with tin roofs and chickens and sheep and cows dotted around them. They were much like the home I had left the day before except they were close together.

After a short while the huts gave way to buildings. Some were one story high, others stretched two or three or even more stories into the air. Most of the buildings had pale facades, white or yellow or gray or blue. They also often had arched doorways and columns thanks to the Italian influence that had made Asmara a great and beautiful city years earlier.

Now the buildings were nice, but their shine had worn away and in some places the stucco had cracks and splits or it peeled from the wall. Many of the buildings were speckled with little balconies. String stretched from one balcony to another and clothes hung limply from them, fluttering occasionally in the soft breeze.

As we walked further into the city the buildings were crammed closer together and the streets grew busy. There were many cars and more people than I had ever seen. Zeray grabbed my arm and pulled me toward him. It was not a sign of affection, rather a sign of possession.

After 15 or so minutes more he began stopping at corners and looking left and right. We turned down one road and then turned down another. I felt like a rat in a maze of buildings and streets.

For practically the entire bus ride and the walk from my home to Asmara, I had wanted to turn and run. This was all so new and foreign to me and now I had to fight my urge to break away from Zeray's grasp and run through the maze. I already missed my home, my family, my life of old.

"We are here," Zeray said.

We walked through a tiny archway and he banged on a door. A woman in a colorful dress answered the door after Zeray banged once more. She wiped her hands on a dingy towel. "Hello Zeray," she said in a neutral tone.

She then looked me up and down, neither smiling nor frowning, and backed away, an invitation to enter.

It seemed I was now home.

Chapter 11

My new home consisted of a tiny room and a doorway and another tiny room. There was no toilet. We had some nice bushes out back between the buildings and that is where we relieved ourselves. It was noisy and the people being on top of each other made me feel uneasy.

The woman turned out to be a relative of Zeray's. His aunt I think, but I was never clear and now I do not even remember her name. She seemed hardened by her tiny existence in the big city and she always looked at me with small untrusting eyes. She also had a habit of constantly placing her hands on her hips, at least when she wasn't carrying around the dish towel.

Zeray was in and out of the house. He was either trying to find work, actually working, or drinking. He started a job at a garage fixing automobiles and other vehicles and it suited him.

Not long after we arrived, Zeray had given us money for groceries for one month. I wanted to go along to the store. I'd been cooped up in this tiny house and felt like I was being squeezed on all sides. I had nothing to do but help clean and try to get along with this woman.

"No," she said. "You stay here and work on the house. I will be back soon."

She left and I wiped down some areas and cleaned some dusty pots, but there was not much to do. After half an hour, Zeray arrived. He came home often to check on me. I do not know what he thought I would do. We had been together for just a few days and I was powerless, yet he already mistrusted me.

"Why are you here alone?"

"She went to the store for the groceries."

An angry look crossed his face. "Why did you not go?"

"She wanted me to stay here to clean."

"Do not be weak, woman. You should have gone."

I nodded as a reply and he approached me. His hair was growing longer in the afro style that was becoming popular amongst some Eritreans. His breath reeked of smoke and he gripped the back of my neck and pulled me toward him. He kissed me and put his hand on my breast. I wished I had gone to the store and I desperately wanted to run from him and this place.

He squeezed hard and pressed his body against mine. After a moment he broke away. His breathing was fast and he looked me up and down. "We will finish this later. I have to get back to work."

He turned and left without another word.

It was not long after this when the woman returned. She struggled to carry the basket that was full of food. I quickly grabbed it from her and carried it to a small table in the corner of the room. The basket was full, but I wondered how on Earth that food was to last an entire month.

After one week I realized that it would not last. And as the second week drew to a close we were almost out. Zeray came home one evening after working. He had already been drinking and he was in a foul mood.

"Where in the hell is all the food?" he asked.

"This is all you gave me money for," his relative said.

"I gave you money for one month, not half a month."

The woman put down the dish towel and placed her hands on her hips in defiance. Zeray's eyes turned into evil slits and his mouth pressed together in a hard line. "Where is my money?"

"I spent it on groceries."

"Liar, what did you do with the rest?"

They went back and forth like this for a while. Finally, Zeray stormed out. I feared his return.

"He's no good," the woman told me. "Why would you even marry him?" Before I answered, she continued. "He is like the devil. You will see."

I did not know how to respond.

Just half an hour later as the city became draped in long shadows from the combination of the setting sun and the tall buildings, Zeray threw the door open. He looked at me. "Did you know?"

"I do not understand, Zeray."

"Did you know about the money?"

I quickly shook my head back and forth. "I do not know what you mean."

He pointed his finger at his relative. "This woman stole my money." He walked toward her and shoved his finger in her face until it touched her chin. She stood, hands on hips, but it looked as if she was about to flinch.

"Did you not think I would find out? All I had to do was ask. You took almost half the money for groceries."

I noticed his right hand, the one that was still at his side, had tightened into a fist.

His relative gritted her teeth. "Get out of my house," she said.

Zeray let out a low rumble in his throat and gripped the woman's chin with his left hand. I stood and watched, too afraid to move. Finally, he pushed her chin away. "You steal from me and then you try to kick me out? We will leave in the morning you no good whore, but if I wanted to stay, we would stay."

The next morning we were out of the house while the streets were still dark. I was not home after all, and as we walked it felt as if we were twisting deeper into the guts of the city.

Chapter 12

The house was not a house at all. It was just a tiny room in the center of the city. It was Zeray's father's room when he came to Asmara for work. Zeray unlatched the door and it squeaked loudly as he pushed it open. It was dark so he felt his way through the room and pulled on a small wooden shutter.

The morning light leaked into the room. I stood at the threshold, suitcase still in my hand, and took in what was apparently now my home. It was nothing but a big closet, maybe ten square meters. A ragged bed on a metal frame barely big enough for two people was pushed up against one wall. The peeling paint threatened to fall onto the worn sheets.

A tiny table was up against the opposite wall. The table held an empty beer bottle that rested on its side. A rickety wooden chair was pushed up underneath the table.

"Here we are," Zeray said.

I looked at him and tried hard to not show my feelings. "Where should I put the luggage?"

He pointed toward the corner next to the open shutter. I walked over and sat the luggage down.

"The toilet is out back. It is shared by the people in this area. I say ten families in all. There is a kitchen there as well. I will be home by noon and expect food."

He placed ten Ethiopian birr on the table.

I started to ask where he was going, but he was already at the door. He turned. "Do not go anywhere except for food."

Where would I go? I did not even know where I was.

The door slammed shut and I was alone.

I searched my new area and found the toilet and kitchen. I asked a lady where the nearest store was. "Who are you?" she said.

"I am Abeba, the wife of Zeray Habtu. We are staying at his father's house."

"I see. You are a young one." The woman pointed toward the road. "Go to the corner, turn right. You will find a store."

At noon Zeray came home and I gave him food. I almost didn't have it ready in time because I had to wait for three other women to finish their cooking in the kitchen. He came home after work and we did things on that dirty bed that I did not want to do. Then he went back out to drink with a friend.

I sat in the bed with the shutters opened and listened to the noises of the city. A car honked. A child cried. A man yelled something that did not make sense. Two women laughed in the distance. It was the end of the first day in my new home with my new husband and I had never felt more alone. It seemed I was a prisoner with only one duty, serve my husband.

Could my life continue to be this way? I tried hard not to think of the answer. It did continue in such a fashion for a few months except for the three times when Zeray left for his village and returned a week or so later. Then one day Zeray came home with papers. The smell of his smoke had always bothered me, but recently it had bothered me much more. "Tomorrow I will go to my village. I will call for you soon."

I had heard from the neighbors that the war was more violent now than it had been before. The planes were bombing many parts of Eritrea and the Ethiopian soldiers had multiplied. His village was a 12-hour walk away. I summoned my courage. "Will I take the bus?"

"No, it is not far and we do not have the money."

"Will it be safe for me to walk?"

He looked at me as if I had just slapped him. "I'm sure you will make it, just stay away from the soldiers."

The next morning he was gone. He left me enough money for food for just a handful of days. I sat and waited and waited. It was good to not have to worry about him. I had grown so tired as of late. After one week a neighbor came. "Your husband called my phone. He expects you in his village tomorrow."

I nodded. There was nothing to say so I packed up my luggage and fell asleep early. In the morning I would walk to his village and pray with each step that I would make it.

Chapter 13

The squeaky door slammed shut and latched. It was a few minutes before six in the morning. The curfew was still in full effect, but I figured I would be okay leaving a little before it ended. It was a half-day's walk and I'd have to hurry to arrive before the curfew returned 12 hours from now.

I wore a dress and carried a small pack that had a few changes of clothes and a large plastic jug filled with water. A smaller pack hooked around my waist had some crackers and two pieces of fruit.

I looked down at the map in my hands and then up at the signs on the street. After one wrong turn I found a main road that led out of Asmara. The city was still mostly quiet. I stayed close to the buildings and tensed before turning each corner. I was desperately hoping that I would not run into any Ethiopian soldiers.

After almost an hour I was nearly out of Asmara. I had seen very few people. The temperature was comfortable, but climbing. I walked at a steady pace. I would remain on the road I was on for another few kilometers before turning to the north.

This was a journey I did not want to make. It was dangerous and there was not a loving husband on the other end. But even though I was just 17 years old and in an unwanted marriage, I was determined to be a good wife. It was my duty and I would do my best to fulfill it.

I had settled into a solid rhythm and was beginning to feel a little more comfortable when a loud rattling sound pierced the morning air. It echoed for a moment and I froze. In an instant of terrible realization I knew I had heard gunfire.

I stood still. My eyes darted to the left and to the right. Dogs barked in the distance. There was another burst of gunfire. It sounded as if it was closer. I moved forward a few steps, and then stopped. I listened again. A single shot echoed through the buildings.

"I have to get off the road," I said to myself.

To my left it was nothing but tiny shacks. To my right was a line of seven or eight old cars. I noticed that one of them was spotted with bullet holes. My life was on the line. I could be dead before ever getting out of Asmara. I flashed back to my family and my old house. I wanted to be there so badly.

Another burst of gunfire, and then another. I heard the rumbling engine of a vehicle and men shouting.

I ran toward the line of cars and ducked between them. I felt naked there. It was such an inadequate hiding place. I saw two men run across the road just 50 meters ahead of me. Again, I looked around. There was a small concrete wall just ten steps away. It ran parallel to the road and some five meters ahead there was a small opening in it. The wall was only one meter high and it looked like it surrounded an old school.

I tried to calm my nerves. I had to think! Could I make it from the car to the opening? What would be on the other side of the wall? A truck skidded into the intersection where the men had been just moments before. A man with a machine gun crouched in the back and fired behind him. The noise blasted into my ears. It appeared they were being chased. To my horror the truck turned toward me.

I was running before I even realized it. The short distance between my hiding place and the opening of the wall seemed to stretch on forever. Another truck burst into the intersection. It was bigger and two men returned fire at the first truck. A third truck followed it.

I crouched behind the wall as the first truck passed. The machine gun continued to spew its bullets. The trucks raced down the road where I had just stood. I crawled on my hands and knees until I reached two palm trees. They were close to the wall and provided a little more cover. I squeezed between them and pressed my back against the concrete. I looked left, and then right. I dared not peek over the wall.

The trucks were long gone, but my heart felt as if it would jump up my throat and out of my mouth. I tried to relax and control my breathing. The reality of my situation hit me. I was on the edge of death with each step I took. If I was caught in a gun fight they would not bat an eye if I was shot dead.

And if I ran into a group of Ethiopian soldiers I was positive I would be raped and killed.

I curled my legs up toward my chest and pressed my back against the wall even harder. I just wanted to be home with my family. Why was I here? Why was I with this man who treated me poorly and did not care if I had to travel through a war to get to him?

"Dear Lord, please guide me," I whispered. "I need you Lord."

I calmed a bit and felt as if I should begin moving again. The gunshots had faded into the distance and all that remained was the barking of the dogs and a soft breeze. But something held me there. I stayed in my hiding spot.

Seconds later I heard boots pounding on the street. A group of what sounded like 20 men ran down the road toward where the trucks had gone. I heard one man yell to the others. "This way, this way...be ready to fire!"

I looked toward the blue sky. It was so crisp and beautiful it hurt my eyes. "Thank you," I said.

The men were soon gone and the dogs had grown quiet. It seemed as if the crazy moments of fighting had never existed. Now I felt as if it was okay to begin moving once again.

Chapter 14

I used the back of my hand to wipe sweat away from my forehead as I sat in the shade underneath a tree. I took a sip of my water and ate a piece of orange. According to the map I was a little more than halfway there. My body had grown so tired. I needed a nap, but knew I could not afford the time. It was already past noon.

From my vantage point of some 25 meters away from the road I could see at least 100 meters in all directions. I had not seen any more soldiers or heard any more gun shots since the skirmish on the outskirts of Asmara. Still, the constant tension and heated walk had drained me.

I took another sip of water and then stood. I had to keep moving. I started toward the road when something caught my eye. Way off in the distance I saw a glint in the sky. I stayed next to my tree and watched the glint. It grew larger and I saw that it was a plane. Then I noticed that it was followed by other planes. They banked to their right toward a hilly area. I had walked from that way just half an hour earlier.

I watched, more curious than scared. Then an explosive thunderclap of gunfire erupted from the hill, and another, and another. The planes wobbled a bit, but none were hit. Seconds later they unloaded their bombs. It looked as if the side of the hill had exploded in fireworks. The planes circled, ready for another run.

I decided I had better move. I jogged toward the road. My weariness and aches had vanished. I hit the road and turned away from the bombing.

Just five minutes later I heard the planes again. It was like they just dropped from the sky and they were almost right over my head. I hurried off the road and squatted next to some bushes. The bombs made a whistling sound and exploded just a half a kilometer ahead of me. The Earth shook. I sunk down further into the bush and waited. What were they bombing?

I didn't have to wait long to find out. A large truck that was covered with a brown tarp came careening down the dirt road. As it passed, I saw a handful of men with guns. They poked their heads out of the back of the truck and fired upward. They were so close I could see their eyes. It seemed fear swam in them. They understood that if they failed to hit the plane they would soon be blown up.

Then I heard the whistling. The piercing sound hurt my ears and I stuck my fingers in them. There was a flash and a sound like none I had ever heard. It made my insides shake. Fire leapt into the air. The truck that had just passed was now nothing more than a burning heap of metal and I felt the wave of heat. I squished my body into the bushes. I couldn't bear to look.

In my mind I saw those men and their scared eyes. Just seconds earlier they were alive. Now they were blown to pieces. I wanted to stay in that bush and cry. I wanted to curl up and let the day turn to night, but I could not do that.

After a few minutes I began moving again. Now I stayed just off the road so I could hide faster if needed. Four hours later I was just a kilometer away from Zeray's mountain village. I had not seen any more soldiers, but I could not get the image of the now dead men's eyes out of my mind. I consulted my map. After one more turn and another incline I would be there.

At five minutes until six o'clock I found Zeray's tiny home. It was a traditional Hidmo, as we called it. It was made with clay that was off-white in color. Two wooden posts held up an overhang above the front door. The roof was made of Earth and piled up sticks and twigs.

I knocked on the door. Zeray pulled it open. He wore a white tank top t-shirt and had a cigarette between his lips. I suppressed a gag at the smell. "Hello, Abeba," he said. "How was your trip you were so worried about?"

I wanted to spit on him. Instead, I said, "Long, and not very eventful."

Chapter 15

The house was dim and the air smelled stale. I entered behind Zeray and found one small room with a damp clay floor and another smaller room that housed a bed and two old chairs. Zeray led me out the back door into an open area that butted up against a sharp rock incline.

There was a small fire with a pot above it. A girl sat not far from the flames and used a rounded stone to crush grains in a pot. She did not look up. A boy sat behind the girl, closer to the rock. He was working with some twine to fix a broken shoe.

"Winta, Kibrom, come here," Zeray said in a sharp voice.

The boy, Kibrom, hopped to his feet and walked toward Zeray. The girl looked up and offered a sneer before reluctantly pulling herself upward. They stood in front of us and Zeray said, "This is your new mother. Her name is Abeba."

My heart stopped beating. I looked at the children and they looked at me. Kibrom seemed indifferent, as if he would just go along with this shocking news and make the best of it. Winta, however, looked as if she wanted to throw the rock into my face.

We stood there staring at each other in an uneasy silence. "Hello," I finally said.

Kibrom smiled. "Hello, Abeba."

Winta turned and sat back down in her spot and returned to mashing the grains.

I did not know what else to say. Just a few months ago I had been a child being taken care of by my parents. I still was a child in many ways. And yet here I was being told that now I had to look after these children. This was one of my biggest fears when my father told me I would marry Zeray. I had protested by telling him that I did not want to raise another woman's children, but here I was.

After we ate a handful of food and sipped on water I talked with Zeray and his father, who had returned just after I met the children. I learned that Winta was almost ten and Kibrom was eight years old. They were from Zeray's previous marriage. There was a baby as well, but he was with Zeray's ex-wife. Zeray had not been divorced for very long when he met me.

I could take no more. I was so tired from the physical and emotional strain of the day. My stomach felt queasy, and as I lay down on a mat on the floor I noticed that my breasts were sore. I thought about the day to try to determine where the soreness had come from. I remembered crawling when trying to get away from the soldiers in Asmara. I must have exhausted my muscles and now they hurt.

Really though, my body hurt all over, not just my breasts. I felt as if my brain hurt as well. It spun with thoughts and my temples throbbed. How could I do this? How could I be a mother to these kids I did not know?

Despite my troubled thoughts, I fell asleep quickly and dreamed of planes and bombs and dead eyes.

The next morning I was expected to be the woman of the house. I did my best, but from the start it was obvious that Winta would not like me. She had a slick way about her that came with years of growing up in this tumultuous land. She was mean as well. She said spiteful things to me and her little brother. She only listened to Zeray because she was smart enough to know the consequences of defying him would be swift. Kibrom was the opposite of his sister. He was sweet and genuine. His hard life had not soiled him yet.

One day turned into another and another. Since we were in the mountains it felt as if the afternoon sun was right next to my face and the nights turned bitter cold. We had next to nothing to eat and I felt weak and tired all the time.

After weeks in this home trying my best to be a mother, I had decided that I would become courageous and tell Zeray that this was not the life for me. We had been together for just five months. It would be best for me to leave now. He was out drinking at a friend's house or I would have told him right then. I was ready for this fight.

I tried to go to sleep and told myself over and over and over that tomorrow morning I would tell Zeray that I was leaving him and Winta and Kibrom to go back home. I had to prepare my nerves.

I had drifted to sleep when Zeray came in. He was of course drunk. The kids were already asleep and his father had left to go back to Asmara a few days earlier. Zeray woke me by placing his hand on my thigh and squeezing. I rolled onto my back, groggy from sleep. He squeezed again and I began to wake up. He smelled of smoke and alcohol and his shirt was off.

He gave me a toothy grin and leaned down toward me. I was so tired. I did not want to do this. He slid his hand up to my breast and squeezed there as well. Abruptly, he stopped. "Abeba, what is this?"

I leaned onto my elbow. "What do you mean?"

"Your breast is bigger than before." He squeezed again. "Do they hurt? Have you felt sick?"

"Yes, but I did not want to say anything."

"Do you not know what this means?"

I did not know. I had no idea. I just stared at Zeray with a blank look on my face.

"You're such a child, Abeba. I cannot believe you do not know."

I felt ashamed, but I did not understand.

"You are pregnant."

The word seemed to echo off the clay walls and I sank onto my back. Any fight I had left was gone. How could I leave Zeray now? His child was inside of me. After such shocking news and the realization that my plans had been destroyed, I did not even have the strength to protest Zeray's advances.

Chapter 16

I used my shoulder to push open the squeaky door. It caught on the cement floor for a moment and then opened all the way. We were back in our tiny box of a house in Asmara. Kibrom sat in a chair and drew pictures on a notepad he had recently received for his birthday. Winta was not in the room. I guessed that she was out back with some of the neighbors' kids.

I sat the groceries down in the corner and separated them into their normal spots. We ate the same cheap food over and over; barely ever did we get a treat.

We had returned from the mountain village five months earlier. For the return trip we took a bus for most of the way since it was the four of us, the kids and Zeray and me. As the bus rumbled along toward Asmara I thought of the walk I had made not long before. Back then I thought things were difficult, and they were, but now they were infinitely more complicated. I was a mother to two kids and I was bringing my own child into this destitute war-torn world.

Since our return I had done my best to take care of Kibrom and Winta. It had gone well with Kibrom. He was a nice boy. Winta, however, had remained angry and hateful. I also visited a woman who supposedly knew about giving birth. She was not a doctor, but she had helped many others in the area. She told me that I was about two months pregnant at the time. I had seen her two more times over the following months. She pushed on my belly and asked me questions about how I felt and what I ate. I told her, and she thought my pregnancy was going fine.

Now, I finished organizing the groceries and then sat aside the cleaning supplies. I was sure Zeray would be very angry that I had purchased them, but I could not take our toilet any more. It was so horribly nasty. My belly was very rounded and I felt more uncomfortable each day. I did not get the morning sickness as much anymore, but smells still got to me.

Our community toilet was like a sewer. It was almost never cleaned and the men peed all over it. Sometimes when I felt especially queasy I would not even use it. Instead I would find a secluded bush or corner.

Kibrom saw the gloves and rags and spray. "What are you doing?" he asked.

"I cannot take the toilet anymore. I am going to clean it."

He scrunched up his nose as if he had just tasted rancid meat.

"I know, it will be nasty," I said.

He put his notepad and pencil on the chair. "I will help you."

"Are you sure?"

"Yes, I do not mind and you are pregnant. You will need my help."

I smiled. "Thank you Kibrom. You are a good boy."

We walked out back and pushed the toilet door open. The flies buzzed everywhere and I kept the door open so some of them would fly away. There was feces and urine caked all over the dark hole where we relieved ourselves. I pulled out a bunch of tissue and shoved it up my nose. I gave some to Kibrom as well.

Before entering the toilet I saw Winta. She was at the back of a neighbor's house with her best friend. The two of them were trouble. She had a look of disgust on her face and leaned over to whisper something to her friend. Her friend laughed. I considered pulling Winta over to help out, but she would cause problems if I did so.

Kibrom and I spent the next half hour cleaning the toilet. It was hot and stinky work and I gagged a couple of times, but in the end we had a toilet that did not make me want to throw up. I knew it would not stay this way for long, but it felt like a little triumph for me.

I was had just finished making food and carried it in from the kitchen when Zeray came home. He stood with his hands on his hips and Winta had a smug look on her face.

"Did you clean the toilet?"

"Yes, it was so dirty and it still makes me feel sick." I rubbed my belly.

Zeray looked at me as if I was a rat. "Did you make Kibrom clean it too?"

"He offered to help me."

"That's not what Winta said." He looked at his daughter and she seemed very satisfied. "You made Kibrom help and would have made her help too if she was not at her friends."

"That is not true," I said.

"I did not lie, Father," Winta said.

I looked at this girl. Why was she this way? Why does she try to cause problems? Zeray stepped closer to me and looked at me as if I made him sick. "You should not clean the toilet anyway. I will talk to Kibrom to find out if you made him do it or not."

"That's fine," I said.

I knew Kibrom would tell the truth.

He did, and Winta of course did not get punished for her lie. The cleaning of the toilet was just a tiny way for me to break up the dullness of living inside that box and taking care of these kids day after day. Now it was not a little triumph, instead I felt as if I had done wrong even though I wanted to do something good.

Later that night, I sat next to Zeray. "I am getting close to having the baby. We should go to my home and I can give birth there."

I fully expected that this would be met with scorn. I knew I would have the baby on my own in the center of Asmara with my family far away. Zeray hated my family and called them names. But then he surprised me. "It would be a good idea. We can leave in a few days."

I could not believe it. I would return home! I would see my family and I would get out of this tiny box in the middle of the noisy city. I was more excited than I had been in a long time.

Chapter 17

I was lying on the center of the floor in the home I grew up in. I stared upward toward the ceiling and tried to find a place to focus on. The contractions were very close, and each one sent shockwaves through my body.

"You have to push, Abeba," my mother said.

I did as I was told and strained with everything I had to get the baby out of me. Four women from the village stood around me. They prayed out loud, asking God to deliver the baby to us safely and asking for my health.

"Push again!" my mother said.

My body felt as if it would break in half and the twisting in my stomach and lower area was unlike anything I had ever experienced before. I tried to continue to focus on the spot but I was mentally exhausted.

"Come on, Abeba, push," my momma yelled one last time.

I pushed with everything I had as I gripped the hand of one of the ladies from the village. She prayed loudly and then I felt immense relief. The baby was out.

"It's a boy, Abeba. You have a boy!"

I lifted my head to see my momma holding a slimy mass of something that kind of looked like a baby. She swatted him on the rear and he began to cry. Moments later he was all cleaned up and I held him in my arms. Joy and fear and excitement all washed over me. Now it was not just me who I had to take care of. I held my son in my hands and he was the most precious thing in the world.

"His name is Fili," I announced to the group.

I did not come up with that name. Zeray did. He had told me that if it was a boy, the name would be Fili. I did not bother to argue. Now I did not care what his name was. He was mine and I would love him and care for him with every ounce of my heart.

Zeray was not there. He came to the house with me and Kibrom and Winta but did not stay very long. He supposedly had work to do. It did not bother me that he was not there. I had my family with me and that was all that mattered.

My momma called everyone into the house to meet Fili. Soon, the living room was filled with people. I looked around at those who surrounded me. There was my very own new little brother, Aman, who was almost three years old. Then there were my sisters, Rosina and Letina, and my brothers, Yafet and Abel. My father was there too, and he smiled proudly. The only one missing from our family was Hiwet. She had gone to Sudan about four years earlier in search of a better life and we still had not heard from her.

It was so nice to be home again. It was not so long ago when I left with Zeray, but so much had changed, at least for me. I was still not even 20 years old and yet I had become the mother of a ten year old and eight year old and now I had a baby of my own.

I looked down at Fili and his big dark eyes looked up at me. He was so beautiful. I knew right then and there that I would become as courageous as I needed in order to keep him safe. I thought of the soldiers and bullets that I hid from in Asmara. I would stand and fight them to keep Fili safe. And I thought of the planes and their bombs when I walked to Zeray's village. I would use my own body to shelter Fili from their blasts.

A little later, everyone was back to work. I sat in a chair in the living room holding my baby boy. Momma came into the room to see how I was doing.

"I'm fine," I said. "It is so nice to be home. The last year has been very hard."

"We are glad to have you here. The family is together."

"Yes, I just wish that Hiwet could be here as well. Do you think we will hear from her soon?"

An expression of sadness slipped onto my momma's face.

"What is it?" I asked.

"We did not want to tell you until after the baby was born." A tear formed in the corner of my momma's eye. "We learned the news not long before you arrived. Hiwet did not make it."

I got a heavy feeling in my chest and I felt as if I could not catch my air. "What do you mean?

"One of those planes with the bombs hit her and her friends as they tried to get to Sudan. She has been gone for a long time now."

I breathed deeply and my chest shook as I did so. Death was all too common in Eritrea, but it had not visited anyone in my family. I knew it was possible that this was Hiwet's fate, but I also had visions of her living somewhere in Europe or even America, safe and sound.

The memory of the planes from a few weeks ago came to me. We were in the house when there was an explosion that sounded pretty close. We looked outside to see streaks of light shooting from the ground, and then there was a distant whistling sound as planes dropped their bombs. The explosions were probably ten kilometers away, but it was as close as the war had been to us for quite a while.

After the planes dropped the bombs my momma had started crying. She told me it was because she knew that somebody had been killed by those bombs, but she cried for a long time. Now I understood why. When she saw those bombs it reminded her of her Hiwet.

I started to cry as I thought of my sister, but I looked down at little Fili and I held it in. I thought back to the last words Hiwet ever said to me, "You are strong and courageous, Abeba."

Whether I felt strong and courageous or not, I would now have to be for my baby boy.

Chapter 18

I sat on the chair and drank the water my father had just given me. As I drank, I prayed to God that He would help me and my baby. Fili was just one day old, but he was very sick.

Yesterday, after everything settled down I went to feed him. My momma taught me how to do it, but for some reason no milk would come. After many tries I was very sore and Fili was getting hungrier and hungrier.

Finally, one of the village women suggested that we give him a bit of sugar water. We were unsure if it was a good idea, but he had to get something in his tiny belly. I took a little wooden spoon and dipped it in a cup of sugar water and then brought it to Fili's lips. He tried to suck on the spoon and some of the water ran down his chin.

I gave him another spoonful and again about half went into his mouth and half down his chin. I dabbed the sugar water away and gave him more. After about five times he got a sour look on his face and did not try to suck on the spoon. I guessed he was finished.

It seemed that the sugar water had done the trick, but an hour later he had diarrhea and then he spit up. Not long after cleaning him up, it happened again. I gave my momma a worried look and she patted me on the shoulder. "Why don't you try to give him some milk again?"

I tried, but still nothing came out, and then Fili had more diarrhea. I did not sleep much that night because I worried about Fili and thought of Hiwet who was no longer with us.

Now, I was tired and my momma had been feeding me and giving me water all morning long. It was almost noon when she suggested that I try to feed Fili again. He had not had any diarrhea for the last few hours and he was hungry and dehydrated. I could tell because his little cheeks looked sucked in and the skin on his arm would not bounce back to its original shape when it was pinched.

"What will we do if I cannot make milk?" I asked my momma.

She thought for a moment. "We will figure something out."

I got Fili in position and he latched on. I prayed once again that he would get milk. Nothing happened for a moment, and then it was there. Fili had milk and he drank thirstily for half an hour. I was so happy and I fell asleep with him asleep on my chest. After that, he was not sick.

I could have stayed that way and in my old house forever, but I knew it could not be. Zeray had phoned and he was going to Ethiopia to get us set up in a house. He was half Ethiopian and half Eritrean. This allowed him to travel between the two countries easily. He said that there would be good work for him and he would call when he was ready for me to bring Kibrom, Winta, and Fili to Ethiopia.

I dreaded that phone call. The idea of moving to Ethiopia after years of fearing its soldiers made my stomach twist. It was like we were going into the middle of a den of lions.

I loved each day with my family. I did some chores, but mostly I just took care of Fili and Kibrom and Winta and I got to know my youngest brother, Aman. He was very little, but always friendly and ready to play. He asked me over and over, "Abeba, I hold Fili now?"

He was too little to hold Fili on his own, so I would sit next to him and place Fili in his lap. Aman spent long stretches just staring down at his nephew and making soft baby sounds.

After a couple of months I had all but forgotten the promise from Zeray that he would call soon. I had only heard from him two other times since he told me of our move to Ethiopia, and the last time was three weeks earlier.

One morning I was lost in thought as I fed Fili when a loud clanging noise made me jump. A phone in the home was still very new to us and it only worked about half the time. I picked up the receiver and heard Zeray's voice. It was crackling and hard to understand, but I got most of what he said.

In two days I would be leaving my home once again. There were bus tickets waiting for us. Very soon I would be in Ethiopia, a country of which we were currently at war with.

I hung up the phone and looked at Fili. He had settled down and returned to eating. I stroked his soft arm and once again became lost in thought, but this time it was ripe with sadness.

Chapter 19

Germany 2011

When I heard the news that I had thyroid cancer and it had spread throughout my body, I was sure that I would die. It was as if I'd been given a slow and painful death sentence, like the Eritreans who had been thrown into prison and then tortured for no reason. Or maybe it would be like the members of the G-15, I would just be gone from this Earth and almost nobody would know what happened to me.

I wanted to be strong, but my body betrayed me. I was sick and I was scared. I believed that I would join my family members in heaven, and that helped, but the fear still picked at me every second of every day. I was rotting away inside this hospital in Berlin.

My children told me over and over that I must be positive. I must try to think that I will be well. The surgery to remove my thyroid was the first step in my recovery.

For so long Zeray had told my kids that I had left them and that I was a terrible mother. He did everything he could to turn them against me. It worked for a while, but now Hannah, Sahra, and

Muse were alongside my bed. Hannah held my hand and Sahra squeezed my shoulder. I had a thin black marking on my neck where the doctor had drawn the spot for the incision, and I was in a paper-thin robe. I looked up at my kids and smiled despite the circumstances.

I had been through many hard times, but I was blessed. I had beautiful and successful children who cared about me. I would continue to fight. The beatings, the war, the prison, the soldiers, the stealing, none of it had been able to beat me. I would do my best to ensure this cancer would not beat me either.

"You'll be fine, Mother," Hanna said as if she read my mind.

"I know," I replied.

The nurses came in to wheel me into the surgery room. My kids gave me hugs and said they would be waiting for me when I came out. The nurses pushed me through double doors that swung open when the gurney hit them.

I was placed underneath bright lights and a doctor appeared. All I could see were his eyes above the mask on his face. They looked serious and focused. Another doctor held up a needle. He pointed to my arm and then placed his hands together in a praying position and put them to his left cheek. He then tilted his head and closed his eyes.

I understood that the needle would put me to sleep. He slipped it into my arm and I heard him say, "Zehn, neun, acht, sieben, sechs..." The words became distant and sounded hollow. "...drei, zwei, eins," and I was asleep.

It seemed like no time had passed when I opened my eyes to a terribly harsh light. I squinted and heard someone speaking. My mouth was as dry as fire and my throat felt as if somebody was choking me.

My first thought was of the floor at Zeray's relatives' house in Ethiopia. I hated that floor so much.

Chapter 20

Ethiopia

It felt like I had landed on an island. I was surrounded by millions of people and yet I was all alone. The bus ride from my village to Addis Ababa, the Ethiopian capital, had been long and tiring since I had Winta and Kibrom and Fili with me. Luckily, Fili had slept much of the way and the kids and I had a bench seat to ourselves.

My body was on the bus, but my soul was still back home. I'd hoped and prayed that I wouldn't have to make this trip, but as I entered the bustling city I couldn't help but look out of the window in awe. It was much like Asmara with the big buildings and busy streets, but here everything was a little bit bigger and busier. I saw a gigantic cathedral in the distance and then another. Almost right next to one of the cathedrals was a giant mosque. There were high-rise buildings that stretched into the sky and blue and white cars and mini-buses zigzagging in and out of traffic.

Now though, the cathedrals and buildings and busyness were nothing but a memory. Upon arrival, Zeray met me at the bus station. His hair had grown thicker with its afro style and I could feel an underlying stress oozing from him. I did not know if it was because of our arrival or for some other reason. He of course had a cigarette between his fingers and he seemed pleased with his new son. He was happy to see Winta and Kibrom as well.

We went to what I thought would be our new house. Earlier, Zeray had told me that he had us set up with a place, but when we arrived I found that we were living with relatives of his. It was a one-bedroom apartment and I had flashbacks to the short stay with his aunt in Asmara, the one that kicked us out. The lady in this house was not like his aunt. She was kind toward me and the kids. She let us have our own business and she kept to herself.

On the night of my arrival Zeray had me walk with him through part of the neighborhood. It was nothing but row after jagged row of box-shaped houses. They were close together and the narrow streets did not have too much traffic. Still, the city was draped in a constant mixture of noises due to all the people and cars.

Zeray stopped at a corner and pointed left and then right. "You see all this around you?"

I nodded that I did.

"This is not yours. These people are not your people. You will stay around our house and you will be there when I arrive."

He was right that none of it was mine, and these people were mostly Ethiopian, not Eritrean, but I could not imagine how he could expect me to once again stay locked away in the house with the kids.

"But Zeray," I said, "I will have to get food and take the kids out and it would be good to know some people."

His hand shot up and squeezed my chin and face. I let out an involuntary gasp of air as my eyes grew big. His pointer finger dug into the skin just below my left eye and it made my vision blurry. He pushed me backwards until my head hit a wall. "You will not talk back to me and you will do as I say. You are not in Eritrea anymore and you are all mine."

As quickly as it began, it had ended. His hand was off my chin and he slid it down to my hand and interlocked his fingers with mine. A cold smile curved across his face and he pulled me along down the sidewalk.

My eye felt dry and it began to water on its lower rim. I reached up and rubbed it with my finger and it felt better. Zeray had been mean to me many times. He had treated me like dirt, but he had never put his hands on me until now. Unfortunately, this was just the beginning.

Chapter 21

It was late and I had just put Fili to bed. He was curled up next to the wall. Kibrom was on the floor doing schoolwork and Winta was next door at her friend's house. It had been two days since Zeray grabbed my face. Since then, I felt his stress had become even more intense. He was on edge and full of mood swings all the time.

I wondered what could be making him so agitated, but there was no way I was going to ask. "It's getting late, Kibrom," I said. "You should get ready for bed soon."

"Okay Abeba." He went into the other room to change clothes.

He was a good boy and so far he had not acted like his father. I hoped that would remain.

The door swung open and Zeray entered. A smell of beer and cigarettes wafted into the room. "You are home late," I said, and then immediately regretted it.

"Shut up you bitch," he shouted. "You don't have the right to know where I was."

"I did not mean anything by it, Zeray," I said.

He flew across the room in an instant. I leaned backwards, but I was too slow. The back of his hand connected with my cheek. I twisted and fell to the floor.

"You slut." Zeray growled.

I got a metallic taste in my mouth and pushed my tongue against the sting. The inside of my cheek was bleeding. I pulled myself up to my hands and knees, determined not to cry. I had flashbacks to my own father and the beatings he sometimes gave us as kids. I could not believe it was happening again.

I started to stand, but Zeray put his foot on my side and pushed. I fell again. My back hit the corner of a table and pain pulsed through it. Now I could not help myself. My body shook and I tried to be silent as the tears fell off my face.

Zeray stood over me. His face was filled with a rage that I could not understand. I hated him and yet I had been good to him. But he was not good to me. I braced for another blow when I heard a small voice.

"Dad?"

Zeray turned to face Kibrom. I looked up at Kibrom and pleaded with my eyes for him to go away. Zeray took a step toward him and Kibrom backed up. "Dad?" he said again.

Zeray stopped and stood halfway between me and his son. He looked at him and then looked at me. "Go to bed, Kibrom," he finally said.

I felt a little tension drain from my shoulders until Zeray turned back to me. "I am not through," he said. But he did not hit me.

He then flopped down across the bed onto his stomach. I remained motionless with my back still pressed against the table. I waited and listened. A few minutes later I was sure that he was asleep. I was glad he did not expect anything else from me on that night.

Silently I got to my knees and crawled toward the bed. Fili was asleep just a few feet away from his terrible father. I grabbed my baby and his worn blanket and brought him down to the floor with me. I rolled up a shirt for my pillow and placed Fili on my chest. I felt his tiny body and his soft breathing and I wondered how some people can be so mean to others.

For my entire life I had been a victim. I had been born into a war-torn land and had been hit by bigger and stronger people. It was unfair, but sadly I knew that I was not alone. There were thousands, even millions, of others suffering worse than me.

Still, it hurt. I just did not understand. Why was Zeray so angry? Why was I stuck in this house in Addis Ababa? Why did I get hurt when I tried to do everything right?

My breathing fell into the same rhythm as Fili's. As I started to slip into an uncomfortable sleep I thought that I just had to keep going. There was nothing else I could do. This was my life.

Chapter 22

One day after another trickled by in that house. None of them brought any peace. Zeray was always agitated and I was living in fear. Some days he would come home and not want to beat me at all. Instead, he'd want to lay with me in the bed. But most days he came home with anger in his eyes and the only way to drain that anger was to ball up his fists and hit me.

I was constantly on edge, never knowing what to expect and it ate at my heart. I could tell that it was bothering Zeray's relatives as well. They had opened up their home to us and we had created a disaster area.

They had stayed out of our problems for quite a while, but one night Zeray hit me and hit me and I tried to get away. I cried for him to stop and he slammed me into a chair and it broke. Finally, after what seemed like hours of rage he had worn himself out. I curled up on the floor with my body feeling broken and my face swollen. That is where I fell asleep because I was too shattered to even move.

I awoke in the morning to a puffed-up eye and blurry vision. My arm had a big bruise and my lip was swollen and it had a cut on it. I slowly pulled myself together and started cleaning the house. It was hard to move, but I managed.

After a little bit, Zeray's cousin came into the kitchen where I was wiping down some dishes. She wore a blue dress and her hair was pulled back and tucked neatly behind her ears. She looked at me with her dark eyes for a long moment. "Do you not have family?" she abruptly said.

"Yes, I have parents."

She shook her head back and forth as she pulled out a chair from the table and sat down. "Did they give you to him without even knowing who this man is?"

I did not respond. I just looked down as I remembered how one day there was no Zeray and the next day he showed up at my house and then I was marrying him.

She went on. "First of all he has been married before and he has two kids. He hit the mother of these children and abused her every day. That is why she left him."

I thought about this and wondered why I didn't just leave him too. I could grab Fili and go. But where? How would I get back to Eritrea? There was a silence in the room as I slowly wiped a dish and the woman stared at me.

"He is not for you." She stood and placed her hands on her hips. "He likes to hit women. You need to contact your parents immediately and get a divorce. If you do not, one day he might kill you."

I nodded, but did not respond. She turned and walked out of the room. I chewed over what she said and I had an empty feeling in my stomach. I did not know how I would even be able to get out of Addis Ababa. I had no money and I knew nobody. But I wondered what would happen if I didn't.

Would he really kill me one day? Would he hurt Fili? That question made me feel so queasy that I almost vomited.

When Zeray came home he asked me if anybody had come by the house looking for him. I told him no. He seemed relieved and then he kissed my cut and swollen lip. When darkness settled over the house and everyone was asleep, he pulled me toward him onto the bed. He did not hit me at all. Instead, he got his rage out a different way.

The next day his cousin looked at me as if I was worthless. I knew what she was thinking. I did not have it in me to stand up for myself and I was weak. Maybe she was right. I was doing nothing to stop the way Zeray was treating me. I let him do as he wished with his fists and in the bed.

Later in the evening I took Fili and Kibrom to the store. We had to pick up a few things for our dinner and I jumped at the chance to get away from the house. Upon returning I heard a commotion as I got to the door. I started to open it and realized it was Zeray and he was arguing with his relatives. I nudged the door open and peeked inside.

Zeray was pointing at the man and the woman. As he yelled at them spittle flew from his mouth. "You cannot do this. I have the right to do what I want."

"Not in my house," the man said.

Zeray stepped closer to him, but the man did not flinch. "I will hit back," he said.

There was a moment of tense silence. I stood there in the doorway with Fili strapped onto my back and Kibrom's hand in mine. Zeray noticed we were there and he turned toward us. "Pack up our belongings. We are leaving this pathetic house."

Soon we were gone, walking through the streets of Addis Ababa. This was the second time Zeray had been kicked out of a relative's house in just over a year. I wished I could kick him out of my life as well. Instead I walked with him shoulder to shoulder through the busy city and wondered where we would sleep that night.

Chapter 23

I did not have to wait long to find out where we would go. We walked through the streets and I summoned the courage to ask Zeray. "Will we stay in a hotel tonight?"

He gave me a sideways look. "No, I have a friend not far from here. We will stay with him until we find another place."

We arrived at a rundown house and Zeray knocked on the door. It rattled with each knock as if it would fall over. I heard somebody on the other side of the door and then I heard a bottle fall and bounce on the floor. It was an unmistakable sound because I'd heard it many times before.

The door swung open and I looked up at a big man with red eyes and a hairstyle like Zeray's. He wore a tank top and there were stains on the front of it. "Zeray!" he said. "Is everything alright?"

"Yes, but we need a place to stay."

"Oh, good, you can stay with me," he said.

He stepped away from the door revealing a dirty beer-bottle-ravaged room. A heavy smell of urine assaulted my nose. There was one bed against the wall and a table with what looked like hundreds of beer bottles.

"I can get an extra bed roll for you to sleep on," the man said.

I did not want to put Fili on the floor. It was so dirty and stinky it made me feel sick. Soon, Zeray and this man left the house to talk. As they walked out the door I heard the man say, "So they have not questioned you yet?"

I did not understand what that meant, but it made me remember what Zeray had asked me the day before about whether or not anybody had come looking for him. He was into something, and maybe this man was into something as well. I did not think about it for long. I did not care.

I was floating from one horrible existence to the next. I'd gone to two homes in Asmara, spent time in Zeray's mountain village, had returned home, and now I was on my second home in Addis Ababa. In the last year I'd moved all over the horn of Africa with no peace in sight. Just get through this day, just get through this day. I had to think that every single day.

I tried to clean the room up a little bit while Zeray and this man were out, but it never stayed clean. Zeray remained tense and he still took pleasure in beating me, but he was so busy with his friend that it became less frequent. However, I was met with other terrible things during my days in that little piece of hell.

The man we were living with was a complete drunk. He put alcohol into his body almost as soon as he woke up and he didn't stop. The drinking was part of him. One night, not long after we arrived in the house, he stumbled through the door. I woke up when he entered because he tripped on something and then cursed loudly. I heard him unzipping his pants. I was squeezed against the wall on our bed roll with Kibrom, Winta, and Fili. Zeray was not home and I did not know where he was.

I hated being alone with this drunken man. He scared me because he was so unpredictable. Sometimes he was a happy drunk and other times he was even meaner than Zeray.

His pants hit the floor and I was now fully awake. I listened carefully and tried not to move. Then I heard a heavy sigh and something splattering against the floor. The man was peeing right in the middle of the room. His urine stank and it splashed off the floor and onto our bed roll. I still did not move. I just wanted him to finish and pass out.

My arm was around the kids and some of the pee splattered onto it. I was thankful that the kids did not wake up to this nastiness.

He relieved himself for a good minute and then let out another sigh. A moment later he was in his bed and snoring. I woke up the next day as soon as the sun rose. I saw the darkened stain on the floor and immediately got my cleaning supplies. I could not walk on this man's pee, so I got on my hands and knees and cleaned it up.

It would be the first of many times when I would clean up his pee.

Chapter 24

I had not been to a doctor yet, but I knew. I was late for my time of the month, and my breasts were full of milk and hurting in a different way than they did before, but what really told me I was pregnant was my nose. The stench of urine and cleaning supplies felt as if it had settled into my nose. Fili was not even six months old and yet I had another baby inside of me.

It had been a few days since I began to suspect that I was pregnant, and tonight I would tell Zeray when he arrived home. I didn't know how he would respond. Would he be happy or angry or indifferent?

It was almost nine o'clock when I heard voices outside. They grew louder and finally I got off the bed roll and opened the front door. I could not believe what I saw. There was Zeray standing in the street. He was surrounded by men in dark brown camouflage uniforms with straight-brimmed hats. Their waste belts held guns and sticks and one of the men was talking loudly at Zeray.

Another one of the men moved in and pushed him against a car. I stood there in shock as he was shoved downward and his hands were placed behind his back. One of the men spoke again. I understood his words. Zeray was being arrested for secretly working with the Eritrean government.

How could this be? He was half Eritrean and half Ethiopian and he did know some people in politics, plus the afro-style hair was supposedly a symbol of those working against the Ethiopians. Still I could not believe that Zeray would do this.

He was marched to a car and thrown inside. As it drove away he turned his head toward me and we locked eyes. There was no emotion on his face and I'm sure there was none on mine. We just watched each other as he was driven away. I realized that if he was found guilty he would probably be killed. I may never be with him again.

This was both scary and exhilarating. What would I do now? Where would I go? I went back inside and explained to Winta what I had just seen. I thought she was old enough to understand.

She looked at me with hard eyes. "What did you do? You did this, didn't you?"

I tried to explain to her that I did not, but she did not believe me.

Some thirty minutes later the man whose house we were in stumbled through the door. I told him what happened. He knew that this was a possibility. He also looked at me in a different way. It looked like his mind was telling him that this could be an opportunity. With his friend out of the way and me already here I could be his.

I thought of his nasty pee and I almost gagged. Luckily, he didn't try anything that night, but as each night passed I grew more and more concerned. I had to get out of this house.

Finally, I took five birr I had saved from my grocery shopping and went to a corner store. I paid them the money to use their phone. I called my home and hoped my mother or father would answer. My momma picked up and I explained what had happened.

She gave me Samuel's address and I asked her to call him to tell him I would come. He was my cousin who now lived in Addis Ababa, and he was my only hope.

I gathered up the kids and left a note for the man so Zeray would know where we were if he ever got out of jail, and then I walked away from that pee-stained house before I would have to clean up that filth again, or worse.

Chapter 25

It had been just five hours since I knocked on Samuel's door. I didn't know what to expect upon arriving. I hadn't seen him for many years and we did not know each other so well. Here I was asking him for sanctuary for me and three children because my violent husband was in jail.

I worried that he would not be interested in helping me. After all, he had his own life here. He was educated and had a good job as an attorney at a big office. Why would he want the burden of us?

Now five hours after knocking on his door I realized I had nothing to be worried about. My cousin had opened the door and smiled big. "Abeba, it is great to see you!" He then gave me a hug.

I introduced him to Winta and Kibrom and Fili and he showed us his house. It was not large, but it was nice and it was clean. It felt like a palace to me and I instantly became at peace. He then showed us to the back. In a courtyard area was a small room.

"I'm sorry Abeba. It is not much but it is what I have."

I pushed open the door and it was the best room I had seen in a long time. It had two beds with blankets, a comfortable chair, and a table and wash basin. "It is perfect for us, Samuel." I gave him a hug. "I cannot thank you enough."

This room was mine and I would make a life here without Zeray. I felt free! I made the room our home and I was getting used to the idea of being on my own. I would need to find a way to make some money. I knew that I could, but it would be tricky because I still had to care for the children and I had another baby on the way.

One day folded into the next, and after the first week I was close to being able to clean a house for a small amount of birr. It was not a lot, but it would be enough for me to get by. On the seventh morning I woke up and felt refreshed. All my bruises had healed, and thanks to Samuel's help and my tiny bit of courage I knew I would make it.

The children were still asleep and I was sitting at a table making a list for the food that I would buy at the store later in the day when there was a knock at the door and then the knob twisted. It must be Samuel saying goodbye before heading to work. I stood up to meet him, but when the door opened, I froze. Standing there with a smile on his face was my husband. Zeray had come home.

"Surprised to see me?" he said.

I did not know what to say. I just looked at him. I had put it in my head that I was now on my own and I would be independent, but that had been squashed in an instant. "Zeray!" I acted as if I was happy. "You are out!"

He walked toward me with a lion-look in his eyes. "Of course, they are idiots." He kissed me hard and squeezed my breast. I tasted smoke and alcohol.

"I do not understand what happened," I said.

"They thought I was working with the Eritrean government on the low-low. They thought I was betraying Ethiopia and giving the Eritreans information about the government."

The smirk on Zeray's face made me believe that he was in fact betraying the Ethiopians. Plus he always seemed to have money to spend. I did not think a man working in a garage would have as much money as Zeray had, but at the moment I realized that it was in my best interest to be on his side. The lion was back in my life and I had to be wise so I did not get bit.

"Those idiots, why would they think that about you? I'm glad you are back."

It was hard to say those words, but I did. Zeray's smirk grew into a smile and he kissed me again. Then he did more than kiss me and I had no choice but to let him.

Chapter 26

My life fell back into the way it was before. Zeray would come and go and I stayed locked away in the very same house of which I had felt so free. Samuel did not really like Zeray and he stayed away from us. Again, I was on an island all alone in the middle of a sea of people and buildings that made up Addis Ababa.

Winta was happy to see her father once again. She immediately started spitting lies about me and she told him that I had been glad he was gone. This earned me a slap across the face. I still had not told Zeray that I was pregnant. I guessed that I was two or three months along, and I might start showing soon. My stomach was queasy to certain smells and I had the morning sickness, not as bad as last time, but it was there.

One late afternoon I was doing laundry so I asked Winta, who was now old enough to watch Fili, to keep an eye on him for a little bit. The sunshine found its way through the buildings and onto my clothes line and there was no breeze. It felt as if the world was not moving because of the oppressive heat. As I hung up a pair of Zeray's pants a piercing scream came from inside the room.

I dropped the pants and ran for the door. I pushed it open and scanned the room. Winta stood in the middle of it. Fili was on the floor by her feet. He screamed in pain. I got down on my knees next to him and franticly searched for an injury. I could not find anything so I looked up at Winta. She stood with her hands on her hips and a smug look on her face.

"What did you do?" I yelled.

The smug look grew. "I did nothing to your baby."

I looked back down at Fili as he continued to wail. I searched his arms and his legs and his stomach and his back. I could not find any obvious marks, but I knew one hundred percent for sure that this evil girl had done something to him.

I stood up. "Tell me now Winta, what did you do?"

Now her smugness turned to defiance. She set her eyes on mine. "I did nothing to your precious baby, *Abeba*. You can't prove it."

Her words dripped with such distaste and my heart got so hard. I grabbed her arm and shook it. "Tell me what you did to him!"

Winta did not respond. Instead, she broke into a scream of her own and started crying loudly. I could not understand, but then I saw that Zeray had just come home. He stood in the doorway with a confused look on his face.

"She said I hurt the baby and now she hit me," Winta said to Zeray.

His confusion turned to anger and he lunged at me. I did not have a chance to even tell him what really happened. He pushed me down hard and my backside slammed into the floor. I felt a shot off pain up my back and my head hit something. Zeray jumped on me and punched me in my face. I saw streaks of light on my eyes and I tried to raise my hands to defend myself.

It was no use. He sat on my chest and pinned my arms down. Then he brought his hands to my throat and started choking. This was it. His relative was right when she said that one day he would kill me. Today was the day.

The rage on his face made me know that this was true. He squeezed so hard and I fought for air. There was none there. He strangled me harder. The light around the edges of my eyes started to go dark. It felt as if I was looking through nothing but a tunnel of light.

Oh dear God, who will take care of Fili? That was what I thought. He would not be taken care of. I knew this. I fought to keep the light there and tried to free my arms, but they were so heavy.

I did not know where it came from. I did not think of it before it came out, but somehow I managed to choke one word out from underneath his strangling hands.

"Pregnant," I said.

His face was fuzzy, but it looked as if a hint of confusion cut through the rage.

"Pregnant," I said again.

His grip on my neck relaxed a little bit and the light started to come back.

"I'm pregnant with your baby, Zeray," I struggled to say.

He released his grip and then punched me on my cheek. I felt dizzy, but he got off of me and I was not dead.

I crawled over to Fili. He was still crying, but not as hard. I scooped him up in my arms and laid there on the floor, bleeding and dazed.

Winta happily walked out of the room with her father.

Chapter 27

Muse, my second son, was born about six months after Zeray had almost killed me. There was no way he would know it, but before he was even born Muse saved my life in a sense. Now he was tucked in next to his big brother, Fili. I fed the both of them and I still took care of Kibrom and his horrible big sister, Winta. My breasts were producing milk and aching all the time.

I checked the door and then slid the envelope out from under the bed and dropped the leftover birr into it. Zeray had just called to check on me so I knew that he would not be home in the next couple minutes. My concern was for Winta. I could not let the devil girl see what I was doing. If so, I'm sure I would be dead before the next sunrise.

The hiding of money that I begged from Zeray for groceries had started some months ago when I was six months pregnant with Muse. I remembered that day so well. My belly was big and I had to sit in a hot and noisy waiting room with Fili on my lap. I was there to get him vaccinated.

Finally, I was called back. "When is your baby due?" one of the nurses asked me.

"In almost three months," I said.

"Why do you do that to yourself?"

I looked down. I was embarrassed but I didn't know why. "What do you mean?"

"Having these babies back to back, why aren't you on birth control?"

"Birth control? I don't understand."

"You don't know about birth control child? You can take a pill that will make it where you will not get pregnant."

I could not believe that there could be such a thing. "Where do I get this pill?"

"You can get it here, but you will need your husband's consent."

It felt as if my heart got heavy and dropped. Zeray would not want this pill. Then again, why would he want me to keep being pregnant and having babies? Maybe he would be glad for me to take the pill.

The next time I saw him I told him about this birth control.

"How much will it cost?"

"It is only ten birr," I said.

"Ten birr each month for some pill?" he scoffed. "That is ridiculous."

Ten birr was not even one U.S. dollar, but that was the end of it. I would not get the pill, but at least I did not get hit for my efforts. For many days I sat and felt sorry for myself. I didn't even need the birth control at that moment, I was already pregnant, but it was a sliver of a way for me to take back a little ounce of control in my life. I wanted that pill.

That is when I came up with the plan. When I got money from Zeray for groceries I would put a tiny bit back each time, just enough so I could get the ten birr each month and he would not grow suspicious. Then I talked my cousin, Samuel, into signing Zeray's name on the paper so I could get the pills.

I had been doing this for many months and it was working perfectly. Of course if I got caught I would face a terrible wrath from Zeray.

Now, after tucking the envelope back in its place under the bed between the metal bars and the lumpy mattress, I fished around next to it for the second envelope. This one was thicker. I found it and gave a tug. It came free from its spot. Before taking it all the way out, I looked at the door and listened for any noise on the other side.

There was none. I opened the envelope and found the small rounded container that held the pills. I popped open the one for that day and quickly placed the pill in my mouth and swallowed. There was a bitter taste on the back of my tongue, but it quickly went away.

As I was returning the envelope to its spot, there was sudden noise outside of the door. I looked that way and the envelope fell to the floor under the bed. Winta came bounding into the room. She saw me kneeling beside the bed.

"Hello, *Abeba*, what are *you* doing?" she asked in a snotty voice.

"Nothing," I said hastily, "I'm just praying for you."

She rolled her eyes as she picked something up off the table. Then she stopped and looked at me.

"I do not need your prayers, if that is what you're actually doing."

"That is okay, I will still pray for you."

Again, she rolled her eyes and walked out the door. She slammed it behind her and the room shook. I didn't realize it, but a little bit of sweat had formed on my forehead. I wiped it away and then slipped the envelope into its place. It appeared I had narrowly avoided a disaster. If Winta knew what I was up to she would run to Zeray in a hurry. She was very clever and she liked seeing me get hit.

That night, we sat at the table. It was one of the few times we were all in the room in the evening. Winta tore a piece of Injera, the bread we ate, and dipped it into a pepper sauce. Before she took a bite she smiled at me. "You know, Papa, Abeba is hiding something from you."

My mouth fell open. Zeray had his beer to his lips. He lowered it and looked at her and then at me.

"Yeah, she has something under the bed."

I could not believe this. How did the devil girl know?

"Is this true? What are you hiding from me Abeba?"

"This is not true. Winta is obviously telling another lie to get you angry with me. I do not understand why you do this Winta. I care for you. I cook for you."

"Shut up," Zeray said in a harsh tone.

"I'll prove it." Winta pushed away from the table and took a couple steps to the bed.

I did not move. I just looked down at my food and waited.

"It is right here," Winta said as she crawled under the bed.

I heard her searching and searching for my envelopes.

"I swear, Papa, she has something here." Her voice had a hint of urgency to it.

"Get back up here, Winta," Zeray said. "It is obvious that there is nothing under there."

I did not say a word.

"I know she was hiding something," Winta pleaded.

"Did you see this thing?"

"No, I did not."

"Abeba is right," Zeray said. "You should not lie just to get her in trouble."

I could not believe my ears and I suppressed a smile.

"She did hide something. She must have moved it," Winta said. "I'll tear this house apart looking for it."

I feigned exasperation. "Please Winta, you are being too ridiculous. I would not hide anything from my husband." I reached over and put my hand on his.

"Liar," she said.

Zeray took a swig of his beer. "Shut up Winta, or I will hit you like I hit Abeba."

It looked as if a tear appeared on the corner of Winta's eye. I had won even though she was right. After she had left earlier I'd started thinking that she just might have suspected something. My two envelopes were now underneath a large flower pot by the back door of Samuel's house a good ten meters away.

When I was sure Zeray was not looking, I smirked at Winta and felt glorious for my little triumph.

Chapter 28

Samuel had been very apologetic when he kicked us out of the house. He just couldn't take seeing the way Zeray treated me and me doing little about it. He told me over and over that I should leave Zeray. I knew he was right, but I just could not make myself do it. I had two kids with him.

I had gotten away from the war when I moved to Addis Ababa, but I was in a war in my own home. Zeray had been working in some politics and he was making money, so when Samuel kicked us out we moved to a different part of the city into a two-bedroom house. It was nice, but it was far away from the clinic where I got my birth control pills. Soon, I ran out and had not figured out where or how to get more without getting Zeray's consent.

My half-sister, Rosina, had come to Addis Ababa to stay with us. Rosina has thick hips and a robust form and she is quiet. We got along fine just as we did when we lived together in Eritrea. She was to help out with the kids, and she did so, but she also went out and about with Zeray to drink from time to time. I did not mind.

It was one of these evenings when they were out when the phone rang. I quickly picked it up and told Fili and Muse to remain quiet. They were playing on the middle of the floor with toy trucks.

The call was from my home and I instantly knew something was wrong. My mom was not her usual self. "What is it? What is wrong?" I asked her.

"It is your little brother, Aman," she said. "He has died."

"What? I don't understand."

"He was killed in an accident." My mom sniffed as she cried on the other end of the phone.

She briefly explained what had happened and then we were off the phone. I looked down at Fili and Muse and remembered how when Aman was a toddler he always wanted to hold Fili. He was just seven years old and he was gone. I had to do something, but I did not know what. I finally just finished cleaning the kitchen and then played with Fili and Muse. I felt numb and confused.

About an hour after the call, Zeray and Rosina arrived. I told them the terrible news. It was decided that I would return for the funeral and Rosina would stay with the kids. It was hard for me to leave them. I trusted that Rosina would take good care of them, but after learning that Aman was gone Fili and Muse seemed so little and fragile.

Now I walked from the bus station toward my old house. It was almost six o'clock in the evening and I had to remember about the curfew. It was the curfew that was partly responsible for little Aman's death.

As I got to the turn for my house I saw the wall. It was big and it was in a crumpled mess. I could not believe that my little brother had been under that pile, and yet I could see it all play out in my head.

Aman was playing hide and seek with the neighbor kids. He hid against the damaged wall and the top part collapsed. He was pinned underneath and the kids started screaming for help. My mother heard the screams and ran to them. She found her son in the pile of rubble. She desperately tried to move the concrete, but it was too heavy. She screamed and begged for help and the neighbors heard her.

Together, they were able to pull the concrete off of Aman. "We have to get him to the hospital!" my mother said.

"It's too late," the neighbor said. "The curfew starts in less than an hour."

My mom hated it, but she knew he was right. If they left for the hospital they would not make it. The Ethiopian soldiers would catch them and shoot them all on the spot. They carried Aman into the house and put him into the bed.

My father was now there. He was in the fields when it happened and came running once he heard. Aman was in and out of consciousness and he started vomiting blood. The pupil of his left eye was dilated very big and his other pupil was small. He slurred his words and did not have control of his body.

He was in terrible pain and my mother and father had to sit by his bed and watch. The night wore on and they comforted him and held him and did everything they could to keep him well. If they could just make it to six in the morning then the stupid curfew would be over and they could get Aman to the hospital.

But they did not make it. At four in the morning my little brother took his last painful breath.

The funeral was horrible. Many people died in Eritrea, but this was a little boy who was not involved in the war. His death was so unexpected and my papa was in terrible shape. I could not ever remember seeing him cry, but now he cried each day.

After the funeral he remained at the cemetery for many hours. He stared down at the freshly upturned dirt that now held Aman. Every day after that for the next year he returned to the cemetery and cried over his grave.

I stayed for a while to help my family get through the terrible loss. I called back to Ethiopia as often as I could and sometimes I got to talk to Fili and Muse. I loved hearing their voices and I longed to see them again. Rosina told me that everything was fine and she was taking good care of them. I was sure this was true, but I wanted to hold them again so badly.

If I'd had any idea about what was really going on back home in Addis Ababa I would have been on the first bus back there, but looking back on that time I don't know how I could have known.

Chapter 29

It was terribly hard leaving my family behind, but I was excited to get back home to see Fili and Muse. On the bus ride to Ethiopia we were stopped at a checkpoint. My hands shook slightly as I showed my papers, not because I was in the wrong, but because it was scary to think that my life was in the soldiers' hands.

Two men on the bus were yanked off. They tried to protest, but the soldiers said they were the men that they had been looking for. The bus drove away, and a few seconds later we all heard the gunfire. I was sure that those two men were now dead, and it was another eye-opening reminder of how fragile life is, whether you are a seven-year-old little boy playing hide and seek or grown men riding a bus.

Upon arriving, I had a short walk through the bustling Addis Ababa. I kept a fast pace because I couldn't wait to get home. Finally, I arrived. I threw open the door and found Fili and Muse playing on the floor. They saw me and jumped up to give me the biggest hugs. At that moment I felt happier and more loved than maybe I ever had in my life.

Rosina, on the other hand, didn't really seem so excited to see me. I guessed after being saddled with watching four kids for a long stretch she was ready to have her break from them. That first night she went out with Zeray to drink. I did not get it. Zeray treated Rosina differently than he treated me. He acted as if she was more of his equal, not a servant.

I quickly settled back into my routine of taking care of the kids and house and struggling to do things that would please Zeray so he would not beat me. One morning, I mentioned to Zeray that it would be nice if some of my other family members could visit us. He got furious. "They are nothing but whores. I don't want them to come here."

I put my head down. "They are not."

I didn't even see it coming. The mug of scalding hot tea hit my shoulder and the liquid splashed all over my face. I screamed in pain and jumped up to find water to soothe the burning. Rosina was in the kitchen, and being always so quiet she just handed me a wet dish towel and looked on with a strange curiousness.

Fili and Muse, however, broke into tears. They had been playing on the floor and they were used to the outbursts, but this one with Zeray throwing hot liquid at me was so sudden.

"Get them out of here. You know I don't deal with this crying," Zeray yelled.

It was my job to keep the kids quiet, and when they were not Zeray made me take them outside. I had not had to worry about this as much lately since Fili and Muse were four and three years old. Now though, I grabbed them by the hand and took them outside while my face still burned as if it was on fire. Zeray could throw hot liquids on me and beat me all he wanted, but I did not want him to lay his hands on my kids.

After Zeray had left for the day I was in the kitchen. I'd put some ointment on my face and it had red marks that glistened. Rosina sat at the table. She had not really said anything since the attack and I was surprised when she spoke.

"Do you know why Zeray treats you that way?"

I stopped cleaning and turned to her. "Yes, because he is an evil man."

Rosina shook her head back and forth slightly. "It is because you let him. You are weak, Abeba."

I did not know what to say.

"It is true," Rosina continued. "He can do whatever he wishes to you because you are not strong."

"He is a bad man," I said.

"Maybe so, but he beats on you because you let him. I don't know why you stay."

I turned back and started cleaning. I didn't want to hear any more because deep down I believed it was true. I thought of leaving Zeray every day and how my life could be without him, but then I thought of my kids. He would not let me have them. Their fragile lives would be in his hands and I could not bear this. They were my babies and I loved them so much. I would endure the hateful words and the beatings if it meant keeping my kids.

Rosina broke into my thoughts. "Anyway, I am going to leave soon to go back to Eritrea."

"Because you cannot stand the way Zeray acts?"

"No, I'm pregnant."

"Pregnant! Who is the father? I did not know you were even seeing a man."

"He is a man I met through Zeray. I don't really like him that much and he will not help with the baby."

"So you are going home?"

"Yes, I won't be any good to you here while I'm pregnant."

I could not believe what I was hearing. I thought of what Zeray had said earlier in the morning about my family being whores. I did not think of my sister this way, but I could not deny what she just told me. Then again, there is no telling if it was really what she wanted. Maybe she was not so strong either and this was forced upon her and that is why she was leaving.

I did not know the answer, but a few days later she climbed aboard a bus and was gone. It would have been good if it was the last time she set foot in our house in Addis Ababa, but it was not.

Chapter 30

I had done my very best to keep up with the birth control. Sometimes I missed a couple weeks or a month here or there because I couldn't get to the clinic or I did not quite have enough money. My cousin, Samuel, still helped me out when he could. I think he felt bad for kicking us out and he was a good man.

For almost four years now I had struggled along through Zeray's beatings and his bed and I had not gotten pregnant again. It was because of the pills, I was sure of it.

I thought back to when I first got to Ethiopia and Zeray beat me and called me names all the time. Back then I thought of killing myself. I could end it all and he would have nobody to hurt. But then I thought of Fili. He was just a baby and I was the only one who would protect him. I could not leave him. After all these years I did not think of ending my own life. Instead, I thought of ending my current life for a better one, but still I did not have any idea how to do this.

One night while Zeray was out drinking, I called Samuel. I'd made friends with a couple of the neighbors despite Zeray not wanting me to talk with them, but I wanted to hear the voice of my cousin. We talked for a while about our family and he told me that he heard Rosina and her new baby were doing well. I remembered the time when I was back home with Fili. It was so nice and I envied Rosina for being able to be there now.

"Samuel, since you are an attorney do you know any people who could help me if I ever needed to leave here?"

"You mean help you to find a place for you to live?"

"No, I mean help me leave Ethiopia all together and go back home with Fili and Muse."

Samuel sucked in some air between his lips and it sounded like a soft hiss through the crackly phone line. "I may know of some people, but it would take a lot of work to make it happen. Are you really thinking of leaving Zeray?"

I asked him because I must really be considering it, but at the same time I could not see it becoming reality. "No Samuel, I am not thinking of leaving him now. I'm just curious to see if it would be possible. I do not want to put you in any danger."

"I am family, Abeba. I will help you if you need."

"Thank you, Samuel. I will always keep that in mind. You are very kind."

We talked a little longer, and then he had to meet with some important client. I hung up the phone and felt a little better. I had taken a tiny step toward taking back my life. It did not move me forward physically, but it helped to shift my thinking. I was reminded of that night in Zeray's village when I learned I was pregnant with Fili. That night I was on the verge of telling Zeray that I was leaving him. That night I had felt strong.

I kept that conversation with Samuel with me as the days and weeks passed. Some days Zeray was normal like a husband and father, other days he was a monster. Winta was now old enough to be out and about on her own fairly often. I was thankful for that, but every chance she got she made life miserable for me. Kibrom, on the other hand, was still a sweet boy. I thought of how it may one day be possible to leave with Fili and Muse. I wondered if Zeray would even care. He had his kids with him and they were now older.

I felt as if I was slowly gaining the courage to go, but then one morning I woke up with a queasy feeling in my stomach. While making breakfast I had to run outside and throw up. Maybe I was just sick with a virus? Maybe I had eaten something bad? But deep down I knew this was not the case. I had missed a few weeks of my birth control pills not long ago because the clinic I went to had a fire. Samuel helped me find a new clinic, but now I realized that it was too late.

I was pregnant. I knew it. I was going to bring another baby into this horrible house and the courage to escape had slipped back into the corners of my soul.

Chapter 31

It was so hard to believe that this was my life. I knew that many other women were suffering just like me, but it just didn't make sense how I had fallen into this without as much as a whisper of protest. My spirit was gone. It was unfair to bring another baby into my life.

Of course when my belly started growing Fili and Muse had a hundred questions. They were excited and looked forward to having a little brother or sister. Zeray was indifferent. He did not beat me near as much, but he still called a few times a day and stopped by the house to check on me. It was like he was my prison guard.

One afternoon our sheep had gotten loose from the side of the house. I was having trouble tying it back up and my neighbor's brother noticed. He came across our little yard with a big smile on his face. "Can I help you with that?"

"Sure," I said. "As you can see I do not know what I am doing."

He started to tie it back up and it was nice to have a man doing something for me. It made me smile and I told him how much I appreciated it.

"It is nothing," he was saying, "I do not mind helping."

And then Zeray appeared.

"What the hell is going on?"

"He is just helping me," I said.

Zeray looked at the man with fire in his eyes. "Get out of here."

"But I was just helping with the –"

"I do not care." Zeray stepped forward.

"It's okay," I said. "You must leave now."

The man looked at me and then at Zeray. Finally, he walked away with an angry look on his face.

"What was that? You are a whore Abeba. You are sleeping with him aren't you?"

"That is ridiculous. He was just being nice."

"Shut up and get inside the house. You see why I check on you. You're a filthy whore."

The words didn't even hurt me, but I feared what would come after the words.

He left for the rest of the day, but I knew he would come home drunk, and I thought of hiding until he passed out like we did when we were kids. Instead, I decided that I was not a kid anymore.

Well after Fili and Muse were asleep, Zeray staggered through the door.

I had hoped that he would be too drunk to remember what happened earlier in the day. I was not so lucky.

"You whore, where are you hiding?" Zeray slurred.

I swung my feet out of the bed and stood. "I am pregnant Zeray. I have to sleep."

I hoped this would slow him down, but before I even had a chance to flinch there was a stinging crack on the side of my leg. I cried out and stumbled onto the bed. He raised his hand up high and I saw that he was holding his belt.

I curled up and turned away just as the belt slapped into my leg. It felt as if I had been attacked by fire ants. Before my cry of pain was finished, the belt landed again, this time on my right knee.

"Zeray, stop it. I'm pregnant!" I screamed between gasping cries.

He did not hear or did not care. The next lash landed on the back of my leg. It hurt the worst of all and I couldn't even scream any more. There was another lash and then another on the same spot.

"This is what you get for being with that idiot neighbor. You are mine!"

I rolled off the bed and crawled toward the table. There was another thrashing on my back, and then another on my leg just above my foot. I barely felt it. I pushed a chair out of the way and rolled onto my side under the table. It was a pathetic barrier, but it was all I had.

"Please Zeray, please. You are hurting the baby. I'll never even talk to him again."

Zeray brought the belt down onto the table and it sounded like an explosion.

"Damn right," he said.

I pushed my back into the wall. "Please God, please help me. Please give me strength," I said.

I heard Zeray walk away. A door slammed and he was gone. A moment later Fili and Muse crawled under the table. They had been cowering in the corner. They hugged me and we all cried together.

The horrible red and purple and black welts were almost healed when I gave birth to Hannah. My first daughter had to be the most beautiful baby on the entire Earth.

Chapter 32

I lay in my bed on my side while nursing Hannah. My back held a steady ache, but I was used to it. Rosina, my half-sister, was in the bed across the room. She had been back for about a week now. During that time I had hugged her and told her how sorry I was. She was dealing with her own terrible tragedy. Her baby had died suddenly and mysteriously. Nobody knew exactly what happened. One night he just stopped breathing.

She had come back to stay with us to get away from Eritrea. She wanted to help out once again and I needed it, especially with the recent arrival of Hannah. As I breastfed my baby girl I could not imagine the pain Rosina must be going through. Losing my baby would break me, I was sure of it. I would not be able to continue with my miserable existence because my kids were the only reason I kept on.

It got very late and I was starting to drift off to sleep when I thought I heard Zeray come in. There was movement and some rustling noises, but in my half-sleep state I didn't really comprehend anything. Then I reached down to put my hand on Hannah. She was still and sleeping in the darkness. She had fallen asleep while breastfeeding. I scooted away and covered myself.

I stayed there and lightly stroked her tiny back. She was so soft and sweet and innocent. I was thankful that she had no idea what the world was really like. Now that I was becoming more awake I noticed that Zeray did not come in. My eyes had adjusted to the dark and he wasn't in the room. I looked at Rosina's bed and saw that her sheets were pushed back. She was not in bed either.

I realized that it must have been her who had gotten up in the night. Zeray was apparently not back from his drinking. I looked at a clock. It was one in the morning. I wondered where she could be and started to worry. Maybe she was like me and she decided she could not go on after the loss of her baby, or maybe she was doing something foolish or dangerous.

I slipped the blanket off of me and tucked it around Hannah so she would not fall. I swung my feet off the bed and got a chill when they touched the cool floor. I walked to the bedroom where Fili and Muse and Kibrom were asleep. Rosina was not there.

Now I was fully awake and I opened the front door. The night was starless and dark, but I could see because there was a thin line of light coming from the outdoor toilet. I looked around the yard. All was still, so I began to make the short walk toward the toilet.

I was about to call for Rosina when the door creaked open.

The light from inside left a long rectangle on the yard, and Zeray stood in the middle of it. He had a lit cigarette between his lips and he was zipping up his pants. Rosina stood just behind him. Her hair was a mess and she too was adjusting her clothing.

It was like a wave had crashed down on my head. My vision went blurry and I blinked hard. Sure enough, what I was seeing was true. I knew Zeray cheated on me, but this was my own sister! I flew across the yard in a rage fueled by complete betrayal.

"What the hell is this?" I yelled.

Zeray had a little smirk on his face as if he was a dog who was happy with himself despite getting caught digging in the trash. Rosina was not smirking at all. She looked shocked to have gotten caught.

"It is not what you think," Rosina said.

"It is not you having sex with my husband in my very own house?"

Rosina started to reply, but Zeray spoke. "It is my house."

I wanted to punch him on his smoke-stained teeth. He was the biggest bastard in the world. I saw my hands on his throat and I saw myself shoving that lit cigarette into his beady eyes. I saw him begging for mercy. All these visions slammed through my head and I was hot with anger.

Her baby, it was from him. I knew it. It seemed as if the world twisted sideways and I feared I would fall over and pass out. That is why she left, and who knew, maybe that is why her baby was no longer alive. This thought sickened me so much.

Rosina was saying something. The words were tumbling out of her ugly mouth, but they were a garbled jumble on my ears. I pushed by Zeray. He seemed to be a cross between confused and amused, but he held no shame. I remembered what Rosina had told me before she left. I shoved my finger toward her face. "Get out of here. I am not so weak that I won't kick you out. You are a whore. Get out! Get out! Get out!"

Her lips had stopped moving and she just looked at me with big fearful eyes. Zeray put his hand on my shoulder. I shrugged it off and shot a look at him. If he tried to hit me now I would fight back with every ounce of strength I could. I'd scratch him and bite him and do my best to rip off his testicles.

"Get your things," I said.

Zeray's hand was back on my shoulder. "Abeba, stop this. It is too late."

The alcohol smell leaked from his mouth and found my nose and I had to stop myself from punching his face. "Too late? It was not too late for you to put that in my sister." I thrust my finger toward his crotch.

His nose scrunched and his eyes narrowed, but he reined it back in, just a glimpse of his bubbling hatred because even he knew he was so wrong.

"Look Abeba, she will stay for a few hours until the sun comes up and then she will be gone."

I was instantly exhausted. My shock and fury was like a day in the sun with no water crammed into one moment. I just wanted them to go away and be gone from my life. I took a heavy breath. The anger that pulsed through me moments earlier drained and settled over my chest. I walked away. I was done.

Chapter 33

Fili and Muse played in the yard and Hannah was fast asleep while strapped to my back. I could feel her tiny weight against my neck and I watched as my boys laughed and wrestled with each other. I looked back at Samuel. I was at my cousin's house and I had just finished telling him what had happened the previous night.

He rubbed his temple with all four fingers of his right hand. It looked like he was trying to push the information into his head. "I knew Zeray was the devil," he finally said.

"So can you help me leave, Samuel? Can you get me back to Eritrea?"

"Maybe, I'll have to call in some favors. A lot is going on with the war right now. The Derg is launching another large attack against the People's Liberation Front, but there is also talk that the Soviets are beginning to consider withdrawing support for Ethiopia. There is a lot of movement and travel is dangerous."

I knew all of this. The Derg had launched many offensives against the Eritrean People's Liberation Front over the last handful of years and all of them had failed. The EPLF had withstood two civil wars with the Eritrean Liberation Front. The second had been going on just five years ago not long after I left Eritrea with Fili. The EPLF attacked the ELF when it learned that they were considering a treaty with the Soviets and Ethiopia. During this time Ethiopia was in the midst of its own civil war and the Mengistu-led Derg battled with its own rebels while millions died from hunger.

It was crazy. The Eritreans and Ethiopians were fighting each other and they were both fighting themselves as well. I was caught up in both the big war and my own little war. Now I did not know if what I was doing would be considered fighting or fleeing, but I knew that I had to do something.

"I do not care how dangerous the travel is," I said to Samuel. "I will get away from Zeray and he will not hurt me or my kids anymore."

"I understand, but the only way to make sure you can go safely is by military plane. It will not be easy and I do not know if they will allow the children."

I felt as if my fighting spirit had been sucked from my mouth. "The children have to go. You know this, Samuel."

"I do. Abeba, I am so glad you are leaving. Do not worry. I will do everything in my power to make this happen. I will just have to make a lot of calls.

"Thank you," I said. "Speaking of calls, do you mind if I call my mother?"

"Please," Samuel said, "I will play with the kids."

A moment later I listened to the static in the line and wondered if my mother would pick up. After many rings there was a clicking sound. "Hello," she said. Her voice echoed slightly.

"Momma, I'm so glad I reached you." Instantly I felt as if I might cry.

"What is it Abeba, is everything alright?"

"The kids and I are fine, Momma. It's Zeray and Rosina."

Over the next couple minutes she listened as I dropped the story into her lap. Finally, I finished. There was a silence on the other end. "Momma, are you still there?"

"Yes, I'm here. Now that I know this I realize that Rosina's baby did look like Zeray."

This made me feel as if I had been stabbed in the stomach.

"You know, Abeba," my momma continued, "you cannot tell anybody about this, especially none of the family.

Now the knife was being twisted. "Why not? Zeray is a terrible man and Rosina is a backstabbing whore."

"He is just that, a man. It is what he will do. It is not right, but nobody can know about this, nobody in the family at all. It will bring shame."

I could not process the words. I looked out the window to where Samuel was playing with Fili and Muse. He already knew. If I were to follow my momma's wishes I would have to tell him to stay quiet as well. He would do as I wished because he was a decent and caring man.

After my momma, I talked to my papa. I told him that it was time for me to leave Zeray. "He is abusing me all the time and he is a terrible man. I just want you to come get me." A single tear slid down my cheek before I even realized it was there. I did not give my papa time to say anything. "Samuel will help me, but if it does not work can you come get me, Papa, please?"

I knew it was an unfair request considering all of the fighting that was going on between the hundreds of kilometers that stretched between my village and Addis Ababa, but Zeray would never sign to let me go. There was silence on the other end of the line.

"Do not worry about it, Papa. I will make it. I am not weak."

Those last four words were probably more for me than they were for him, and I did not know if I believed them or not. It did not matter though, I was doing this. I was leaving this hell behind and I was taking my babies with me.

Chapter 34

Addis Ababa is like a giant beast waking up each morning. It stretches and yawns and then growls at the world. I quickly walked through the growling city and realized that this was the last time I would wake up here.

My friend from around the corner was holding all the papers that I would need for the flight. I had received them just three days earlier and considered keeping them in the house like I had done with the birth control pills, but I did not want to risk it.

It was still early morning when I walked back to my house with the papers safely tucked inside a small pouch that rested on my hip. The papers allowed room for me and one other. Samuel apologized over and over when he gave them to me. He knew I was desperate to take all my children. I had cried at first and told him that there was no way I could go. Finally, though, I came to a realization that Samuel had done everything he could to get me home, and me plus one of my babies was the best he could do.

Of course I had no intention of leaving any of them behind. I would take them all and beg for leniency as I boarded the back of the military plane. I knew that Samuel had called in favors and paid money on top of those favors, and I hoped that the soldiers would recognize this. After all, my kids were not big and we would not take up much space.

I had a strange feeling of euphoria mixed with sadness as I made breakfast that morning. A stream of sunlight slanted into the room and dust seemed to dance on it. It was dirty but beautiful, much like my life. Now I had to get my beautiful kids away so they could flourish.

We ate breakfast and I talked with my kids. I had a small bag under the bed and I'd packed some of Fili and Muse's favorite toys in it the night before. The flight was at noon. I needed to leave within the hour and I hoped Zeray came home to check on me before then. Once he left he would not come back for some time.

Winta was there. She was now 17 years old and she did not spend much time at our house. I did not want her there, but sometimes she showed up. She was her usual snotty self. I was glad that I would not have to put up with her for much longer.

As I cleaned the plates, Zeray came through the door. "What are you doing?" he asked.

"The dishes, Zeray."

He had become like a dog guarding his bone after I caught him with Rosina and then asked for a divorce. He turned me down and then watched me as if I was a criminal plotting my escape.

He ate a piece of bread and then sat down with a paper. I did not know how he got any work done with all this checking on me. I looked at the clock. It was almost ten in the morning and I would have a long trip to the airplane.

"Are you not going back to work?" I asked in as relaxed voice as I could muster.

"I do not have much to do today," Zeray said.

My heart quickened. I could not have him here. There would be no escape if he remained. Then I had an idea. "I have to go to the store for some groceries. I will take the kids so you do not have to deal with them."

He lowered his paper and looked me up and down. "The boys are playing outside, just take Hannah," he said.

"I do not mind. Muse loves going to the store."

"The boys can stay here," Zeray said sternly.

This was it. I had to go now. As Zeray read, I glanced at the bag with Fili and Muse's toys. It rested under the bed, but it was visible. I wondered if I could grab it before pretending to go to the store. Finally, I decided it was not worth the risk.

I strapped Hannah to my back and walked out the door. Fili and Muse were playing in the dirt and I looked at my boys. They were so sweet and I loved them so much. "Where are you going, Momma?" Muse asked.

"To the store."

"I want to go. I want go," Muse said.

"No, you stay here," I said.

My plan was to walk away as if I was gone so Zeray would relax, and then I would come back a moment later and grab Fili and Muse.

"But Momma, I like the store," Muse said.

"I know. I will be right back for you." My eyes watered, and this triggered Fili.

"Momma, will you be right back?" It was like he knew this was more than a trip to the store.

"I will. I love you."

I turned and walked down to the corner of the busy street. Once there, I pivoted and walked back to our house. I looked around the corner. Fili and Muse were still in the yard and they were back to playing. I tried to get their attention but they did not hear me. I stepped around the corner and felt naked. Our doorway was just ten meters away and the window next to it was wide open.

"Fili, Muse," I whispered urgently.

Both of them looked up at me. "Come on," I beckoned with my hand.

"I thought you were at the store, Momma," Muse said.

I put my finger to my lips, "Shhh!"

Fili took a step toward me, Muse followed. We were so close! But then the house door was flung open and I saw Zeray. He had a wild look on his face and he was holding the bag of toys. "What is this?" he yelled.

My eyes went from him to my babies. They had stopped walking toward me and Zeray yelled at them to get in the house. They hung there between us, unsure of what to do. Tears filled Fili's eyes when Zeray yelled at him again and then strode towards us. "Get inside, now!"

Fili and Muse turned toward the house. I stood by the street just steps away from freedom. I had Hannah on my back and Zeray's face turned into a mass of rage as he truly figured out that this was my escape attempt.

The plane awaited, and Samuel had done everything he could to get me on it. This was my only chance. I had no other choice. I looked at my beautiful boys one last time. "I love you!" I screamed. Then I turned and ran.

Zeray immediately gave chase, but I had already mapped out my route. After just ten steps through the crowded street I made a quick left between two buildings and then a right. I went through a narrow passageway and heard Zeray yell my name. He was not far behind.

The passageway opened onto another busy street and I turned left. The people were thick here and I knew I had to blend in because I would never outrun Zeray. There was a shop with an alcove leading to its wooden door. I slipped into it and waited.

Before I could catch my breath, Zeray raced past me. I watched as his eyes searched the crowded street. As soon as he was by I left the alcove and walked into the traffic. The cars moved slowly because there were so many of them. I weaved my way until I reached the other side. After fifty meters I found the taxi stand. I slipped into the back seat thankful that Samuel had given me one hundred birr, and told the driver where I needed to go.

He pulled away into the growling city of Addis Ababa.

I had left Zeray behind. But I left my babies behind as well.

Chapter 35

My blue and white taxi got swallowed up with the other taxis on the busy street. There was no way Zeray could find me now, yet I still looked behind me. Of course he was not there. Hannah had started to cry. I was sure all of the jostling from the running was not good for her. I put a cloth over her and gave her my breast. She slowly quieted down.

I stared out the window as the waves of people and cars slid by us. My body felt tired and my thoughts were split in two between happy and heartbroken. I was away from Zeray. I had finally had the courage to leave the abusive bastard. Then I thought of Fili and Muse. Zeray was probably just arriving back at the house now. I feared he would take his anger out on my boys. They were little and innocent and now I was not there to protect them.

I leaned forward in my seat. I had to tell the driver to turn around. The flight was my salvation, but I couldn't accept it while knowing that Fili and Muse were not safe. Besides, Zeray wasn't always bad. He didn't always beat me and he didn't hit the kids. Sometimes he was friendly and he played with them and sometimes he was nice to me. Even though he didn't show it in the right way, he had to care a great deal about me. Why else would he be so possessive?

I opened my mouth to tell the driver to go back. It was the right thing to do. But no words came out. Instead I sat back against the seat. I closed my eyes and slowly raised my hands and pointed my palms toward the sky. "Dear Father, guide me, tell me what to do. I can only get through this with you," I whispered.

I kept my eyes closed and waited for something, anything, to happen. God would give me a sign about what to do, go back or go forward. My body was so heavy and I could feel the connection with Hannah as she rhythmically brought out my milk. The sign would come. I knew it.

The taxi braked and turned and I opened my eyes. I was surprised to see that we were at the airport. Had I drifted to sleep? I had received nothing to guide me and yet here I was. It seemed that the final decision was made without me even recognizing it. Hannah and I were leaving.

My instructions were to find a gate along the north end of the airport. I walked toward it with my papers in my hand. Two unfriendly-looking guards stood at the gate and each had a machine gun draped across their shoulder. They looked mean in their brown camouflaged uniforms and helmets. As I got closer, their stances seemed to subtly change and they grew more alert.

"Hello, I am Abeba Habtu. I have papers and I was sent by Samuel, my cousin."

Neither of the men acknowledged that they heard me. I slowed my approach and held the papers out in front of me. "I am supposed to come to this gate for the military flight at noon."

This time, one of the men stepped forward. The other adjusted his gun and I thought of how so many people in Eritrea and Ethiopia had been gunned down in the last two and a half decades. I hoped that Hannah and I would not be the latest to be given the bullet.

"Here, these are my papers." I was now just five steps away.

"Stop there," the man who stepped forward said.

I stopped. The soldier approached. He grabbed the papers from my hand and looked them over. "Where are you going? What flight?"

"I am going to Asmara. I was just told it was the flight that left at noon."

The soldier walked over to his partner and showed him the papers. They talked quietly for a moment and then went to a little shack next to the gate. The man who took my papers picked up an old brown phone. He spoke, but I could not hear.

The second soldier approached me. "I need to search you. Raise your arms."

I did as he asked and he rubbed his hands over my shoulders and arms and down my sides and my legs on the outside and then back up on the inside. He reached around and felt behind my back and wrapped his hands around to the front. "What is in the bag?" he asked.

I opened the small bag that was attached to my hip. He spent a few seconds looking through it.

The soldier who was on the phone came out of the shack. "Okay, he said. "Walk to that building over there and you will be taken to the plane."

"Thank you," I said.

He opened the gate and I started to walk. The day had grown hot and little pellets of sand blew along the ground and slapped against my ankles. This was it. There was no turning back now. I felt as if I was drifting in some kind of dream. A jeep picked me up before I even got to the building that the soldier told me to walk to.

It drove for a half a kilometer up to a big gray plane with four large spinning propellers. The whining sound it made reminded me of the bombs from the planes when I walked to Zeray's village. I had never been inside a plane and I became filled with dread. I would soon be many kilometers above the Earth with nothing really holding me up.

I showed my papers to another soldier and he walked me up a set of stairs into the door at the back of the plane. I ducked through the door to find a pile of green bags and a line of crates. I had no idea what was in any of them and I did not want to know. The soldier showed me to a tiny seat behind the crates. "Here, do not get up from this seat," he said.

I sat down and looked through a tiny rectangular window. It made the outside world look distorted. Hannah had finished eating and had fallen back asleep. I held her in my arms and thought of what Fili and Muse were doing at that moment.

The plane began to move. I closed my eyes tight. We bounced along and I reached up to grab a strap that hung from the ceiling. Then it felt as if my stomach dropped and we were in the air. I looked outside and saw the buildings of Addis Ababa grow smaller and smaller.

I was free, but my boys were down there somewhere in that maze of buildings. I held Hannah tight as streams of tears fell silently from my eyes.

Chapter 36

Germany 2011

I slid my fingers back and forth along the thin scar on my neck. The surgery to remove my thyroid was a week earlier. It was a success. I guessed it may be of help to stop the spread of the cancer, but it did nothing to help with the pain in my back and hip, and my neck was now very stiff and sore as well.

Sahra came back into the room. "How do you feel?" she asked.

"I am fine, just hungry for something besides this hospital food." I pointed to my IV. "I'd even eat a bowl of sauerkraut right now."

This made Sahra smile. "I do not believe it."

Moments earlier she had been the translator between the doctor and me. My back was in a very bad way. I was to be fitted with some kind of brace that would make it where I would be unable to move. It would be this way for about one week until I had surgery. "It is your spinal column," Sahra had translated to me. "It has been eaten through by the disease and you are on the verge of being paralyzed."

My body felt so weak. The thyroid surgery had exhausted me and I was still unable to eat solid foods. The best I had done was vanilla pudding. The thought of another surgery so soon worried me greatly. It was like I could just feel that my body was ready to shut down even though my spirit still held some fight.

I remembered that terrible day back in 1998, when we were forced to leave Ethiopia. The bus we were on was packed with refugees and it stumbled and groaned along the road until finally it just shuddered and came to a stop. We were just two kilometers from our port and they made us pile off and walk the rest of the way through the cold darkness.

Back then, it was my spirit that felt broken, and yet I somehow kept on. I had to be brave now and do my best to make my spirit lift up my body. Hannah always talks about the power of positive thinking and how it is really that our thoughts shape our world, not that our world shapes our thoughts.

I tried my best to use this concept as each day passed and I got closer to the surgery on my spine. The doctor had told me that without the surgery, I would be unable to walk, and with the surgery there was still a chance that I would have to be in a wheelchair. Over and over I told myself that I would be fine and I pictured myself walking on my own two legs.

Then I took it a step further. I pictured having Selemon and Michael and John with me here in Berlin even though they were thousands of kilometers away and stuck in Sudan. In my imagination they would get away from there soon. I saw them smiling and laughing as we all hugged at the airport. And finally I thought of little Fili. He was not so little anymore, and I saw him safe and sound in Ethiopia and raising a family.

I did my best to keep all these positive thoughts with me even as the doctor wheeled me into the surgery room. "We will be right here for you," Hannah said. "The surgery will go perfectly."

I was groggy from the medication and her voice had a hollow sound, but I was still able to squeeze her hand. "I know you are right," I said.

A moment later I was in the room where I had been just two weeks earlier. The doctor stuck the needle into my arm and I heard the countdown, "zehn, neun, acht, sieben, sechs..." The light faded and my eyes began to close. My last conscious thought was of the rough landing of the military plane some 25 years earlier.

Chapter 37

Eritrea

They were there, just around the corner. I could not even remember who told me, but I felt it with every inch of my soul that Fili and Muse were in that building. I ran toward it as fast as I could and wished I could go faster.

Finally, I was there. I slammed into the large metal door and it bent inward, but did not break. There was the faintest sound from inside. It was Fili's voice! I slammed into the door again and it busted open.

It was as if the sun had erupted in the room. I squinted against the light and called for my baby boys. "Fili, Muse! Momma is here."

I heard Muse this time. I ran into my blindness and called their names over and over. The light dulled and I saw them in a courtyard much like the one back at the home I had left in Ethiopia. They were on their knees, but they weren't playing. Instead they scrubbed into the dirt with their bare hands.

A woman stood over them. She wore a wicked smile. As soon as she saw that I saw her she brought her hand down at my boys. The piece of metal she was holding lashed into Fili first, and then Muse.

I moved toward them, but it was like being in mud. Then I heard a laugh. In the shadows I saw Zeray. He smoked an impossibly large cigarette and a chimney's worth of smoke bellowed from it. In between laughs, he said, "Hit them harder."

"No!" I yelled, and then I was sitting in a dark room. I could not catch my breath and my body was sweating. For a moment my head felt twisted. Where was I? And then my world came back to me. I was on the floor asleep in my old house. I brought my knees up to my chest and stared into the darkness of the room. I knew I would not sleep the rest of the night.

I had been having these terrible dreams since arriving in Eritrea a few weeks earlier. When I boarded that military plane to fly away from Ethiopia my body had broken away from Zeray, but my spirit was back in Addis Ababa with my kids.

My mother said I would get along better as time went. I did not see how this could be possible, and if the dreams along with my every waking thought were any indication, I was not getting over anything. I had tried to settle in and work around the farm. I took Hannah out in the fields and showed her the vegetables and I did some housework, but nothing could take my mind away from my kids.

Earlier, Zeray had called the house a couple of times. He begged my father and mother to talk to me. I told them I would not. Now though, if he called I felt I would have to talk with him just to find out about Fili and Muse.

At least I did not have to worry about dealing with Rosina. After I kicked her out of the house she ended up going to Assab, a port city at the southern tip of Eritrea. It had an oil refinery, but it was most known for its nightlife. Rosina got a job in a bar there and I figured she would find a man and be out of my life for good.

My mother had pulled me aside the day after my arrival. "Will you follow my advice? Will you keep what Rosina and Zeray did a secret? Please do not bring shame to the family?"

"Me bring the shame?" I stepped away from her. "It is not me who did the deed with one of my sister's husbands. It was Rosina. She has brought shame."

My mother saw that the anger bubbled in me. "I understand," she said calmly. "But nobody knows about this."

"Except for Samuel," I said.

"You told him?"

"Yes, before I told you. He helped save me many times."

"But he will tell others."

"No he won't. I asked him not to and Samuel will keep my wishes."

My mother did not respond for a moment. Instead she stood with her hands on her hips, thinking. "Will you keep it a secret, Abeba?"

Now it was I who did not respond. I was angry enough to want her concern to linger for a moment longer. "I will not say a word. It brings more shame to me than anybody else."

That was the end of our conversation about it, and the weeks since had carried a certain tenseness that had not been between my mother and me before. Really though, it did not bother me so much. Compared to being separated from my boys it was just a trivial matter. I was glad to wake up unworried about getting beaten up, but even Zeray's fists and belts were trivial when compared with leaving Fili and Muse.

Chapter 38

Being back home in Eritrea I heard so much of the awful stories about how so many people just like me, people who were not fighters, had been shot down to the ground. I saw the effects of the Napalm, the fiery gas that the Ethiopians had used on my people, when I bumped into two men in the village. Their bodies were disfigured with hideous scars. One of them had a scar from his hairline to his chin and the place where his left eye used to be was now an ugly pinkish patch that looked like it belonged on a pig knuckle.

I had also seen the burned fields and the dead cattle on the sides of the roads and the starving people begging for bread. I saw a village just 20 kilometers from mine that looked as if it had been stomped on by an angry giant.

I kept all these images with me. They sank to my soul and settled. It would be best to forget them, but for a reason I could not quite comprehend, I wanted them there. I did not need a reminder of the fragility or brutality or unfairness of this life in Africa. I had lived in the middle of it for most of my days.

It hit me one morning after being home for a couple months. I stood outside of our backyard kitchen in the blistering early-summer heat and turned my face to the heavens. All of these images and horrors were part of me because they were something of a compass. The horrors of my days side by side in the same soul that held so many beautiful moments showed me that things could be better, or things could be much worse.

I had been pulled through hell and I was going through it at that very moment, but how could I not be thankful. I was weaker than so many others, and yet I had been able to survive and even find moments of happiness. If I could do such a thing, others must be able to do it as well. I thought back to the man with the burned eye. He was in pain. His body was destroyed, but he had smiled at me.

That morning and those thoughts etched a tiny thread of hope into me. I would get through this. Fili and Muse would get along without me as well. It was not what I wanted, but it had to be.

Just an hour or so after these thoughts, a man came to our house. As he walked up the road I thought he looked familiar. And then I noticed it was my long lost friend, Tedros.

I ran toward him and we embraced in a strong hug. "My Goodness, Abeba, you look even more beautiful than you did before!" His whole face, even his eyes, seemed to smile as he spoke.

I had a rush of hotness to my cheeks. "You look well yourself, Tedros."

Moments later we sat at the table in our house and talked over cups of tea. Hannah was asleep next to me. "She is beautiful," Tedros said. "She looks just like you."

Again, I blushed.

Years earlier, I had worked with Tedros for a short time. He lived a ways away, but he always insisted on walking me home. He was a gentleman and I had liked him, but I was a girl back then. I never thought of him as being anything more than a friend. Now as he sat across from me I could see that he was very handsome.

"What are you doing here in Eritrea?" I asked.

"I'm visiting."

"But it is dangerous."

"Maybe, but I have to see my family. I am not staying long."

"I am glad you came by," I said. "So tell me, how are the United States?"

"They are more than I imagined. People are free and there is no war. There is money and jobs. People are either friendly or they leave you alone. I am not doing it justice. You must see it to believe it."

"Maybe one day I will be able to see it for myself," I said, even though I did not believe it.

A serious look crossed Tedros' face. "I want you to see it too. I want to take you there, you and Hannah." He reached across the table and placed his hand on mine.

I looked down at it. I knew that the hand on top of mine would never swing at my face or hurt me. "I, I don't know what to say."

"Say yes! We will be so happy there together. I have not been able to stop thinking about you for so many years now, Abeba. I should have been the one to ask for your hand. I was a fool."

"No, you were not. I was the one who made the mistake," I said.

"So say yes. We will fix our mistakes and be happy."

I felt as if I had been given a drug. My head swam with thoughts. They swirled around and I could barely keep track of them. This was a way out with a man who would care for me. It would keep Hannah safe. It would change our lives in an instant. This war with its bombs and guns and dead people and smashed villages and men with burned eyes and broken limbs would be thousands of kilometers behind me, but Fili and Muse would still be here in the middle of it with Zeray.

"This is so much to consider."

"I understand, but please think about it, Abeba. I know how wonderful life in America will be with you and Hannah."

He was right. I knew it. I had to do this for Hannah and for myself. It was a sudden and unexpected new beginning. I looked up at Tedros. His eyes were pleading with me to say yes, but there was no harshness in them. My lip trembled slightly and I bit down on it. I would go with him. I just had to get the words out of my mouth.

"I know we would be happy in America," I said.

A cautious smile spread across his face.

"I know it," I continued. "But I cannot go."

I did not even know where those last four words came from. The look of hurt and surprise on his face could only be matched by mine.

"I don't understand, Abeba."

"My boys are still with Zeray in Ethiopia. I have to stay here for them. I have to find a way to protect them."

For a while longer he tried to convince me otherwise, but now that I had said it I knew that it was the only way. Fili and Muse had trumped the freedom and safety of the United States and the love of a good man. On the one hand I could not believe that I was turning down this chance for Hannah and me, but on the other it made perfect sense.

With my rejection, Tedros had lost his aura of happiness. I tried to explain that it was not because of him at all. I think he understood. Finally, it was time for him to leave. He gave me a hug and then kissed my cheeks. His warm lips felt nice.

He walked away and I watched him go. Why couldn't Zeray even be a little bit like him? I sat down and poured another cup of tea. At that moment I felt so sorry for myself and my children. Why could I not have the life with Tedros? Why had I been given to Zeray?

The next morning I woke up with those very same thoughts in my head, and then while I was cleaning, the telephone rang. "Hello," I said.

"Hello, Abeba," the voice on the other end replied.

It was Zeray.

Chapter 39

My bags were packed and I waited at the table. Hannah was strapped to my back and my father was lingering in the house. I knew he had the fields to tend, but for some reason he had not disappeared into them. Zeray had begged and begged me to take him back. It did not take too long for me to give in because I had decided that I had to get back together with Fili and Muse.

It was almost mid-morning when Zeray knocked. My mother let him in. I looked him up and down. I had seen him just two months earlier, but he seemed older and more worn down.

"Would you like a drink?" my mother asked.

"A beer," Zeray replied.

My momma brought a beer for him and another for my father. He still sat next to me at the table, but he had not said a word.

"Hello, Abeba," Zeray said.

"Hello."

"I am glad you have decided to come back home. Fili and Muse miss you."

There was a pause and Zeray took a big swig of his bottle of beer.

"You'd better not touch her again." It was my father and his voice was harsh. I could not believe it. When I was younger he beat me with his own hands. Now he was trying to protect me.

Zeray seemed equally surprised and I saw a hotness roll through his face. He did not like being challenged. He glanced at me. "I will not." He took another swig. "I have learned a lesson."

The words must have tasted like vinegar to him. "You're damn right you won't," my father said.

This time Zeray's rolling anger went to his hand and he raised his bottle as if he was about to hit my father with it. My father pushed away from the table and stood. Zeray quickly composed himself.

"Thank you for the beer," he said. "Let's go Abeba."

I said my goodbyes, and once again I was gone. Zeray had a car waiting for us and it whisked us away to the airport. Obviously his work in politics was paying off. We did not talk much on the drive. He did not say he was sorry for all the beatings he had given me, nor did he act mad for me leaving him. I took this as a good sign, but I feared that his attitude would change before long, and I steadied myself to deal with his hand soon. If he hit me I would take it as long as it got my boys in my arms.

The plane ride was much less eventful than the military flight I had taken. We were back in Addis Ababa by evening time and Zeray had still not thrown any anger at me. In fact, he had remained almost apologetic. "I will try to change, Abeba," he said on the plane.

Now as the taxi exited the highway and slipped into the city traffic I began to get excited. I scooted to the edge of my seat and looked out the window. The streets became familiar and I could not believe I was about to see my boys.

"You are looking forward to this," Zeray said.

I turned to him. "Of course."

He put a crooked smile on his face and did not reply, so I turned back to the passing buildings.

After one more turn the taxi came to a stop. Across the street I could see the entrance to our house. I jumped out of the car and hustled through the slow-moving traffic while holding Hannah in my arms. The gate caught for a moment before breaking free. I remembered the crushing feelings of fear and sadness and desperation the last time I stood in this place. Now it all was washed away like day-old chalk on concrete.

I burst through the front door. "Fili, Muse," I said, as I scanned the room.

They were on the floor, playing. They stood up and both wore confused looks. "Momma?" Fili asked.

"Yes baby, it's me. I'm home!"

I dropped to my knees and hugged them tight. I had given up freedom and a new life in the United States with a caring man for this moment, and I knew it was the right choice. I had my boys back.

Chapter 40

It was late summer of 1985 when I returned, and I began to feel that my life was taking a positive turn. I was in my mid-twenties and Zeray was almost 40 years old. My leaving him had maybe helped him grow up because he said he would be nice and not hit me, and for the most part this was true.

Upon returning to Addis Ababa, Fili had asked me why I didn't love him and Muse. I told him that I loved them so much and I came back just for them.

"But Papa told us that you left because you didn't love us."

I hugged him. "That is not true. I love you both with all my heart."

For a while it seemed that he was not so sure, but he eventually came around.

Month after month I prepared for Zeray to change back to his old ways and start swinging his hands or belt at me, but it did not come. We had our rough patches and two times when he was very mean to me I went to stay at Samuel's house for a night. Both times Zeray apologized and I returned.

I became pregnant again and had another girl. I did not think it could be possible, but Sahra was just as beautiful as Hannah, who was now almost one and a half years old.

I had four children with Zeray: Fili, Muse, Hannah, and Sahra. I never would have thought this would be possible some five years ago because I figured I would leave Zeray or he would beat me to death. But here we were, our own little family in the Ethiopian capital doing what we could to carve out a life.

The horrible famine that had killed hundreds of thousands of Ethiopians had come to an end, but the war between the two countries still went on. The Ethiopians, with the backing of the Soviets, had tried many times to end it, but the Eritreans proved to be very resourceful and dragged the war out. I wanted it over so badly, and even though I lived in Ethiopia I wanted Eritrea to claim its independence. When that happened there would be true reason for celebration.

Right now though, the only celebrating I did came from watching my children grow and having a husband that could now just be considered as less than ideal, not a tyrant who beat me every chance he got.

For nearly two years Zeray had maintained his promise, and during that time I had gained courage. I had more self-worth and confidence. I had a purpose to live and did not have fear constantly running through my veins. Unfortunately, that was all about to come to an abrupt end.

Alganesch, my good friend and Godmother of my children, had invited us to a celebration for her brother's wedding. A couple weeks earlier I'd asked

Zeray if we could go. He could tell this meant a lot to me and he approved. Now it was Sunday morning, the day of the celebration, and I had my hair done nicely with extensions and I was very excited. It was not often we did something like this.

Zeray woke up after a hard night of drinking and looked at me as if I was somebody he had never seen before. At first I thought he was just surprised at how nice I looked, but then I realized that he had forgotten about the celebration. "Remember," I said, "today is the celebration for Alganesch's brother's wedding. It will be so much fun."

He looked me up and down. "We're not going," he said.

"I do not understand."

"What is there to understand? We're not going."

"But Zeray, why? You said we would go."

"Now I say we are not going," he said again.

"I have to. Alganesch and I have talked about it and she is very excited. I wish you would come, but if I don't at least go she will be very upset with me. I do not want that."

Zeray stepped closer to me and pointed his finger in my face. "I don't allow you to go. If you do I'm going to break your legs."

I crumpled down into the kitchen chair feeling defeated. We had been doing so well and now Zeray was threatening to hurt me. He did not say another word. Instead, he changed clothes and was gone. He could go wherever he wanted. He had no keeper who threatened him for wanting a simple thing. I sat there and felt so powerless. All of that self-worth and confidence had been pushed down in one instant.

For the next hour I sat and seethed about this unfairness. Finally, I made up my mind. To hell with Zeray! I would go to the party for a little bit and return before he came home. At around three o'clock in the afternoon I slipped out the door and hurried to the celebration.

Once there, I had a good time and Alganesch was happy to see me. However, Zeray's leg-breaking threat sat in the back of my mind. He usually did not come home until late at night, but I had a bad feeling. I left the reception area and found a phone in the hotel lobby. I called the house and talked to Kibrom. He confirmed my fear. Zeray had called home and asked Winta if I was there. Of course she gladly told him that I had gone to the wedding. Now Zeray was to be home any minute.

I left the celebration and ran home with my beautiful dress slapping against my legs and my extensions fluttering behind me. With each step my fear grew. By the time I arrived at my house my heart felt like it would explode. I turned the corner and prayed that I would not see Zeray's car, but there it was.

I stopped at the gate. I did not want to go in. Zeray had not hit me in so long. Maybe this time he would not hit me either. Maybe he would yell at me and call me a dirty whore and threaten me, but he would not lay his hands on me.

These thoughts could not get me to move, and then I saw little Hannah. She came into the courtyard to play. She sat in the dirt with one of her dolls. I stood and watched her for a moment. She was so sweet and innocent. Then she looked up and saw me.

"Momma, Momma," she said. "Momma home."

I did not move, and she turned toward the house. The door was halfway open and her little voice barely carried to my ears.

"Momma home, Momma outside," she announced to everyone.

Now I had no choice. It was time to face Zeray.

Chapter 41

I stood just inside the doorway and braced for the fury that I was sure Zeray would release. He did not do anything though. Instead, he just walked out the door. I knew he was going out to drink, and this time it felt different. It felt like old times when Zeray would return and put his fists on me.

I considered getting the kids and leaving for Samuel's house, but for some reason I decided to stay. Maybe I thought this was one final test, if Zeray did not hit me now then he had truly changed. Or maybe somewhere deep down I thought I deserved it for disobeying him. I put on a thick shirt and a thick sweater to prepare myself, and then I waited. It was almost one in the morning when Zeray finally stumbled home.

He locked the door and then glared at me. I just sat there on the bed, not knowing what to say or do. Zeray went to a drawer and flung it open. The contents made a rattling sound as he fished for something. After a moment, he turned around. My breath caught in my throat. He was holding some long and sharp scissors.

I kept my eyes locked on him and my hands in my lap. This would be my defense unless he started slashing me with the scissors. Then I would do everything I could to stay alive. I still held a sliver of hope that he would remember the last year and a half and do nothing.

I was not so lucky though. He slipped his fingers in the scissors and brought them close to my head. I remained still. He gripped my extensions and pulled hard. I winced, but did not cry out. I felt the scissors against my hair. Zeray cut and cut on my extensions. Tears began to well up in my eyes, but I did not give him the satisfaction of seeing them fall.

After my hair, he turned to the beautiful dress I had worn to the celebration. It was on a hook against the wall. He ripped it off the hook and started cutting it into pieces. I watched as the bright colors tumbled through the dimness and onto our floor.

"Why are you doing this?" I finally asked.

Zeray threw the dress down and slammed the scissors on a small table. He then ripped off his belt in one motion and swung the metal part at my back. It hit with a thud. He reared back and swung again. Despite the extra clothing, it still hurt.

I had taken it for too long. I reached for the belt and grabbed it. Zeray's face twisted with surprise. He tried to push me and I clawed at his arm. He abandoned the belt and swung his right hand at my face. He wore rings, I think on purpose so he could hurt me worse, and his ringed knuckles drove into me just above my left eye. My skin split wide open and blood poured into my eye.

I became like a wild animal. I had to get away from this bastard. I struggled and clawed at his eyes until I got to the window and flung it open. As I jumped through it I heard screaming, and then realized it was coming from me. I took five steps in the darkness.

I felt Zeray behind me. He gripped my remaining hair and yanked me to the dirt. He started kicking and stomping on me like he wanted to bury me right there.

I screamed and curled up in a ball as he stomped and stomped. I was sure this was the end. I took blow after blow and prayed to God that it would stop.

I was saved by a noise at our gate. Men's voices cut through my screams. Zeray stopped beating me and I realized it was the police. They had been to our house other times. They knew the situation and I guess my screams alerted them along with everybody else in the neighborhood.

They looked me over and said I'd have to go to the hospital. This made Zeray unhappy, but he followed their instructions.

At the hospital the doctor looked at the gash above my eye and the bruises on my face and body. I was going to need many stitches to fix my wound. The doctor was a slender older man and he had an air of confidence about him. After he surveyed my face he let his eyes fall on Zeray. "Who is this woman?"

"She is my wife," Zeray replied.

"And you did this?"

Zeray did not answer. He just looked toward his feet.

"Why would you do this?" The doctor raised his voice. "She is a human being like you and me."

Again Zeray was silent for a moment. The doctor kept his eyes locked on him. "She disobeyed me." Zeray mumbled.

The doctor shook his head in disgust and then turned to me. "Let's stitch you up and take care of you."

It felt good to have a man stand up for me, and it felt good to see a little bit of shame from my horrible husband. We did not get home from the hospital until five in the morning. My body ached and I curled up in bed next to Hannah and Sahra. Their warm bodies and soft breathing gave me a little bit of peace.

It had been so long since Zeray had hit me. It was like he stored it up for almost two years and unleashed it on me that night. I ached inside and out, but now the fact that I was with my kids and not dead made me feel grateful. Still though, I needed a miracle to happen, and thankfully one was not far away.

Chapter 42

After a couple hours of restless sleep I woke up with sore ribs, a splitting headache, and my eye throbbing with pain. I popped one of the pills the doctor gave me into my mouth. It was supposed to help with pain. I hoped it did its job.

I got the kids ready and fed them a quick breakfast. At eight in the morning I called Samuel and his friend and asked them to come get me. My cousin had been there so many times for me. I knew he was tired of this craziness between Zeray and me, he had told me to leave him many times, but he had always helped me in the past.

The kids were subdued. I think the shock of what happened last night and seeing me with my eye swollen and stitches in my head got to them. Fili asked me a hundred questions about getting the stitches. I tried my best to answer them casually.

Zeray woke up before the kids and I left. I'd desperately hoped he would stay asleep. "Where the hell are you going?" he asked.

"The kids and I are going over to my cousin's for a little bit."

"No, the kids can stay here," he said.

He must have thought that I would go if the kids were with me. Maybe he was right.

"So you are going to take care of Sahra? You will change her and feed her?"

He scratched his chin and yawned. "Take Sahra, but the others can stay. After all, you will be back later today, right?" He smirked, and I fought the urge to spit on his face.

I did not want to leave my kids with him, but I also needed to go to Samuel's to get away from Zeray for a little bit.

Sahra and I settled into my old room and I fell asleep for many hours that afternoon. When I woke, I called my father. I told him what happened and that this was it.

"I will come to you now," he said.

"It is too dangerous," I said. "I will be okay."

"I will be there in a day or two."

There was no use arguing. When my father made up his mind to do something he was going to do it.

Sure enough, the evening of the very next day he showed up at Samuel's house. In the meantime Zeray had called numerous times to apologize and beg for me to come back. He even showed up once but I would not open the door.

As soon as my father arrived, he talked with Samuel and his friend and then we all went to my house.

Fili and Muse were in the courtyard playing. They were both very happy to see me. Little Hannah was inside with Winta, and she too was happy. Zeray, he was not so happy. "What is this?" he asked as we walked through the door.

It was evening time and he was already drinking.

"You need to divorce my daughter," my father said.

"I told her I was sorry. It was just a one-time deal."

"Liar!" my father yelled. "You do this over and over."

Zeray's anger rolled through him again and I saw his fist, the same one that had cut me open, tighten around his beer bottle.

"You are a hypocrite," Zeray said. "You used to hit her too and now you are mad at me?"

My father's own anger boiled. He stepped forward. Zeray's eyes narrowed until he looked like a snake. His hand that was holding the bottle coiled, ready to strike.

"You shut up." My father stuck his finger into Zeray's face.

The bottle was brought up so quickly that I barely saw it. Beer spilled as Zeray brought it down toward my father's head. He raised his arms to protect himself, but before the bottle ever crashed into him Samuel stopped Zeray's arm. His friend rushed in too and pushed Zeray against the wall.

Hannah began to cry softly, breaking a tense silence. My father wiped beer off of his arm. "Divorce my daughter."

"I will not. She is my wife and you gave her to me."

"You are pathetic," my father said.

Zeray erupted against Samuel and his friend in an effort to break free. He growled and spit at my father and Samuel slammed his forearm into Zeray's neck. I could not take it. I ran out of the house and started yelling for the police. They knew us well and happened to be close by. A minute later they were there. Samuel and his friend released Zeray. He pushed them away and grabbed his now almost empty beer and took a drink.

My father and Zeray and the police went back and forth. It was obvious that Zeray would not budge. He had no desire to allow me to leave him. My father shook his head in disgust and backed away toward the door. I started to follow him, but I turned and scooped up Hannah. I hugged her tight. "I love you," I said. "I will be back soon."

I walked out the door and gave Fili and Muse hugs as well. Samuel and his friend stayed behind for a moment. We were already out the door and to the street by the time they caught up to us.

Back at Samuel's I noticed my father looked very tired. He was older now and the stress of the trip and the confrontation had drained him. "You and Sahra can still come home with me," he said.

"Thank you, Papa. I cannot leave my other children behind."

"Why can't you? Look at your face. Be smart, Abeba. We can come back for them soon."

"It would be too dangerous for us to go, and I would worry about my kids." I said feebly.

"It would be dangerous, but really that is just your excuse," he replied.

My father was probably right, and maybe I was being stupid, but I felt that I could not just leave Zeray. He would come back again. He would keep begging and I would still technically be married to him. I looked at Sahra and thought about the others. Fili, Muse, and Hannah were Zeray's kids too. I had said over and over again that this time I would leave him, and one time I actually did leave him, but I was too weak. Something inside of me kept me chained to Zeray even when he treated me badly and beat me.

The next morning my father left to go back to Eritrea. He was upset with me and I understood why. He had risked his safety to come save his daughter and I did not allow it.

That afternoon, I sat at the table sipping tea with Samuel. After the confrontation with Zeray he had been strangely distant. He was usually friendly and concerned for me, but now it seemed his compassion had run out.

He took a sip of his steaming tea and looked at me over the rim of his mug. He set it down and said, "I cannot do this anymore, Abeba. This back and forth with Zeray, these beatings, this trouble, either you divorce and leave him or you do not come back here."

I did not know what to say. Samuel had been my rescuer so many times, and now he could take no more. He continued. "Leave him or go back to him and take it and raise your kids. Obviously you must enjoy what he is doing."

The words stung so deeply. Of course I did not enjoy Zeray's beatings. Couldn't he see that I was just not strong enough to break free? I could not sleep that night. My thoughts churned through my brain. I should just leave and start over. I could even sneak back and try to get the kids and then go. My father was right, Samuel was right, and I had left Zeray before. I could do it again, and if I had all my kids with me I could be okay.

Deep down though, I felt that chain. For a long time after I returned Zeray had been a better man. He had not hurt me and had provided. He was making money and connections with his job in politics and he had begged me to return repeatedly over the last few days. This could very well just be a one-time deal. Before I drifted to sleep I knew that in the morning I would return to him.

When my eyes opened, my decision had not changed. I felt a great deal of shame as I packed up our things and returned home. I knew something had to be wrong with me. Here I was going right back to Zeray, right back to a hell I had longed to escape for many years.

Chapter 43

I had been back in the house for a week or so. We were right back into our daily routine. We acted as if the horrible incident had never happened. It had been this way for so long. Zeray would beat me and I would run away and he'd tell me he was sorry and beg me to return. Every time I eventually gave in and sickened myself for doing so.

The stitches had been removed. Now a pink line ran above my left eyebrow. It was tender to the touch, but other than that it did not hurt. My ribs had healed too, but I could not twist without pain shooting into my back.

I could not look at any of my neighbor friends. It was obvious that they did not want to look at me either. I was a blot on the landscape of the neighborhood. I was the woman who let her husband beat her over and over and still stayed. I am sure they wanted me to be stronger, but I was not.

Zeray was much nicer, however just like before he called to check on me three or four times a day and stopped by the house at least once. He did not have to worry about me going anywhere or spending time with my neighbor friends. It wasn't that they were unkind to me. It was just that I was too ashamed.

Still, he checked up on me. That is why I found it odd that it was already lunch time and he had not called or stopped by. I fed the kids and we played in the yard. By the middle of the afternoon I had still heard nothing from Zeray. I began to worry and I was angry at myself for doing so. Why should I care about him not checking in on me? I should be happy.

It wasn't until the evening time when the telephone rang. I was nursing Sahra so I awkwardly leaned over and plucked the receiver off of the base. "Hello," I said, expecting to hear Zeray's voice.

"Abeba?"

"Yes, this is Abeba?"

"Hello, I am one of Zeray's friends and I have important news for you."

I instantly became anxious. Was Zeray in trouble? Was he hurt, or even dead?

The man continued. "He has been arrested. He is in jail and you need to call a number I will give you."

"In jail? Why?"

"The Ethiopian government says he is working with the Eritreans under the table."

This was not a new thing. It was why he was detained years earlier and I thought it was probably true at the time. Zeray was a cruel and dangerous man. He was not above breaking the law to get what he needed, and he had been getting deeper and deeper into the politics.

"Is it serious? Will he be put in jail for a long time?"

"You will find out more when you call the number, but yes, it seems serious."

The man gave me the information and I hung up the phone. I sat and thought as I finished nursing Sahra. I had four kids of my own to raise and then there was Winta and Kibrom. I had no money for food or rent. I did not have access to any of Zeray's bank accounts and did not know how I would get by if he was locked away for any length of time.

Sahra started making a soft humming sound. This was her signal that she was getting tired and full. I gently sat her in the bed and then stood in the middle of the room. I turned a circle and raised my hands. It started slowly, but got faster with each second as I did a spontaneous little dance.

It was wrong for me to be happy that Zeray was with the Ethiopian police, and yet I could not help myself. The future may become very difficult, but there was one thing I knew for sure, he could not hit me from behind prison bars.

Chapter 44

Germany 2011

I awoke from my back surgery to a foggy room and distorted faces. The fog lifted and the faces came into view. There were two nurses standing over me and working on one thing or another. At first I could not remember what had happened, and then it came back. I'd had surgery on my spine.

There was no pain in my back. It felt as if I had been lying on a block of ice, it was tingly and numb. And then I realized that it was not just my back that was numb. I looked down my body and could see my legs underneath the thin sheet, but I could not feel them. It was like my body stopped at my waist.

I began to panic, and then had the idea to try to move my toes. If they wiggled I would be fine. I consciously told myself to wiggle them. I focused on the sheet that draped over them and waited to see it move...nothing.

I tried again. Still there was no movement. The panic swelled within me and I tried to tell the nurses. Of course I was not speaking German and they had no idea what I was saying. I knew this was a possibility, and now it had become a reality. I was paralyzed. My legs were useless.

The nurses worked for a moment longer and one of them did something to the needle that was stuck in the back of my hand. The room grew foggy once again and then there was darkness.

When I awoke again there was only one nurse. She was accompanied by my two daughters, Hannah and Sahra. Both of them had relieved looks on their faces. I did not feel relieved at all. I remembered that I was unable to feel my legs or move my toes.

In my head I told myself to wiggle. This time, my toes responded. The sheet that was covering them moved slightly. I also realized that I could feel my legs. They were numb, like my back was earlier, but they were there. I was no longer half of myself.

"How do you feel, Momma?" Hannah asked.

"My back and my legs feel funny. Earlier I could not move my toes."

"The surgery was very hard," Hannah said. "They were worried that you would not be able to walk, but now they say that you will regain feeling."

"Oh, that is good. I was so scared earlier."

"Remember how I said the surgery would go perfectly. It was a challenge, but it did go well," Hannah said. "You are going to be fine, Momma."

"We knew you would be okay," Sahra added. "This cancer won't get the best of you. You're too strong."

"Thank you," I replied. "I love you both."

The numbness in my back had faded, and now it felt as if a tennis ball was pushing into my spine. It hurt a little bit at first, and then quickly grew into an almost unbearable burning. I shifted in the bed and the burning scorched the entire backside of my body. I winced in pain.

"What is it, Momma?" Sahra asked.

"My back has started hurting so badly."

Sahra spoke to the nurse in German. She nodded and did something with the bag that dripped clear fluid into my veins. My daughter's beautiful faces seemed to fade away. I was asleep once again.

Chapter 45

Ethiopia

Being arrested in Ethiopia was not like being arrested in the United States or other parts of the western world. Zeray was guilty without any real trial and thrown into prison immediately. He had been in for two weeks.

I now walked toward the foreboding building to visit him. It had a mountain of a gray metal wall that was topped off with sharp wire. Beyond the wall there were two towers where guards stood with long guns. Beyond the towers I saw the top of a dirty building that looked as if it had sprung from the Earth.

It had been a long morning. I had to take a bus and then walk for a couple kilometers to get to the prison. Luckily, my only true friend, Hilina, was watching the kids. She lived right around the corner from us. Her husband, Jemal, was good friends with Zeray. I didn't understand this because Jemal was unlike Zeray. He was kind and friendly. He had a truck and delivered supplies throughout Addis Ababa and the surrounding area. He'd even given me money to get Zeray cigarettes and food. I spent a little more than half of the 80 birr and kept the rest. I would need to save as much money as possible to survive.

I approached the prison gate and a guard asked me what I was doing. "I'm here to see Zeray Habtu," I said.

A moment later I was inside the fence, but another large gate kept me from moving forward. Two guards searched me and my bag. It reminded me of the day I flew back to Eritrea with Hannah. Back then I was running from Zeray, and now I was going to him.

Finally I was allowed to enter. The air in the prison had a smell to it that seemed to leak from the walls. It was as if the trash needed to be taken out. I was directed to a small table in a windowless room. I sat there for a few minutes and tried not to fidget. I opened my bag and sat the cigarettes and bread on the table.

A creaking sound and then a loud clang came from the other side of the door, and then it swung open. Zeray wore dirty blue clothes and he had already lost some weight. His face carried a sickly look and his wrists were bound together by a chain. Underneath the chain his skin was raw and bloody. As he slowly approached, I noticed that his left ear was caked in blood and he took each step with great caution.

I didn't know what to say. I just stared at him with my eyes wide. I hated him for all he had done to me, and yet looking at this sad creature made me feel sorry for him.

He sat, and the guards left the room. "Hello, Abeba," he said.

"Hello, Zeray. I brought you cigarettes and bread. Jemal gave me money for it."

"Did you spend all the money?"

I was unsure how to answer. Did he expect me to save money or spend it all on him? "I kept a little bit of it," I finally said.

"Good, keep the money that is given to you. Save it up."

I just nodded in response as I slid the box of cigarettes across the uneven table.

"What have they done to you?"

"They beat me and try to get me to say I am working with the Eritreans. They want me to tell them who I work with."

"What do you say?"

"I say nothing. I am innocent."

I did not know for sure, but I highly doubted this was true. However, I let it go.

"Why is it hard for you to walk?"

"They beat the bottom of my feet with sticks and then made me walk on rocks."

I imagined how painful this must be and my emotions battled each other. I did not think anybody deserved such treatment, but Zeray was very close to deserving it. I felt sorry for him and strangely satisfied at the same time. I did not let him see my satisfaction.

"I'm sorry Zeray. I know how it feels."

"No you don't," he said, but then stopped himself and looked down at the cigarettes.

"Do you think you will get out of here?"

"I don't know. There were 33 of us arrested. They did some kind of sweep and attempted to find traitors. We will need some help to get free."

I didn't know what else to say to that. I changed the subject and talked of Winta and Kibrom. Winta was still a horrible person, and sadly Kibrom, who had been such a sweet boy, had begun to take after his sister and father. But I spoke of them fondly when talking to this beaten down version of my husband. I talked about Fili and Muse and Hannah and Sahra as well. A slight smile curled onto Zeray's lips when I mentioned that Fili missed him.

Our words slowed to a trickle. This was the most we had talked to each other in some time. The silence between our words made it feel like there was a vast distance between us. A couple of times the silence was interrupted by a slamming door or a far-off scream from a prisoner.

The entire place gave me a sick feeling, especially because now I saw the effects of it on Zeray. Without warning, our door was pulled open. The guards didn't say anything; they just walked in and grabbed Zeray by his arms.

"Thank you for the cigarettes and bread," he said, and then he was gone.

I made my way back out of the prison. I did not know what to think. I ended up not having to run to get away from Zeray, but I could not come to grips with the horror of this place. The bus ride home took a long time and I didn't want to have to visit the prison again. But I would end up visiting it many more times.

Chapter 46

Sometimes in life we simply do not recognize just how kind others can be. We think that others do not care for us or do not want to help us or even wish that we were not around them. This is what I thought about my neighbors. There was no way they would ever want to help me. Zeray and I had caused a great deal of unrest for them with our fighting through the years.

With Zeray in prison I learned that I was mistaken. I couldn't believe how helpful my neighbors were, especially Hilina and Jemal. They knew that I had no means for making money. I had offered to wash clothes or clean or do other tedious tasks for those who helped me, but they all just said that they would let me know if they needed help.

Every time Hilina and Jemal went to the store they brought me some groceries. The kids and I did not eat much, but at least we had some food. They also gave me money here and there. Other neighbors gave me money as well. I worked very hard to save as much as I could and only bought exactly what we needed.

Fili was now ten years old and Muse was nine, Hannah was three years old and Sahra was two. Fili and Muse were old enough to understand what was happening. Fili did not think it was fair that his father was thrown into prison. We had many long talks about it. He was a little bit angry, but mostly confused. He was just learning about Eritrea and Ethiopia and the war.

The war had just experienced a huge turning point. The Eritrean People Liberation Front had attacked the Ethiopians in December of 1987. It was a violent battle and many soldiers from both sides were killed. Afterward, the Derg executed one of its main Generals and this news was shocking.

Then in the spring of 1988 the EPLF attacked again, this time in the town of Afabet in Eritrea where the Ethiopians had their headquarters. The fighting raged for three days, some 15,000 Eritreans attacking about 20,000 Ethiopians in an effort to reclaim Afabet.

In the end, the Eritreans claimed victory and almost half of the Ethiopian troops were killed. This was the first big defeat for Ethiopian President Mengistu.

I was far removed from all this fighting and killing and I even had peace in my own home. A lady who lived down the street was not so lucky. She had lost her son in the battle. Her name was Milena and after Zeray's arrest she had given me 50 birr. I did not even know her very well and yet she reached out to me.

I saw her at the market about a week after she learned of her son's death. We bought fruit together and she tried to smile and seem as if she was okay, but it was obvious that she was suffering greatly. My heart hurt for her.

I just wanted all of the violence and fighting to stop. Why couldn't we live together side by side in peace? It was obvious by the actions of my Ethiopian neighbors that we would not hate each other. They saw I needed help and they treated me well even though I was an Eritrean.

It was now the summer of 1988, and there were rumblings once again that the Soviets would not continue to support Ethiopia. It seemed that the Ethiopian army's morale was very low, and yet the war kept going.

A month or so after seeing Milena in the market I was in Jemal's truck. He had offered to give me a ride to the prison so I would not have to take the bus. We talked about the war and he had the same feelings as me. It needed to end.

It was my fifth time to the prison. It had almost become routine for me, but I still had a hard time stomaching the misery of the place. Zeray was worn down to his bones. His eyes were sunken into his skull and his skin seemed to stretch across the angles of his face. "Are you okay?" I asked as I gave him his cigarettes and bread.

"I'm still alive," he said.

"You look well considering everything."

"You are not a good liar, Abeba. I know I look like death. They continue to beat my feet and they stick my head into buckets of dirty water and hold me there until I'm on the edge of death. They hit me with sticks and whip my back."

"I'm so sorry, Zeray." I meant it. Even with my anger toward him I did not think it was right for him to go through this.

We talked a while longer and he thought the only hope for release was for Eritrea to begin to win the war and demand his and the others' release.

The door opened abruptly. As the guards picked Zeray up and marched him toward the door, he said something to me in a mumbling voice. I could not quite make it out at first, but as I sat there in the echoes of the slamming prison door I decided that what I heard from Zeray was, "If I get out, I won't hit you anymore."

Maybe it was wishful thinking, and Zeray being released was a big if, but I clung to those words as I trudged through the upcoming months on my own with the help of my Ethiopian friends.

Chapter 47

The weeks and months turned over, one after the other, and I continued to struggle through life on my own with my four kids and Winta and Kibrom. I had developed a nice system for getting everything as cheaply as possible and we never spent money unnecessarily. The birr was piling up. I sat at the kitchen table and counted it. I guessed I had 2,000 birr, but as I counted I realized I had underestimated.

In all there was 3,160 birr! I had visited Zeray a few times since I thought he said he would not hit me anymore if he ever got out. He didn't mention it, but he repeatedly talked about the money I was saving. I had not given him an exact amount, but told him I was doing the best I could.

As I folded up the money and put it back into its two envelopes I thought that Zeray would have to be impressed with this amount. I sure was. It showed that I could save it, and it showed the incredible generosity of others. Even though I was willing I had not worked for any money, and yet in 14 months I had been able to save so much.

I slipped one envelope into its hiding place behind a box, and the second envelope underneath a thick carpet next to the table. I figured it would be best to keep the money divided in case anything ever happened to one of the envelopes.

I poured myself a cup of hot tea. I felt good at that moment. I was showing that I could make it on my own. I could take care of my kids and manage the money. The first part was expected of Eritrean women, the second part, the money managing, was absolutely not expected. We were not supposed to know about money at all. I do not think it was because we could not take care of money, it was more of a way for the men to have more power over us. It worked.

Right now though, my husband did not have power over me. He was locked away. I was here taking care of my life. I scooped up the drawings that Muse and Hannah had done for Jemal and Hilina. The pictures were a small way for us to say thanks to them for all they had done. Later in the day we would take them over to their house.

I looked at the drawings. Hannah's was a bunch of squiggles, but she proudly told me that it was all of us at a park. Muse's was of Jemal's truck. Jemal sat in the driver's seat with a smile on his face and all of us stood along the side of the truck.

I started to walk outside when the telephone rang. It had been at least a week since the phone had rung the last time. I placed the pictures back on the table and reached for the phone.

"Abeba Habtu?"

"Yes."

"I know your husband, Zeray. We have learned that the Eritrean government is working to get him and the other prisoners set free."

I just sat there staring at the pictures while gripping the phone in one hand and my tea in the other.

"Hello, are you still there?"

"Yes," I managed. "Why are you telling me?"

"So you will be prepared." Again, I did not know what to say. The man continued. "Do not mention anything about this yet."

"Okay," I replied, and the line went dead.

I had not planned to visit the prison for another two weeks. I now realized I would be making a trip to that dismal place much sooner than that.

Chapter 48

I gave Zeray his cigarettes. He took them then leaned in close to me. "I am not supposed to talk to the other prisoners, but I have. There is a persistent rumor that the Soviets will stop backing Ethiopia. Eritrea is starting to win the war and the government is working to gain our release."

I kept my eyes locked on Zeray's. The white part was yellowed and it looked as if his eyes were slowly falling backwards into his head. It was an interesting thing because with his face so skinny I figured it would make his eyes bulge. Now, they weren't bulging nor falling, instead they carried an intense look in them.

"Do you know of this, Abeba?"

I considered not telling him of the call, but then I said, "I received a phone call yesterday. That is why I came so I might learn more."

"I told you what I know. So the rumor is true?"

"It seems like it."

"You are saving the money?"

"Yes, I am only spending just enough to feed us."

Zeray nodded and stared down at the cigarettes in thought. I noticed his wrists now looked pencil thin and the raw red areas had turned into a grayish calloused stretch of skin. One of his finger nails was missing. I did not want to imagine how that happened. Earlier, when they brought him into the room he could barely walk.

"Zeray, one time when they were taking you away from this room you said something to me. You said that if you ever got out of here you would not hit me again. Is this true?"

He looked up from his cigarettes and started to speak, but the door was flung open and the guards marched in. They pulled him to his feet. "Save more," Abeba," he said as they dragged him away. He did not answer my question and I probably did not want to hear his response anyway.

A few months went by with no news about Zeray and his possible release. There was news in the war however. The EPLF had continued to build on its victory at Afabet, and the Soviets were no longer supporting Ethiopia. It seemed that Eritrean's independence was only a matter of time, and yet despite having their morale beaten to the ground, the Ethiopians continued to fight. There were still horror stories of their napalm and cluster bombs.

It was almost 18 months to the day since Zeray had been thrown in prison when a man showed up at our door. He towered over me and he was as thin as a rail. I looked up at his shifty eyes as they darted left and then right. He handed me a piece of paper and then told me what it said. He probably figured I was illiterate.

"You should be at the prison tomorrow at noon to pick up your husband, Zeray Habtu."

I took the paper and walked back inside where I plopped into a chair. How could this be?

Even with the earlier rumor of a possible release I had grown used to the idea of being on my own with my kids. I had not had to worry one time over the last 18 months about getting hit, and I had grown stronger and more confident.

Zeray would be free tomorrow. I couldn't help but wonder if it would mean that I would be a prisoner once again. I could not sleep that night. I stared at the ceiling and listened to the breathing of my children. I had not told them the news yet. I decided I would do so the following morning. Fili was becoming a young man at 11 years old, and Muse was not far behind. Hannah was almost five years old and Sahra was almost four. She really did not even know her father. She was just a baby when he went away.

I was unsure whether they would be excited or not to hear that their father was coming home. I was unsure how I felt as well. After going through what he had gone through I hoped that Zeray would be a changed man. But I feared that it would make him that much angrier, and in the past when he was angry there was one person he especially liked taking it out on, me.

Chapter 49

My hands were folded together on the table. My palms felt damp and I wanted to fidget, but I stayed still and watched as Zeray opened the envelopes. It was surreal to have him back in the house. He'd walked through the door five minutes earlier. He greeted the kids with a brief hug as if he'd been gone for one week instead of a year and a half, and then he snatched a beer and sucked it down. I made sure there was beer in the house for him.

He pulled the money out and spread it across the table. He wanted to count it even though I had told him how much was there. He spent a couple minutes thumbing through it while taking breaks to drink his beer. He'd been unable to have any in prison, and his thirst had obviously built up.

Zeray was definitely a changed man, at least physically. Now that he was sitting at our table instead of in the gray prison, it was even more apparent. He had to have lost 25 kilograms and his clothes hung loosely off his skinny limbs. His face was withdrawn and his cheekbones looked like sharp ridges below his eyes.

His eyes, however, still held that look of angry fire. That look did not do a very good job of hiding a brain that was popping with dangerous emotions. I looked across the table at those eyes and tried to read them. It was amazing how fast I had fallen back into that state of being on the edge. Now that the last year and a half of freedom had ended I had to reacquire my instincts for survival, or at least it felt that way. I still held out hope that after taking such brutal beatings in prison Zeray would not hit me anymore.

He took another long gulp of his beer and finished thumbing through the money. I expected that he would be very happy with such an amount. I could not believe that I was able to accumulate it while he was away.

After another gulp, his beer was empty. He looked at me as if I was crazy. I quickly got up to get him another one. He continued to count as I opened it and handed it to him.

I sat back down and said, "Jemal was here for me. He gave me a lot of money and food. Your other friends helped as well."

"You should have saved up more money then," Zeray spat the words out of his cracked lips.

I sat back in my chair. "I saved everything I could. I promise."

"It is not enough."

I did not know how to respond.

"And why did Jemal give you so much money?" His tone dripped with accusation.

"Hilina helped as well. We spent a lot of time together."

"You two were whores!"

I gritted my teeth and squeezed my fists together. The tension pierced every muscle in my body. "How could you say that?"

"Did you sleep with Jemal? You must have slept with him if he gave you all this money." He picked up a handful and tossed it across the table at me.

I locked my eyes on him. This bastard had not changed, but I had. I would not take it anymore.

"You are wrong, Zeray. I did everything I could for you. I remained faithful to you. I could have left you to rot in that horrible jail."

His face curled up into a ball of anger. I did not cower. Instead, I stared at him and let my contempt show.

I was prepared. He would hit me and I would fight back. I did not go for 18 months on my own to go right back to this.

The room grew silent as we sized each other up.

Finally, he took another long drink. "It will have to do," his words sounded soft on their edges. The alcohol was already affecting him.

"I did what I could for you."

He did not respond. He just started corralling his money, the money that I gave him thanks to his friend. He did not hit me either. He was mean, but his violence stayed locked away like a guard dog behind a tall fence. I wondered if the fence would hold.

Chapter 50

After the money incident and Zeray's accusations, we managed to slip back into life with him being around. The days and weeks and months came and went and he was not exactly nice, but he did not hit me. I was sure it was because of his time in prison. He still walked with a slight limp and something inside of him was a little bit different, not much, but just enough to keep him from swinging his fists.

Our relationship with Jemal and Hilina was strained after Zeray accused Jemal. I felt ashamed and saddened. They had done so much for the kids and me, and even for Zeray, and he put stress on our relationship. He told me I could not be friends with Hilina, but I did not think this was fair.

Before he went to prison I probably would have abided by Zeray's wishes. Now though, I just kept my friendship with Hilina hidden from him. One day I was at her house. She lived just around the corner and I could see part of my house from her window. My heart leapt into my mouth when I saw Zeray. He had come home early. I immediately left to go home, but he saw me come out of Hilina's house.

He stood at the front door with his hands on his hips and a cigarette hanging loosely between his lips. "I told you not to see this woman ever again," he said. "I know you were whores while I was in prison."

"I just went to pick up my cooking pots." I held them up to show him.

He replied by grabbing a bucket of water that was next to him and dumping it on my head, and then he stormed off. The water did not bother me that much.

After being released from prison, Zeray sent Winta and Kibrom to Germany. He wanted to make sure they did not get stuck in the Ethiopian army and decided they could make money in Germany. They had been gone for a while and wanted us to send them family pictures.

Zeray asked a friend of his to come take the pictures. I think his name was Dagna. He was a nice man and arrived right on time. He got his camera ready and everyone was there and all dressed up, except Zeray. Dagna waited for two hours and then decided to take pictures of me and the kids. In the middle of the photo session, Zeray came home.

"What is this?" he growled. "Why did you start without me?"

Dagna did not know what to do. He fumbled with his camera and started to speak, but Zeray beat him to it.

"I don't need your pictures. Give me the film." Then he turned to me. "Why the hell did you take the pictures without me? How stupid are you?"

A spark of fear shot through me and I could not answer him. He whipped around toward his supposed friend. "Give me the damn film."

"If I take it out it will be bad. We will lose all the pictures I took," Dagna pleaded.

"I don't give a damn!"

Zeray continued to pressure Dagna until he handed over the film. As soon as he did Zeray kicked him out of the house. He then grabbed a hammer and smashed the film. During this whole time, Fili, Muse, Hannah, and Sahra stood quietly next to the wall. They understood that it was best to not get involved. Zeray walked over to Fili. "Put out your hand," he said.

Slowly, Fili raised his hand. It shook slightly. Zeray placed the broken film in his palm. "Give it to your mother."

Fili turned to me and looked down as he offered me the broken film. I noticed a tear had formed in the corner of his eye. I quickly took the film and did my best to give him a reassuring smile.

Two days later, when I was in my house clothes and my hair was a mess, Zeray showed up with a different photographer. He made me gather up the kids and we all took family photos. Of course he was the only one who looked nice, but obviously looks can be deceiving.

It was not long after this when my mother had gone to the United States for my little sister Letina's wedding. On the way back she stopped in Ethiopia to see me. She had the wedding tape, but we had no VCR. I borrowed one from a neighbor and he hooked it up for me. While my mom and I were watching it, Zeray came home.

"Where did you get this?" He glared at me as he pointed to the TV.

"From the neighbor," I replied.

He walked to the VCR and ripped the cords from the TV and wall. "I don't want you to watch this in here."

My mother tried to protest. I knew it was of no use. I took the VCR back to the neighbor and then my momma and I went to Samuel's house to finish watching the wedding. My mother had three days left in Ethiopia, but she refused to stay in our house. She went back to Eritrea upset because of Zeray.

After watching the tape, I was afraid Zeray would hit me when I returned. I asked Samuel to go with me. "You decided to stay with this man. There is nothing I can do. No matter what he does to you, please don't ask me to help you ever again. As I told you before, Abeba, I have already helped you many times. I am done."

I could not blame Samuel for still feeling this way, and I went home with nothing to protect me. Luckily, Zeray did not hit me.

Despite these cruel moments and Zeray's insanity, we marched on through our life. The war marched on as well, even though it seemed like Eritrea had the momentum. I had lived my whole life with war.

Chapter 51

The port city of Massawa stretched out along the Red Sea. It was an Ethiopian stronghold that allowed the army to shovel supplies to garrisons in Eritrea. There were no rumors of the attack. One morning in February of 1990, the Ethiopians held the city. The next morning it was under attack. The Eritrean People's Liberation Front blasted away at the Ethiopians from both land and sea. In just three days the EPLF had captured the city and driven the Ethiopian army away.

This battle, also known as Operation Fenkil, was a big turning point in the war. The Ethiopians were now landlocked and had to fly supplies to the fragmented army. Not long after the defeat, the Ethiopians retaliated and bombed both Massawa and Afabet. There were thousands of people killed in the bombings, and most of them were not soldiers. It gave me a hollow feeling in my stomach because it felt like the war was close to ending and yet so many people were still killed. The bombings did little to hurt the EPLF though.

The war continued on in spurts and spits for another year, but then Mengistu's regime began to crumble and he fled to Zimbabwe. There was some unrest in Addis Ababa as the EPLF and TPLF (Tigrayan People's Liberation Front), led by Meles Zenawi, conspired to take over the newly vacated leadership role. It was hard to believe, but the

Eritreans had won the war. It had raged for all my life, and then on May 29, 1991, it appeared to be over.

With the defeat and exile of Mengistu, delegates from the United States came to Asmara to help with the process of setting up the new government for Ethiopia. Eritreans were awash with excitement because of the newfound freedom. I was as well, but it was odd because I lived in the heart of Ethiopia. I would not dance in the street or sing songs at the top of my lungs.

There was a great deal of anticipation, and positive expectations flooded through the Eritrean people. I just kept on living quietly. Zeray had his malicious moments, but he still had not begun hitting me again, and then something else happened that I did not think would happen again.

Not long after the end of the war, I became pregnant. In 1992, I gave birth to Selemon. From the first moment I laid eyes on him I knew he carried a sweet heart and he would be a beautiful soul.

Now it was the seven of us, Zeray and me, and our five children: Fili, Muse, Hannah, Sahra, and Selemon. Sahra, who was now six years old, was ecstatic with the new baby. She was no longer the little one and she took it upon herself to take care of her little brother.

In 1993, two years after the end of the war, the Ethiopian government recognized the right of the Eritreans to hold a referendum for independence. The numbers in favor of independence were staggering. Less than one percent voted against it.

In May, Eritrea officially became independent. Two years earlier, the leader of the Eritrean People's Liberation Front, Isaias Afewerki assumed the role of President of Eritrea. Once our independence became official he continued in that role. Afewerki was obviously a tough and capable leader. He had made many hard and bold decisions en route to Eritrea's independence, and it was said that he had a decent relationship with Ethiopia's leader, Meles Zenawi.

At the time of such excitement in the early 90s, we never could have guessed what President Afewerki would do in the coming years. We were about to walk through a hell that would rip our family apart, but before that I got another terrible shock, this one was from my husband.

Chapter 52

The Eritrean People's Liberation Front had renamed itself. Now it was the People's Front for Democracy and Justice. Our President Afewerki had been outspoken about the need for a multiple-party political system and a committee to draft a constitution was created. On the face of it Eritrea was on its way to being a shining light in the horn of Africa.

Eritrean people are strong and caring. And despite all that we had been through we were brimming with optimism. Our country was on the verge of huge change.

It was now 1995, and my family was about to change as well. One evening I was cleaning clothes outside. Hannah, who was ten years old, was in the house preparing dinner. Fili was 17 years old and he was a hard worker with big plans of making a splash in business. He was at work at the time and Muse was gone as well. Sahra was in the house playing with little Selemon, who was now three years old and bubbling with energy.

There were long shadows across the yard and a slow breeze licked at my skin. The humming of the city as it churned along provided almost a soothing sound. It was a pleasant evening and I felt content. Then Zeray came through the gate. He'd let his hair grow longer again and of course he had a cigarette between his lips. After all these years I still had not gotten used to the smoke and the way it seeped into his clothes. Because of this, I scrubbed extra hard when doing his laundry. As he approached, I was cleaning one of his white shirts.

I stopped and looked up. "Hello Zeray." I smiled.

"I've been thinking." He pulled smoke into his mouth and then slowly let it loose in lazy circles toward the sky.

"What have you been thinking about?"

"Hannah and Muse." He made the smoke rings again.

"Why are you thinking of them?" I tried to hide the concern that crept into my chest.

"I think it is time for them to go off to Germany."

I dropped his shirt into the bucket and stood up. "What do you mean, Germany?"

"They can stay with Winta and go to school there and work."

"But they are just kids. They should stay with their family."

Zeray rolled his eyes.

I could not think of what else to say at the moment. More smoke rings came from Zeray's mouth. "They will have a better life there. There is so much more money in Europe. They will even be able to send us some."

"I don't want them to go," I said weakly.

A smile of sympathy slipped onto Zeray's face. "I know," he said. "But I can get them there and it is where they need to be. You don't want them to get stuck here if Eritrea and Ethiopia begin fighting again do you?"

I picked up his shirt and started scrubbing again. I had to do something before tears forced their way into my eyes. "No, I don't. When will you send them?"

"In a week."

I nodded and blinked hard.

At dinner I looked around the table. Fili and Muse had just arrived and we all were there. I sat across from Zeray and the boys sat on each side of him. Hannah sat next to Muse, and Sahra was on the other side right next to Fili. Selemon squirmed in his chair between me and Sahra.

My whole family, all together and all happy. This was all I could ever hope for, but now I realized that it would not last. Zeray dipped a piece of bread into a spicy sauce and shoved it in his mouth. After he finished chewing he took a swallow of his beer and then looked at Muse and Hannah. "I have decided that you will both move to Germany and live with Winta."

Muse glared at his father. He had a streak of meanness in him and had gotten in a handful of fights over the last year. "Why?" he asked.

Zeray leaned forward. "Don't question me," he said. "It will be best for you to go there."

Hannah looked back and forth between me and her father. It seemed as if she was pleading with me to tell her this would not really happen, but I could not. I had been thinking about it for the last hour. It hurt me deeply, but it would be best for them. They would not have to go through the same difficulties I had to go through and Europe really would offer a better life.

"Momma?" Hannah said. "I don't want to leave here."

"I know, but it will be a great opportunity for you."

She put her head down and wiped her small hands over her face. I waited for her to protest, but she composed herself and took a bite of bread. At that moment I knew she was strong enough to make it, but the thought of her being away from me made my stomach hurt. She was my first girl and she was only ten years old. I did not want to lose her so soon.

Muse pushed away from the table and headed for the door. Zeray said nothing to him. Instead, he took another drink.

"Muse, wait," I said.

He did not turn around and the front door slammed behind him. I knew that this moment would be one of the last times my family would all be around the dinner table and my earlier contentedness was now long gone.

Chapter 53

The week leading up to Muse and Hannah's move to Germany was full of conflicting emotions. I only had seven days to tell my little girl everything I needed to tell her. Really, I did not know so much. She was going to a place I had never been and she would find a life I could not comprehend.

The first night after finding out, we sat in our courtyard underneath the stars. "Momma, please don't make me go."

I sighed deeply. I was desperate for her to stay, but I knew it would be best for her to go. "It will be so hard at first, and I want you to stay here so badly, but you have to understand that it will be a better life for you."

"Momma, I will help out around the house. I will clean even harder."

My heart hurt for her. She was already responsible and helped out so much. "That is not it," I said. "You have to go so you can have a better life. You will have more freedom and what has happened to me will not happen to you."

"I just don't want to go."

"I know, Hannah." I pulled her close and hugged her.

She was so scared, but she was brave as well. One of her biggest fears was living with Winta. Her half-sister was a mean kid and she had not gotten any nicer as she aged. I thought back to the time so long ago when she hurt Fili on purpose and then lied. Zeray almost killed me that day.

Hannah knew that Winta was selfish and cruel, but I warned her to watch out anyway. We also talked about things a mother and daughter usually would not talk about until later. I told her about getting her period and the things she could expect. And I told her what little I knew about relationships with boys.

Then there were the times I told her and Sahra stories about when they were babies and we laughed at some of the things they did. It was a beautiful week of bonding with both Hannah and Sahra, but it was bitter sweet because Hannah would soon be thousands of kilometers away.

Muse did not want to talk so much. He was still angry, but he had accepted his fate. He even wondered what it would be like in Germany. I could not give him any answers so we speculated about what the foreign land would hold.

Zeray went about his business as if nothing was changing. I didn't understand this and I didn't try. He was always distant when it came to his family.

All too quickly the day came. I had packed everything I could think of for Hannah. Muse did not let me pack for him, but I gave him suggestions. I looked at their cases and they were so small. How could I send two of my babies off with so little?

The ride to the airport was quiet except for Selemon singing songs and smashing his toy car into the seat. I felt that there was so much to say, and yet very few words came to my lips.

It seemed like I was moving through a dream as we approached the counter and got their boarding passes. I somehow dulled my senses in an effort to not tumble into hysteria. I kept putting my hand on Muse's shoulder and rubbing Hannah's back. I knew this was best for them, but it was so hard. For almost two decades I had been with my kids and done everything to keep them safe and with me, now I was turning two of them loose. It was a completely different circumstance, but I thought of the time I went back to Eritrea and left Fili and Muse behind.

We walked along a dirty corridor until we found the gate. I held Hannah's hand. Sahra walked with Selemon. Fili walked next to his father and tried to remain as unemotional as possible. Muse was next to his brother trying to do the same.

At the gate we had to wait for a while. We stood and talked and I tried to think of any last minute advice I could give to my babies. No great wisdom came to me. After all, I knew a life that was full of survival and little else.

There was a voice over the speaker. It was hard to hear, but we all knew it was time for Muse and Hannah to leave. I hugged Muse so tight and he hugged me back. "Be strong and good, Son," I said.

He pulled away from me and his eyes glistened. "I will," his voice was almost inaudible.

"I love you." I kissed his cheek.

Then I squatted down to my beautiful little girl with her perfectly smooth skin and bright eyes and a smile that could part the clouds. I squeezed her and she almost climbed right into my lap as she hugged me back.

"Hannah I love you so much," I said. "I know you will be strong."

"I will, Momma," she whispered in my ear.

"I know," I replied.

Her little arms squeezed even harder. "I love you," she said.

And then she was hugging her brothers and sisters and walking away. I followed her and Muse to the counter. Muse got his paper stamped and Hannah followed. She took a step toward the door and then glanced back at us one more time.

"I love you," I yelled.

She gave me her smile and then vanished into the tunnel.

Sarah hugged me and we cried together. Selemon ran around the airport driving his car over chairs, and Zeray and Fili stood a few steps behind us. After what felt like forever the plane backed away. Sahra and I pressed up against the window and waved at the plane as it carried my children away.

Chapter 54

Our small house felt so empty without Muse and Hannah. Often I found Sahra sitting and crying silently. She was close with her sister, and the crying continued for two months after Hannah had left. It made sense because they were so close in age and had been through the same things together: the craziness of Zeray and his abuse, my pain and heartache, the threat of war reaching our home, and then Zeray's prison time. They had formed a very tight relationship and that had been pulled away from Sahra when she was only nine years old.

It hurt me badly to see her so upset, and every day I wondered how Hannah and Muse were doing. I had wanted to call them at Winta's, but Zeray would not allow it. "Do you know how much it costs?" he said in a grating tone.

I'd hoped that they would call us, but of course that was not going to happen because of who they were staying with.

After a month I was finally able to call. I talked to Muse for only a few minutes and Hannah for not much longer. It was so good to hear their voices, but the information I learned scared me so much. Winta had been horrible, and now she was taking them to a group home in Germany where they would live. I imagined them all alone and unable to speak the language in a strange place. No child should have to go through such a thing, and mine were.

As sad as I was, there was nothing I could do. They were now in a group home instead of with me, and I was powerless. It felt awful. I had to stay focused on being the best mother I could be for the children who still lived with me: Fili, Sahra, and Selemon. I tried to do this as we went on living our lives.

It was very hard at first and it didn't really get any easier. It was just that we all adapted and moved forward. We had no other choice.

One thing that did set our minds at ease was that the committee to develop a constitution had been successful and there was also a commission to help resolve any problems that might arise between Ethiopia and Eritrea. It seemed as if my home country and the one I currently lived in had become friends after years of war.

Then in May of 1997, the Eritrean constitution was ratified. It was a great moment, but the constitution was not put into effect because we had to wait for parliamentary and presidential elections. They had been scheduled for 1995, but were pushed back to 2001. Still, it felt good to think that my country that had fought for its independence for so long was for all intents and purposes now free.

Unfortunately, the countries could not remain friends. Just months after the constitution was ratified, a border dispute that had been brewing for some time had grown more intense. I carried a heavy feeling with me as the two governments that used to get along so well argued with each other about the border.

The commission to solve disputes such as this had tried, but they were unsuccessful. The governments even looked back at what the border was when it was between Italy and Ethiopia even though this had gotten washed away when the war had started. Nothing helped.

The city of Badme was the major problem. Afewerki said it was Eritrea's, and Zenawi said it was Ethiopia's. The two former friends had become enemies and the border area turned violent.

I remember that day when I learned that Eritrean officials had been killed at Badme. I was talking with a friend in the courtyard of our house. She told me of it and I felt sick. The peace would end soon. I was sure of it.

I just never could have expected how bad it would get and that I would soon lose another child.

Chapter 55

It was an early summer day in 1998, and just a few weeks ago waves of Eritrean troops had attacked at Badme in an attempt to claim the city. The Ethiopians were not ready at first, but quickly regrouped and responded with their tanks and planes. There was intense fighting and we kept getting reports of thousands and thousands of terrible deaths.

It was hard for me to stomach, but I did take solace in the fact that at least two of my children were far away in Germany. Life had been hard for Muse and Hannah. They were separated and placed in different group homes and basically on their own for the last couple of years. I rarely got to talk to them, but each time I did it made me so happy at the moment, and then sad for days after we hung up the phone.

Now I was concerned for my family in Addis Ababa. We had heard rumors that Eritreans living in Ethiopia were being branded as spies. Of course this was ridiculous. The Ethiopian capital had been my home for so many years.

Despite the war and these terrible rumors, life went on for us, and this day was no different. Zeray had come home early and he was tense as usual. I folded clothes that I had just washed and Sahra and Selemon were inside the house watching a cartoon on TV.

I had just finished with the last of the folding and carried them into the house. I was thinking that I should start dinner soon when I heard a commotion outside. I placed the clothes on the couch and looked out the window.

I backed away from it with my hand over my gaping mouth. A group of soldiers stormed toward our house. Some of them held their sticks and two of them had their guns in their hands. "Zeray!" I yelled even though he was almost right next to me.

He jumped up. "What is it?"

"The soldiers."

Immediately after I got the words out of my mouth there was a banging on the door. Before I could move, the door burst open. The men in their military fatigues crammed into our house and yelled at us as if we were dangerous criminals. I scooped Selemon up and then put my arm around Sahra. They both looked so scared, and Selemon's lip trembled with fear.

"What is this?" Zeray said in an authoritative tone.

"Shut up," one of the men said.

I counted five soldiers in our tiny room. I had no idea why they would be here. Did Zeray do something wrong again? I looked at him and saw that he was about to lose his temper. "I will not shut up! Why are you in my house?"

One of the soldiers stepped forward and shoved Zeray. He fell backwards into the wall. Before he could recover, two more had their sticks pushed up against him.

The apparent leader spoke. "This is no longer your house you Eritrean scum. You are being kicked out of Ethiopia."

I couldn't believe these words. Kicked out?

"Momma, what is happening?" Sahra asked.

"It's okay, Baby." I rubbed her head.

"You get one small bag. We'll give you two minutes to pack."

The words thundered into my head. Dear Lord, they were making us leave right this minute.

"Now?" I asked. "But we are not ready to leave."

"Your clock is ticking. Pack your bag you slut," the man said.

"My son, Fili, he is still at work. We have to wait for him."

The man abruptly turned on me and pushed me hard. I stumbled and almost dropped Selemon. "You have one damn minute before we all walk out the door."

Now Sahra and Selemon were crying. "Get the bag," Zeray said.

"No, we cannot leave Fili behind!" I yelled.

"Dammit Abeba, we don't have a choice."

"He is right," the man said.

"I am not leaving my son." I stood with my feet planted firmly on the floor.

The man shook his head, and in an instant one of the guns was pointed at me. "Then you will be dead in the next minute."

"Abeba!" Zeray yelled. "Get the bag right now."

I remained still and locked my eyes on the man with the gun.

"Momma, please," Sahra said.

This made something shift in my head. I could not be killed in this room. I would lose all of my children and they would lose their mother. "Get some things as fast as you can," I said.

The kids started grabbing their stuff and I did the same. Less than one minute later we were being shoved out the door. The clothes were still folded on the couch and the silly cartoon was still on the TV.

Chapter 56

We were pushed through our courtyard to the busy street. Our neighbors looked on in a sad silence. As we approached a large truck with a covered back, I stopped and scanned the street for Fili. He would be coming home soon. I prayed that I would spot him. I prayed that he would come running toward us before we were thrown into the truck.

"Keep moving," a soldier barked at me.

I felt a tug. It was Sahra's little hand urging me forward, but I stayed still. "Fili!" I yelled.

The soldier pushed me in my back and I fell forward. He pushed me again and I almost fell to my knees. Another grabbed my arm and they pulled me into the back of the dark truck. It had a distinct smell of sweat and fear. A handful of other somber faces stared at us. The back door was slammed shut and the engine roared. I feared that I had lost my son forever.

After just 15 minutes or so the truck came to a halt. The back door opened and light streamed in. We were ushered into a large dirt field outside of an industrial building. My eyes adjusted to the brightness and I saw the tents and the large fence that gleamed against the sun in the distance. We were at some kind of camp.

There were already a large number of people moving about in the confined area, and we were led to what looked like a check-in area. There were so many of us we had to move at a turtle speed. I looked around the crowd for Fili, but it was no use. I decided to start calling for him. After all, there was a good chance he would be here. I yelled his name over and over. A few others took cue and yelled the names of those they had lost as well.

At the check-in area they took our names and gave us a blanket and two pillows. "Go find a tent," the man said.

"My son, his name is Fili. We have lost him," I said.

The man just stared at me.

"Can you see if he has been checked in?"

"Go find a tent," he mumbled.

"But my son, you have to help me find him."

"I don't know where your son is. Now go."

Zeray grabbed my arm and gently pulled me away. "What kind of person are you?" I yelled at the man.

A guard with a machine gun appeared. "What's the problem?" he said.

"No problem," Zeray replied, and led me away.

We found a tent on the outskirts of the camp. There were two toilet areas and some large tanks for water, other than that we had nothing else. I settled the kids into the tent and then started to leave.

"Where are you going?" Zeray asked.

"To look for Fili. Stay with the kids please."

Zeray nodded, and I set off to find my son.

I walked all over the camp calling his name and asking people about him. Twice somebody thought they might have known where he was or thought that they had seen him, but both times proved fruitless.

By mid-morning of the second day it was obvious that they were not going to feed us. I had circled the large camp one more time calling Fili's name, but had no luck. Then there was a commotion at one of the large fences. I noticed that maybe one hundred people were lined up on the outside and people on the inside were streaming toward the fence.

Could Fili be on the outside? I hustled over to the fence and fought through a noisy crowd. I noticed that it was Ethiopians on the other side. They had food and were giving it to us. It was not Fili, but with two starving kids in our tent it was the next best thing.

I forced my way along the fence looking for somebody I knew. Finally, I saw a group of our neighbors. "Abeba," they said, "we are so sorry you are in here."

They shoved bread through the fence.

I quickly grabbed it. "Have you seen Fili?"

"Yes," one of them said. "He was at your house just moments after you were taken away. Hilina told him what happened. He was very upset for a while, but then he went in and gathered some things and left."

I did not know what to make of this. "Thank you so much for the bread and the news of Fili," I finally said. "If you see him, please tell him where we are."

They agreed to do so, and I fought my way back through the crowd with some bread for Sahra and Selemon.

We remained in the camp for another day. I continued to search for Fili, especially when new buses arrived. Then on the third day a long row of white and blue buses pulled up outside of the gate. From a distance I could see they were empty. I guessed they were for us.

Chapter 57

It was the middle of the afternoon. The dirt was scorching hot, and everybody was so tired. They pushed us toward the buses and we shuffled along in the mass of fellow Eritreans. I held tight to Sahra's hand and carried Selemon on my hip even though he was now getting pretty big. I didn't want him to get lost in the crowd.

My stomach rumbled with a desire for food. I'd eaten two pieces of bread, but that was all I'd had since being taken from my home.

After walking up the bus steps, I quickly found a hard seat in the middle. I wiped away the grime from the window and desperately searched for my son one last time. I yelled for him through the window as the bus became packed.

Now Selemon, who had just turned six years old, was on my lap, and Sahra was squished in next to me. Another woman sat on the other side of Sahra, and Zeray stood in the aisle of the bus. I continued to search for Fili in the slow-moving crowd outside. I screamed his name over and over. The bus was hot and sweat got in my eyes. I blinked it away and screamed for my son until the bus slowly pulled away.

I sank into the seat and pushed my head back. I stared upward at the white ceiling and fixed my gaze on a rusted bolt. Literally in an instant I went from folding clothes in my home and thinking about dinner to becoming a refugee and losing my son. Now we were on a hot and stinking bus and I guessed we were on our way back to Eritrea. The emptiness inside of me threatened to burst outward.

This had to be some kind of strange nightmarish dream. I'd been through so much, but this was more than I thought I could handle.

"Momma, are you okay?" Sahra asked.

"I'm fine," I said. "How are you doing?"

"Okay, but I'm worried about Fili."

I reached over and patted her leg. "Me too."

The bus crawled along toward the northeast and the sun dropped behind us. After four hours we learned that we were being sent to Assab, the port city where my half-sister Rosina had lived after having an affair with Zeray. There, we would be met by Eritrean troops and put on a boat to the north until we would reach Massawa, and from there we would go to Asmara.

With every kilometer I feared I was getting further and further away from Fili. I pictured him coming home to an empty house. I saw him looking at the folded clothes and the cartoon on the TV and wondering what had happened. I saw the neighbors tell him and I saw the sadness on his face.

He was 19 years old and really more a man than a boy, but to me he was my little Fili who had been through so much with me over the years. Selemon fell asleep on my lap and Sahra dozed as she leaned against me. I adjusted until my shoulder pressed against the bus window and I fell into a troubled sleep as well.

We arrived at Assab in the middle of the night, and as we entered the city our bus broke down. We had to walk through a stiff breeze that came in off the Red Sea for the last kilometer or two. The chilly darkness cut into my skin and made my bones ache, but it was nothing compared to the ache I felt in my soul.

Again, I searched the crowd at the port, but could not find Fili. Soon we were on an old boat. We chugged along the coast for almost a day. After another bus ride we were in Asmara. Many people did not have families to go. They were placed in a large camp not far from the airport where black smoke still drifted into the sky thanks to the recent Ethiopian bombings.

We were at least lucky enough to be able to go back to my home. As we made it to the old farm I could not believe I was there. It was the second time I had returned home without Fili. As soon as I got through the front door I hugged my mother and then collapsed on the floor. I was too exhausted to cry.

Chapter 58

Germany 2011

A constant dull throbbing leaked through my bones and made my body feel like it was a factory that produced pain. Weeks earlier when I came to the hospital I thought I was terribly frail. That was nothing like what I felt now. I did not want to move any part of me.

It had been five days since the surgery on my back, and now I just found out that I had to have another surgery to remove the tumor on my left hip. The doctor had said that it had to be removed as soon as possible because it was spreading fast, but I did not know if my body could take it. Hannah repeatedly told me how my thoughts can produce real things and I could use my thoughts to survive this cancer and all of these surgeries, but as I laid in my bed I kept thinking that I would not make it through this one. My body was just too broken.

I thought about my young sons, Michael and John. They were now with Selemon and I hadn't seen them for some time. I didn't know if we would ever be able to get them all out of Sudan. Hannah and Sahra had worked tirelessly to raise the money for their rescue, but there was no way to know if it would ever happen.

I could not watch TV and I didn't have the strength to do so anyway, so I just spent my time talking to God. I'd always had deep faith. Even though it might seem to some that my life had been a series of one terrible event after another, I didn't see it that way. I had survived them all and I had a beautiful and loving family. What more could I ask for?

Now, I worried and wondered if I had been a good enough Christian. I asked God about heaven and I told Him I was sorry for all the sins I had committed. I walked back through my life with Him and I thanked Him for all that I had received.

It was time for the surgery. Once again my kids were right alongside me. Hannah told me I would be fine. Sahra told me I was too strong for this to take me. Muse agreed with both of them.

The doctors gave me the all too familiar countdown in German. Soon I was out. I could have no idea what was happening. I was asleep as they cut me open and started sawing away at my hip bone. I was asleep when my blood pressure dropped and my pulse got rapid and weak and my life began slipping away. I was asleep when the doctors hastily removed the tumor while struggling to keep me alive.

I would stay asleep for a long time, clinging to a slender thread of life while my kids prayed for the best, but prepared for the worst.

Chapter 59

Eritrea

I was so physically and emotionally exhausted that I slept right there on my parents' floor for 12 hours. When I awoke it took me a moment to understand where I was. I stared at the stained ceiling as the past few days flooded back into my head.

I was at my farm with Zeray and Sahra and Selemon. Fili was somewhere in Ethiopia. I sat straight up and pushed my aching body off the floor. I had to start trying to figure out how I could locate my baby boy.

I found Sahra and Selemon playing in the fields. I talked to them about all that had happened. They were worried, but they had already been through so much and they were resilient. "Do you think Fili is alright?" Sahra asked me.

It was a hard question. I hoped and prayed that he was, but there was no way to know for sure. "I like to think that he is, and I'm going to do everything I can to find him," I replied.

My momma yelled to us that she had some soup ready. The kids ran for the house and I followed them.

Over the next couple of days I gained my strength and began searching for ways to find Fili. I tried to call our old house in Ethiopia and got nothing but a dead line. I then tried to call our neighbors. Again, nothing. I started asking around and learned that the phone lines between the two countries had been completely severed.

I talked with an old friend about taking a bus to Ethiopia. He was something of an expert when it came to finding ways to move around the region. He looked at me as if I had lost my mind. "It is absolutely impossible to drive into Ethiopia right now. If you tried you would be killed for sure."

I thought back to my cousin Samuel and how he got me a military flight from Addis Ababa to Asmara some two decades earlier. I asked about the possibility of a flight and quickly learned that this was even crazier than taking a bus.

I wondered if I could make it back to the port at Massawa. It might be possible to take a boat south until I reached Ethiopia. Again, I received incredulous looks.

After a week of searching for a way back into Ethiopia I began to realize just how hopeless it was. There were thousands of soldiers along the border and I had already been thrown out of Ethiopia. Besides, even if I was able to get there I would not know where to begin when it came to finding Fili. Who would know if I could even make it all the way to Addis Ababa and our old house?

I slipped into a deep despair. I had to keep telling myself that at least Muse and Hannah were safe in Germany and Sahra and Selemon were still with me. But this only helped a little bit. I could not help but think of all the nights I had held Fili when he was a baby and how he would fall asleep on my chest. He was my first child and we had gone through a world of pain and happiness together.

My father had set us up with a small room not far away from their house. He had also rented out some rooms to others. And then there was Rosina. My half-sister who had slept with my husband was living right next to us. I had never said anything to the rest of my family so they did not know, but of course I knew and Zeray knew as well.

I had put it behind me and decided to forgive Rosina. She was family and family meant everything to me. Zeray's behavior was odd. He talked badly about her, and the rest of my family, even though they were giving him so much.

The war along the border was raging on. The armies had built trenches like the armies from the first world war had done, and they launched their missiles at each other. We were not close to the war, but it had already affected us so greatly. I'd hoped it would end quickly so I could find Fili, but it was obvious this would not be the case.

One evening we gathered around the small TV. President Afewerki was to make an important announcement on the state-run Eri-TV. The broadcast was our only source of news.

His voice crackled through the TV speakers and we all listened without making a sound. He talked about how we had worked so hard for our independence and now Ethiopia was trying to take it away. He talked about how he would not let this happen, and then he made the announcement that all young people that were at least 17 years old were being called to duty. The National Service, where all able-bodied boys and girls of age had to serve for one and a half years was still very new. And this announcement changed things considerably.

Kids from all over the country were being called on to take up arms and fight against Ethiopia. At the time we had no idea where this national service would lead and how much pain it would cause.

Chapter 60

Many young Eritreans were sent off to war, but nobody from our family. Selemon was still much too young, and thankfully Muse was in Germany. I wondered if Fili was at the border fighting, or if maybe he was hiding out somewhere in Ethiopia. There were many other terrible alternatives, but I tried hard not to think about them. My fragile spirit could not handle it.

Zeray was in his own funk. He was angry and mean to everybody, especially Rosina. He drank all the time and did nothing around the farm to help out. I tried to think about what it was like for him. He had lost his son as well and he was ripped away from his life in Addis Ababa. He'd had some influence politically with the Eritrean government, but now it was like he had been crumpled up and thrown to the side of the street.

Still, he was such a jerk that it was hard to even be around him. Despite this, we fell into our new life on the old family farm. I started helping my momma, who was much older now and not nearly as able as she used to be. Sahra was by our sides almost every moment of the day. And Selemon divided his time between playing with some new friends and helping my father in the fields.

It was as good as it could be, but every night I went to sleep worrying about Fili, and each morning I awoke with the worry still there. One day we were told that there would be information in the village about those who had been sent off to the war.

"I am going to go," I told Zeray.

"Why? You will not find out anything."

I glared at him. "I will still go. There is always hope."

He responded by rolling his eyes and taking a long swig of his beer.

Selemon made the walk with me and we talked about Fili and where he might be. Selemon had big ideas that he was living in a castle in the desert or that he was flying a plane in the war. I smiled when he came up with these wild scenarios and replied with a simple, "Maybe so."

His plane scenario bothered me though. Both sides had dropped bombs on the other and I thought back to the airport in Asmara and how I saw the black smoke billowing into the sky, and then I thought all the way back to my sister, Hiwet. She had been gone for so long now. We had heard many terrible stories. One family had to send all five of their children to the warfront. And then came the horrific news that all five of them had been killed. I could not imagine this, and when I heard the story I stopped and prayed to God with everything I had.

Selemon and I arrived at the center of the village and there was a large group of people there. The men wore their farming clothes or tan pants and button shirts and talked in a serious tone. The women mostly wore their colorful dresses and talked amongst themselves in the same tone. A thin cloud of dust had been kicked up and it hung around their feet, but nobody seemed to notice. They were all too engrossed in their conversations about their loved ones and the war.

I was surprised to notice that the beating of my heart had sped up as I approached what looked like an information table. Selemon must have felt the tension because he gripped my hand a little tighter. I approached the table and a man looked up at me. "How can I help you?"

"I do not know. I am looking for my son. We were kicked out of Ethiopia and we were separated."

A frown spread onto the man's face. "I don't know if I will have any information. We really just have information about those from this region who have been hurt or killed. We also know where some people are stationed, but there is no way to know how long they will be there."

"I would appreciate it if you would look."

"Of course," he said, and looked at me with sad eyes. "What is your son's name?"

"Fili Habtu," I said.

He flipped through one paper after another and scanned the names. After a long moment he looked up. "He isn't on the injured or killed list."

He then scanned some more. "I have a Fikru Habtu here."

"His name is Fili," I replied.

He scanned for another long moment. "I'm sorry," he finally said. "There is no Fili Habtu on my lists. Maybe he is serving somewhere or still in Ethiopia?"

The words had a hollow sound to them and I knew why. This man did not believe either of his suggestions. I thanked him for his time and turned away.

As we walked back to our farm Selemon continued to come up with crazy scenarios, but all I could think about was that I might never find out what happened to Fili.

Chapter 61

Despite my prayers and faith, I'd began to lose all hope that I would ever see or talk to File again. The not knowing was so hard. There was nothing I could do though but keep living my life on the farm.

Zeray had gotten a little better, but not much. He hated my family and they all hated him. I felt as if I was walking on hard rocks all the time. I had to tiptoe between my husband and my family and constantly try to keep everything as peaceful as possible. There was never any real hope of total peace amongst them.

On the warfront there was at least a little hope of peace. We'd been hearing of the Organization of African Unity and how it was calling for a cease to the fighting. The United States and Rwanda had also been working on some kind of plan. As 1998 gave way to 1999, nobody was exactly sure how it would play out.

We continued to get plenty of news from Eri-TV. We were constantly told how dangerous Ethiopia was and how our neighbors were desperate to destroy us. Our president often came on the TV and radio to assure us that he would not let this happen. He would work tirelessly to defeat our oppressors.

I found his words to be contradictory because it was he who had initiated this war. Maybe it was true to at least some degree. Maybe Ethiopia was a huge threat to Eritrea. But these thoughts made the faces of my Ethiopian friends who had had helped me so much through the years pop into my head. The last time I saw them they were giving me bread. They could not be a threat. It wasn't the people. It was the governments.

One evening we had just finished watching one of President Afewerki's announcements when the phone rang. I hurried over to it. Every time it rang I had a quick thought that it just might be Fili. It was not my son, but I was excited nonetheless. I heard Hannah's voice on the other end.

"Hi Momma," she said, and I could feel her smile through the phone.

"Hannah! It is so good to hear from you."

"I'm at Winta's for two weeks during the winter break. How are things there?"

"They are good. Still no word from Fili," I replied.

It was not very often when I got to talk with Hannah or Muse. They had been separated now for some time, Hannah in one group home and Muse in another. Despite their struggles they were both doing well and this made my chest swell with happiness.

"I am sure he will contact you when he can," Hannah reassured me.

"I know he will. How is it going in Germany? How is school?"

"It is good," Hannah said. "My grades are good and I just got a job delivering papers."

"That's wonderful!"

"Also, I don't think I have talked to you since I got into a fight."

"A fight?"

"Yes, this boy has been so mean to me and he threw my backpack into a tree. I had enough so I confronted him. He threw a book at me and got kicked out of school."

"Are you alright?"

"I'm fine. He got what he deserved."

"Hannah, you cannot do this. What if you were the one who got in trouble?"

"I know, Momma, but I just could not take it anymore."

I couldn't help but picture my little girl off in a completely foreign world having to get into a fight to protect herself. It stung because it hit home with me that life was not exactly easy for her either.

"I am just glad you are okay, Hannah," I said. "I love you very much."

We talked a little more about the war and the rest of the family. The conversation was too short, as was always the case, but it was so good to hear from her. I longed to have her with me again. I longed to have Fili and Muse with me as well.

I did not know if this dream would ever come true with two of my children in Europe and another lost in Ethiopia, but I still prayed for it every day.

Chapter 62

Zeray took a long drag of his cigarette and then blew the smoke into the air. "I'm taking Sahra to Germany," he said.

The words hit me hard, but I did not flinch. "I understand," I replied.

I hated the idea of having my baby girl leave us, but it was much like when Hannah and Muse left. It was a very difficult way to give them the opportunity at a better life. After talking with Zeray, I sat down with Sahra and explained this to her.

"I don't want to go. I need to be here to help take care of Selemon," she said.

Her response made me remember Hannah's response some five years earlier. She too had wanted to stay to help protect her siblings.

"I know Sahra. Of course I do not want you to go, but it will be for a better life. You will probably get to see your brother and sister often."

Sahra looked down at her hands and then back up at me. Tears glistened in her eyes. "I will miss you, Momma."

I reached over and hugged her tightly. "I will miss you too."

The following morning Selemon came up to me before school. His gentle spirit was quiet as well, so when he talked, I listened. "I should go with Sahra," he said in a very serious voice for an eight year old.

"Do you want to take care of her?" I asked.

"Yes, I can make sure she is okay in Germany."

"It is not time for you to go yet, but maybe soon you will be able to protect all your brothers and sisters in Germany."

Saying this made me wince with hurt. I did not want my family so far away, but I didn't have much of a choice. Our country was at war and I knew there was a better world out there. Afewerki had been working feverously to build up our army. Boys and girls were being pulled from their families to join the fighting. He'd told us over and over that it was a must since Ethiopia was building up its army so it could crush us.

The war was not on my mind though on the morning I hugged my little girl. She was 14 years old and much more prepared for Germany than Hannah or Muse had been, but she was still my baby and I was letting her go. Zeray held her suitcase and impatiently stood to the side. He was going with her to Germany so he could see his kids, Winta and Kibrom, as well. I of course asked to go along so I could see Hannah and Muse, but he quickly shot down that idea.

"I love you so much, Sahra. You will do wonderful things. Have courage and believe in yourself." My throat felt so tight as I squeezed the words out.

"I love you too, Momma. I will have courage," she replied.

Then I watched Sahra give Selemon a hug and she walked away. I watched until I could see her no more, and then Selemon and I went inside and cried.

Now it was just me and my little Selemon. The rest of my children were either thousands of kilometers away or lost. My whole adult life I had bounced from one house to the next and endured the beatings from Zeray in order to keep my family together. Now I felt as if I had failed.

Chapter 63

In February of 1999, the tension had grown and the armies were ready to really unleash on each other. Then Afewerki rejected the US/Rwanda peace plan and the war spiraled out of control.

Ethiopia attacked with everything it had. Eritrea fought back, but in a matter of a week the Ethiopian army had pushed the Eritrean army back into Eritrea. Now, both countries accepted the Organization of African Unity's peace plan, but that didn't exactly stop the fighting.

It kicked up again later in the year and it was just as fierce. We continued to hear of families we knew who had lost loved ones, and I continued to wonder if Fili was out there fighting somewhere or if he was somewhere in Ethiopia.

My brother, Yafet, and his wife came back onto the farm. It was strange because so many members of my family from childhood were together, and yet my own family was fragmented. Of course Yafet and Zeray did not get along very well either. One day while I was washing clothes outside of our room I watched them almost get into a fist fight. I don't even think they knew why they were fighting.

It was a late summer day when I was washing farm equipment and Yafet came up to me. "Zeray is pathetic, Abeba. He does not deserve to live here and he definitely doesn't deserve any land for a house."

I stopped cleaning and squinted up at my brother. "Land for a house? What are you talking about?"

"Don't try to pretend like you don't know."

"You do not make any sense," I said.

"Papa is giving you land so you and Zeray can build a real house on the farm. He says, 'They should not live in such a small room.' I don't know why he would do such a thing for Zeray."

"I had no idea. Maybe he is doing it for me and Selemon, not Zeray?"

"Yes, you are the chosen one." Yafet rolled his eyes and then turned to walk away.

I did not know what else to do so I finished cleaning. About an hour later I saw my father coming in from the fields. He was slightly stooped over and his shoulders seemed to just hang from his neck. The years of coaxing food from the fields had been hard on his body. Still, he worked for hours on end every day. I walked toward him and we met in front of the barn.

"What is this I hear of land?" I asked.

He rubbed his glistening creased neck with his hand. "I'm giving you land to build a house over there." He pointed off into the distance. "It will be good for you."

"But it will make the rest of the family so mad. You know they hate Zeray."

"I hate him too, but you need a house and not a single room. You are almost 40 years old now."

That evening after dinner I told Zeray about my father's plans. "Good," he said. "I'm tired of living in this hole in the wall."

He did not show any gratitude and I did not expect it.

The next day it seemed everybody was especially tense. The family was so angry and it made me both sad and mad. My younger sister, Letina, was back to visit for a wedding. She had been living in the United States for many years. "Why the hell is he giving you land? Build your house where your husband is from."

"This is my family," I responded. Letina did not like hearing that.

And then we got news about the war. There was heavy fighting south of Asmara. The Ethiopians attacked and the Eritrean army pushed them back. There were claims that up to fifty Ethiopian tanks had been turned into smoldering piles of broken steel and that hundreds of Ethiopians were dead.

All this did was give me an empty feeling. It seemed that my life was full of empty victories and constant turmoil. But I could have never guessed the shock I would soon receive.

Chapter 64

My mouth hung open as if my jaw had been broken. I looked at the doctor and wondered if he had lost his mind. "There is no way," I said.

"There is a way, because you are definitely pregnant."

I had felt sick off and on for a while and feared I might have some kind of disease. That was apparently not the case. I was going to have another baby. That just didn't sound right, but it must be true. I thought back to the times Zeray and I had been together. He was not nearly as demanding or aggressive as he once was, but he was still a man.

"You are one hundred percent sure?"

The doctor nodded in answer.

My youngest son, Selemon, was now eight years old and Sahra and Hannah were teenagers. Muse was on the verge of being a man and Fili was already a man. I thought I was done with diapers and breastfeeding, but it seemed God had other plans.

The news hit everyone with surprise, and it only added to my troubles. We had the land from my father and would soon start the process of building the house. The tension between Zeray and my family was still high. My belly grew and my feet swelled and I was beginning to come to terms with the fact that I was going to have another baby.

My family was very nice to me and I was so grateful to have them. Zeray was focused on the house and making money as he began to rebuild his political connections. He was able to do this because there was finally a break in the war. The Algiers Peace Agreement had been signed and both countries were left in shambles. Thousands and thousands of young men and women had been killed, food was scarce, and our fragile economy had been broken. And really the peace agreement did not lead to peace. The troops still lined up along the border and Afewerki continued to tell us how dangerous Ethiopia was.

Zeray almost never talked to me about political things, but one night he was very drunk after spending hours with an old friend. I was not yet asleep because my swollen feet ached so badly. He started talking about the government. "There is a lot of turmoil. I think many officials are upset with Afewerki."

"What do you mean?" I asked.

"The war and the prisons and the aggressiveness..." His words slurred and he just kind of drifted away from them. A moment later he was asleep with his shoes still on.

We had all heard about how Afewerki had thrown political rivals in jail and many people had been executed or just disappeared, but nobody really talked too much about it because we were afraid. As the war had unfolded there were rumors that Afewerki feared there were Ethiopian spies in

Eritrea. He started a network of Eritreans to spy on their own people.

Nobody knew exactly what to believe, but it did seem that there was some sort of struggle amongst our political leaders, the very same ones that had worked to gain independence during the first war with Ethiopia.

This border war had been terrible and so many Eritrean people were hurting because of it. We were fortunate that we still had food to eat, and I needed it as I got closer and closer to giving birth. Finally, one day I knew it was time. I was on the very same floor where as a young woman I had given birth to Fili over twenty years earlier. I looked up at the faces. My mother and my sister, Rosina, were there, and two mid-wives were with them.

I feared the birth would be hard because I was 40 years old, but it was not. After a short time of painful pushing my sixth child, Michael Habtu, came into the world. One of the mid-wives toweled him off and handed him to me. He was just as beautiful as all my other children and I made a silent vow that I would take care of this one until my last breath.

Chapter 65

The rumblings which Zeray had drunkenly spoken of seemed to be growing. The rumors of political trouble trickled through our country because each person remained careful about what they said to the next. Despite this, it was generally believed that the other high-up officials of President Afewerki's government were pushing him toward democracy. They were tired of the fighting, and felt that the border war with Ethiopia made no sense.

Our president did not see it this way. He believed that a very centralized group should control the rest, even though he'd said numerous times that his government would not be that way and the constitution would one day be implemented.

I was busy taking care of baby Michael at this time and Selemon was doing his best to help me. He loved the idea of being a big brother. For so long he was the little one, now he was the big one.

Zeray was working his way around the political networks and digging himself into that life once again. And then something happened that shook the world.

We rarely got information about other countries except for our now sworn enemy, Ethiopia, and maybe Sudan. And after the

US/Rwanda peace treaty was denied we certainly did not get much news about the United States.

Then September 11th happened.

The planes hit the World Trade Centers and the Pentagon and the world's eye was turned to the United States. Even us Eritreans were drawn to the unfolding events in New York and Washington DC, and this gave Afewerki the right moment to capture total control.

Just one week after September 11th, he shocked us all by imprisoning the other members of his inner circle and all the independent media. In a two day period the landscape of our government changed significantly.

The world was too preoccupied with all that was going on with the terrorist attacks to really notice what had happened in our tiny country in the horn of Africa.

At the time I don't think any of us realized exactly what would happen because of this. It was the beginning of the end of what little freedom we had. It was obvious that those who opposed Afewerki would be dealt with in the harshest of ways, and hopes of instituting our constitution and getting the freedom that we worked so hard to earn had vanished in an instant.

Over the months to come the national service was in full swing and pretty much all adult men and women could be subjected to it. First, there was a six-month stretch at Sawa military camp that was pure hell. Many people could not even make it through these camps and died or committed suicide by hanging or burning themselves.

Many other people were rounded up for no reason and they just disappeared. Some believed they were sent to secret prisons in the desert and others believed they were simply murdered. There didn't even have to be any reason for it either. Maybe a spy had told somebody that a person had talked badly and then poof, they were gone. The spy network had exploded and everybody was afraid to say anything bad about our president.

Many Eritreans decided to try to flee the country, but it was forbidden. If they were caught they were shot dead and left in the sand. Our country was now a hellish prison. It happened with amazing speed and everybody was reeling with fear and confusion.

As Afewerki's iron fist slammed down upon us with all its might, I was also about to have to deal with many more problems right in my own home.

Chapter 66

We were in our new home. It was much bigger than the room we were in before. It had the same metal ceiling and thin walls, but it was definitely nicer as well. Michael was now a year old and Selemon was almost ten years old. I worried for him so much. The government had decided that nobody who was at least eight years old could leave the country.

Selemon was stuck in the country and I continued to hear horrible stories about the military camp and the national service. A son of our friend returned after the camp and he had lost at least ten kilograms of weight. He had been a happy boy full of hope. Now he was hardened and his childhood joy had been pulled out of him. One day at the village bar he sat outside and started telling us his story.

"The food gave everybody diarrhea," he's said. "One skinny kid kept getting sicker and sicker. The guards did not care and they kept pushing him. He fell down and they hit him. Finally after a week of this I thought he might die. And then we were outside in the sand being put through drills. He fell to his knees and pulled a match from his pocket. He lit his shirt on fire and it became engulfed in flames. He screamed and screamed and fell to the ground, but the fire didn't have any gasoline and it went out. The smell of his burning body was terrible and the sounds he made will never leave me. The guards just stood by and watched until the boy's breathing became labored and then stopped. He was taken away and a moment later we were back to doing drills as if it had never happened."

It was stories like these that haunted me when I looked at my sweet and innocent Selemon. Just the day before he'd come home with swollen hands. "What happened?" I asked.

"I forgot to do my homework and the teacher hit my hands with a stick."

This beating of children was a normal practice and I hated it, but to see my sweet son with bruises and swelling made me furious. "They should not do this! They are helping to create the violence and abuse in our country."

Selemon just offered me a small shrug. "It is okay, Momma," he said. "Next time I will get my homework done on time."

He was gentle and he reminded me so much of Fili. They both had kind and caring spirits. I wondered if Michael would be like them or if he would lean toward Muse's personality. Muse was a fiery kid who wasn't afraid to mix it up with others.

It was a cool morning when I was in the field and thinking about all of my kids when I got a sudden wave of nausea. It came as fast as it went, but I almost instantly wondered if by some miracle I was pregnant again.

I went into the village to see the doctor. I was told he had been taken away just two days earlier. The soldiers said he was treating people who were traitors to Eritrea. I could not believe this news. The doctor was nothing but a doctor. He was a kind, elderly man. Now he was gone and he would surely never be seen again.

I walked down to one of the mid-wife's houses and she was able to see me. "I cannot be one hundred percent sure," she said, "but I believe that you are pregnant again."

I thought she was right, but it was still shocking. I was almost 42 years old. I should be a grandmother, not a mother once again, but seven months later right there on the floor of my momma's house I gave birth one more time. Everything was fine except for a growing pain in my hip.

John came into the world in 2003, and now I had three boys in the home, three children in Germany, and one lost in Ethiopia. I had a big family, but it did not feel like it.

It was not long after John's birth when my own family and I began to really fall apart, and it would be more than I could ever bear.

It started when my momma got sick. She had always been so kind, and she was strong in a silent way. She'd tried hard to protect me for my whole life. Her sickness happened so fast. She'd had diabetes and high blood pressure for years and had been in some pain, but she went from being herself to being bed ridden in a matter of days.

The doctor came and gave her some medicine, but when we walked outside he stopped and looked at my father. "It does not look good. I think her conditions have done a lot of damage to her body. I will get another doctor and we will try to get her to the hospital within the next day. I have given her medicine for the pain, but I am very concerned."

He never came back with the other doctor. The night after he left I was sitting in a chair by my momma's bed when she made a loud groaning sound. "Momma, are you okay?" I asked.

She did not answer. Instead, the air seemed to just slide from her lungs. I went to her and put her hand in mine. Her eyes fluttered, and then she was gone.

Chapter 67

It was just the family and a few friends at the funeral. There was a lot of screaming and sobbing as my mother was carried to her burial place. Then we stood as the man of God talked about how kind my mother was. He had known her for many years, but he did not know her as I did. He did not know just how much she did for me and my siblings. The morning was cool and my dress fluttered in the slight breeze. For some reason I focused on the feeling of the material as it hit my leg. Maybe it was my way to try to keep from breaking down.

Others said a few words and there was more crying. I did not feel like doing either. I just stood there with a numb feeling while thinking about my momma's life. Soon, she was gone and the funeral was over. I looked to the left and my heart was filled with a strange mixture of comfort and grief. My momma was laid to rest right next to her little boy, Aman, who had been killed so many years ago when the wall fell on him. I hoped that they were now together once again and I said a quick prayer to God asking Him to make sure that they were. Then I gripped my father's hand and we walked away.

It was a hard few weeks for us, but despite the terrible loss of my mother and the country continuing down the road of complete chaos, my father did fine, just as he'd always done on the farm. It had been in the family for so long and he was an expert at bringing forth the crops. He had a little bit of money saved and life for him was okay. I could tell that it was now harder for him since Momma was gone. He spent so many hours in the fields, and I think it comforted him.

We had started receiving money from Muse and Hannah and Sarah. They were now out of the orphanage and had all found jobs. Muse was working in construction in a city called Hamburg. Hannah and Sahra were working in the hotel industry in a town called Heidelberg. They had sent money to us for many years, but now they were able to send much more.

I was so proud of them and amazed by them. They had grown up on their own and now they were together and making it. And they gave me a sliver of hope that one day we would all be together and happy far away from the prison that President Afewerki had created.

As the years passed we were able to get some gold thanks to the money they sent. Gold was being mined in Eritrea and it seemed that it could become a very good product for making more money, or at least that is what Zeray thought. At the time it was inexpensive and he thought that soon it would be worth much more money. I knew that we would need a lot of money because we had to find a way to get Selemon out of the country. By 2007, he was 15 years old and each day brought him closer and closer to being sent to the Sawa military camp for his national service.

This so called service had really become more a form of slavery, and now kids were sent to the camp to complete their last year of school, but of course most of them could not complete it because they were forced to do military activities instead of study.

The border was still being guarded and we were still bombarded with words about the threat from Ethiopia. Tension and small uprisings of violence erupted every so often and Afewerki continued to tell us that he was the only one who could really protect us.

He was really a master of brainwashing us into inaction by creating one crisis or another. That way we would be preoccupied with survival instead of thoughts of trying to force him out of power.

The stories of sickness and death and brutality rolled out of Camp Sawa like waves on the beach. Some had escaped it and told stories of running from machine gun fire and being cut up on barbed wire. Many others tried to escape but could not outrun the bullets.

Now though, in November of 2007, we all tried to put the violence and pain behind us as we attended my cousin's wedding. Our gold was in a small brown pouch hidden in the corner of the room. I wondered if I should just leave it there, but then I feared that with all of us gone it would be easy for somebody to come in and steal it.

I slipped the pouch with the 150 grams of gold into my bag. I did not want it with me, but decided it would be safer.

The wedding was a tiny moment of freedom that I relished. We sang and danced and laughed. As I danced, I kept feeling a sharp pain in my hip. I did not think too much of it. It was only a few years ago when I'd had John. Now he was four years old and I laughed and laughed as I watched him and his big brother, Michael, as they danced around the room.

In the middle of all the fun, Zeray came up to me. "I'm ready to go home. Let's go."

"Oh Zeray, let's stay a little longer. It is so much fun."

Anger flickered in his eyes, but it was so much weaker than it used to be. I did not doubt that he still wanted to hit me from time to time, but he had not done so since he was thrown in prison in Ethiopia.

"I'm ready now," he said in a firm voice.

"I want to dance one more time."

"Fine, dance all you want. I am taking the kids home."

A moment later, I hugged Michael and John and they left with their father and Selemon. I felt sad that they were unable to stay, but soon I was dancing once again.

It wasn't until midnight when I arrived home with my sister, Rosina, and my brother Yafet and his wife, Weini. Because it was so late and we did not want to disturb anybody, we decided to sleep at our father's house.

I remembered the gold and pulled the pouch from my bag. "We need to put our gold somewhere safe," I said to her.

"I know a good place," she said.

I handed her the pouch and watched as she put it on the back of a shelf in the small closet and then locked the door and slipped the key in her purse. "It is safe now," she said.

I fell asleep in a hurry, and woke up bright and early at six in the morning. I did not want to wake anybody else so I slipped across the street to my house. Later that morning, I saw Rosina. "Is the gold alright?" I asked.

"It's fine," she replied.

"I will come get it later."

I was around the back of my house doing laundry. Michael and John were playing in the yard and Selemon was across the way at the barn working on a piece of farm equipment. It was a nice day and the music from the wedding still played in my head when I heard commotion and somebody was running through my house and yelling. I quickly sat down the clothing and wiped my wet hands on my towel. I headed for the noise and found Yafet coming out of the door.

"Abeba, come quick."

"What is it?"

He was already leaving, so I followed him.

We got to my father's house in a matter of moments. Yafet burst through the door. Rosina and Weini were standing in the room. There were streaks of tears on Weini's face. "What is going on?" I asked in a frantic voice.

"Our gold, yours, mine, and Weini's, is gone!"

"Gone?" I felt my world tilt a little bit. "How?"

"It was stolen."

I started to reply, but flashes of Selemon setting himself on fire in Camp Sawa flooded my brain. Everything spun around in a big circle and my knees gave out. I collapsed to the floor in a heap.

Chapter 68

Germany 2011

I was in surgery and then fell into a coma so I was unaware that my hip surgery had proved too much for my fragile body and it had started to shut down. The doctors worked feverishly as my pulse grew weaker. They cut away at the bone and pumped medicine into me in an effort to keep me alive.

Hannah and Sahra and Muse sat outside of the door. They knew by the frantic sounds and the calls for medications and doctors that I was in serious trouble. Hannah later said that there was a time that a nurse rushed through the door. "How is my mother?" She asked.

The nurse looked her straight in the eye. "We are trying to keep her alive." The Germans were not ones for dancing around a serious topic.

My children could do nothing but wait to find out my fate. After many hours, a doctor entered the room in which they were sitting. "We have removed the tumor. Your mother was very weak and for a brief time we lost her pulse. We were able to revive her, but she is now in a coma."

My children were able to come into my room in intensive care. "It scared me," Sahra later said.

"The machines and wires and beeping, I didn't know if you'd ever wake up."

One hour after another passed, and I remained motionless in my bed. My kids waited just outside of the room, none of them willing to leave the hospital for even a moment. I do not remember if I dreamed. I do not remember if I had any idea about the state I was in. It seems that I was in some strange place teetering between life and death.

It was 27 hours after I had come out of surgery when light flooded over me. I didn't know what was happening or where I was. My body felt strangely numb. The light flickered and I heard something in the distance. And then it went black again.

A moment later the light returned. This time it was clearer, and when it flickered I realized it was because my eyelids were fluttering up and down. I heard the noise again. It was a voice. I listened harder and realized it was Muse.

"Momma, Momma, you are awake! You were in a coma."

I felt a hand on mine and it squeezed gently.

Soon, other people were around me. Nurses worked on the machines and asked Muse to ask me questions. I learned that I had been in a coma for 27 hours after serious complications with the surgery.

My mouth was so dry and my lips felt as if they were split into a thousand pieces, but I managed a smile when I heard two more familiar voices. Hannah and Sahra rushed into the room moments after I awoke. They had been in the cafeteria to get coffee. Neither one of them had slept since I went into the coma.

I remained in the intensive care room for an entire week. The doctors told me that they had to put in some kind of metal fake bone into my hip because they had to completely remove the other one. They got the cancer in my hip bone, but there was more cancer around it and in my body. After I became stronger I would begin radiation.

Of course this scared me, but I remembered how my children had told me over and over that I was too strong for the surgery to take me. Besides, I still had to get my other three children out of Sudan.

I talked to God a lot in the week after the surgery. I thanked him repeatedly and told him that I would do whatever I needed to show how grateful I was for the life he had given me. Now I wanted to give a life to Selemon and Michael and John, a life that was a long ways away from Eritrea and Sudan, a life that they would be grateful for as well.

Chapter 69

Eritrea

The words bounced around in my head and seemingly turned my brain into mush. "It was stolen," was what Rosina had just said to me, but I couldn't believe it. I was now propped up on one arm and sitting on my right hip. I took a deep breath as Yafet helped me into a chair.

"I don't understand." I said.

"We don't either. Look at the door. It is not even broken."

"But nobody knew about the gold except us."

"Somebody must have known," Yafet said. "All our gold is gone!"

"How did it happen?"

Rosina stepped toward me. "Weini and I went to the grocery store. We were not gone very long. When we returned we found the closet unlocked and the gold was gone."

This had to be some kind of bad dream. What would Selemon do now? We would not be able to help him escape from the country without the money. He would be forced to go to Camp Sawa and I would lose him. I just knew it. I thought of Fili as well. My oldest son had been lost to us for almost ten years now. I just could not lose Selemon too.

"You look very sick, Abeba," Rosina said. "Let's get some air."

We walked through the door into the sunlit afternoon. I felt as if I'd had too much to drink. I was still a little bit disoriented from hearing the shocking news.

As we crossed the yard, I looked at Rosina. "Who do you think stole it?"

She hesitated for a brief moment. "I believe it was my brother."

"Really? You think Yafet stole it?"

"When we were gone he came home to eat lunch and was already gone when we returned. He knew where the key and the gold were. And there is nothing else missing. A thief would take other things and not even know about the gold."

This made a lot of sense. "So what do you think we should do?"

"I think we should report it. The police will figure it out."

With the current state of our country there was never any way to know how something like this could turn out. "Are you sure that is a good idea?" I asked.

"I don't know, but what else should we do?"

I thought about it for a moment and decided that we should take the risk. Rosina agreed, and we walked to the police station.

It was just an old white building with peeling paint and a beaten up police car sitting by the front door. We entered, and the wooden door squeaked loudly as I pushed it. A young policeman who sat at a desk shot us a wary look. "What do you need?"

"We had our gold stolen," Rosina replied.

We explained the story to the man. He nodded as we talked and seemed somewhat interested. Afterward, he stood and asked us to wait where we were. I watched him walk away and felt that we should run. How could we know if he believed us or thought we were liars? Were we about to be thrown in jail and accused of horrible things?

He returned after only a moment with two younger officers.

"They will go to the house with you."

It seemed they believed us and I sighed with relief.

We rehashed the story as we walked back to the house. We arrived and the officers looked around the room and then turned their attention to the closet. They asked us a few questions and we answered them the best we could.

Finally, one of them said, "Who do you suspect took your gold?"

Rosina and Weini exchanged a glance, and then Rosina spoke up. "I think it was my brother, Yafet."

"I agree," Weini said. "I believe my husband did it."

I could not believe what I was hearing. Maybe he did steal the gold, but the way they both told the officers so quickly that they thought it was him surprised me.

"Do you live here?" the officer directed his question to me.

"No, I am a married woman. I live across the street with my husband."

"How much gold did she give you?" the officer asked Rosina.

"About 150 grams," she replied.

The officer asked some more general questions, and then he asked where Yafet was.

"He is in the field probably. He will be here soon," Weini said.

A moment later the officers walked toward the field. Yafet and our father were walking toward the house. The officers cut them off and informed Yafet that he was being arrested for stealing the gold.

He wiped away the sheen of sweat on his face and kind of shook his head back and forth. "Arrested?"

"Yes, we believe you stole the gold."

It seemed Yafet was too bewildered to do or say anything else. A moment later he was in handcuffs and the officers led him away.

There was no way I could have known what trouble this would cause for me.

Chapter 70

Zeray threw his still-lit cigarette against the wall and stepped toward me. "How the hell was it stolen!" he yelled.

I stepped back and prepared for his fists to launch at my face. "I was trying to protect it," I said.

"Your family is pathetic," he yelled. "They are snakes and thieves."

He had the look in his eye that he used to have just before he unleashed his hatred on me. I backed up a little bit further. "Yafet is arrested," I said in an effort to settle Zeray. "He is in jail and we will get the gold back."

"You don't know that. You don't even know if it was Yafet who did it. It could have been your slut sister, Rosina!" Spittle flew from his mouth as he yelled.

He spun away from me and toward the door. "I'm going over there," he said.

I was glad to be spared from violence, at least for the moment, but I knew that if he went over there he would release his fury . I quickly followed him. "Zeray, don't do this," I begged.

He did not listen and marched across the street with his fists clinched. He got to the front door of my father's house and shouldered it open. It swung in and banged against the wall. I was just two steps behind him. My father sat in a wooden chair working on a small piece of metal. He shot to his feet. "What the hell are you doing, Zeray?"

"I want my damn gold," Zeray demanded.

"I don't have your gold. And it's not yours anyway. It's Abeba's."

"Where is your slut daughter?"

"Shut your mouth," my father said.

Zeray got real close to him. His eyes had a crazy look in them. "It's my gold if I say it's my gold. Your thieving family is worthless."

"You're living on my land, on my farm. You are the worthless one," my father shot back.

Zeray got right into his face and I was sure they would fight, but then I noticed my father had brought the piece of sharp metal up. He stuck it right against Zeray's neck.

There was a moment where we all stood in silence. It reminded me of the time they had a confrontation in Addis Ababa many years ago. Zeray let out a long breath that had a slight growl with it. He stepped backwards and shook his head in disgust.

"I'm going out," he said.

I looked at my father and he looked at me. He had the hard eyes that I remembered from my childhood when he would come home and beat us.

I left the house without saying a word. By the time I got to the street, Zeray was already gone.

After the confrontation, there was so much tension around the farm. Nobody was very happy with anybody else, and I felt like a trench had been dug between me and my family. Zeray had his thoughts and they had their thoughts. Mine fell somewhere in between. I was worried sick for Yafet, but also mad at him. He was still in jail and yet my gold had not been returned.

After two weeks of being completely on edge, my family called me over to my father's house. I noticed they waited until Zeray was out drinking. I entered the room and saw my father and Rosina and Weini sitting around the table. They all wore uneasy looks.

The table had a piece of paper and a pen on it. "What is this?" I gestured to the table.

"Sit down," my father said.

I sat and looked around the table.

"We should forget about the gold," my father said. "We should drop the charges and get Yafet out. We all agree and we've signed this." He pushed the paper toward me. "We need you to sign it as well."

I stared at it, uncertain about what to do.

"We've all already signed it," Rosina said.

I glanced at her and then back down at the paper. "I'm not sure. If he took it I do not think I should sign. How can you just give up your gold?"

Rosina shifted her weight to the side as if she was uneasy with this question.

"Just sign it," my father said.

"I think I need to talk with my husband before I make this decision."

My father leaned forward and placed his forearms on the table. "Why do you have to go to him? It's your gold anyway." His voice rose as he talked. "And besides, if he doesn't like it you can leave him and live with us."

This was an option that I might have jumped at years ago, but now I was already living here and I needed the gold to set up Selemon's escape. "If you give me my gold back, I'll sign."

It was a bold thing to say, but I just had a feeling that there was much more to this story than what was going on. Maybe Yafet had taken the gold, but with the others being so willing to sign this paper to get him out I had an itch in my brain that told me they were involved somehow as well.

"We are not going to give it to you," my father said. "Even if it is missing it's just a material thing. You should sign to get him out."

"I'm not going to sign until I find out exactly WHO took the gold." It was the first time I had raised my voice in a long time and I never raised it to my father.

He sat back in the chair with an angry look on his face. "You are no longer my daughter from this point forward, and we will say that you stole it and get you arrested."

Hot tears started to fill my eyes, but I held them in. My family was everything to me, but this was not right. I pushed the chair backwards and stood. Without a word, I walked out the door.

Chapter 71

The following weeks were absolutely horrible. I started having a hard time sleeping at night and I felt sad all the time. I barely ate any food and never felt hungry. My kids and I were separated by continents, one would be forced to go to Camp Sawa soon, and now my father had disowned me.

No of this mattered to Zeray. He acted as if he had really achieved something special. For so many years he had tried to drive a wedge between my family and me. He'd even moved me all the way to Ethiopia to split me from them. Now we lived right next to each other, but I was not a part of the family.

It was so unfair. I had done nothing. My gold was stolen and then I stood up for myself. That was it. Maybe I should have just signed the paper, but I'd lived so long in an unjust household and now our whole country was unjust. It was as if I could take no more of it.

Zeray was still very angry that the gold was gone, but not because it changed our plans to get Selemon out of the country. He just liked having the money available.

I had told him we should tell Hannah and Sahra and Muse. They would send money. "No," Zeray said. "They should not know about this. They will be too worried about you and not be able to work or get in an accident because they are so stressed out about it."

I understood what he meant, so I did not tell them.

After three months, Yafet was transferred to a different prison and we were able to visit him. Even though Weini and I now did not talk much at all, we went together to see Yafet. We sat at a table that reminded me of the one I sat at when Zeray was in the Ethiopian prison.

Yafet came through the door. I don't know what happened, but as soon as he entered the room I burst into tears. I felt so terrible for everything. I did not know if he took the gold or not. The others, including Weini, had signed the paper saying that they dropped the charges. I was the one keeping Yafet here, and it made me sick. But at the same time I felt that it was the only hope I had of ever getting the money to free Selemon.

It seemed that Yafet did not blame me, and I appreciated that. We all talked for a while. He would soon be sent back to the military. He was on leave for a month when the gold was stolen. I guess they figured that the Eritrean military and Eritrean prison were similar enough to punish him so they planned to send him back.

Before leaving, I gave Yafet 200 nafka. It was not much money, but I figured it might help him a little bit. As we walked away, Weini looked at me. "Drop the charges Abeba. You are being ridiculous and your family hates you."

"I do not see it that way," I replied.

That night I could not sleep at all. The next morning I talked Zeray into returning to the prison with me. We did not have very long with Yafet, but we did give him 200 more nafka. This time when we left, Zeray looked at me and said, "I am pretty sure he took the gold. And Rosina or Weini came up with the idea."

Maybe Zeray was right, but I couldn't stand the thought. I had already lost a lot of weight and I felt ten years older than I did just months earlier. I thought back to that night when we danced at the wedding. It might be my last happy memory ever.

The next few months of my life seemed to confirm this. My family still hated me and of course they hated Zeray too. Selemon was getting closer to being sent to Sawa, and although my other children had sent more money, it would not be enough. I felt helpless, and I continued to toss and turn through sleepless nights and eat just tiny amounts of food.

My family had stolen from me, and yet it was they who had branded me as the bad one, the outcast. Finally, Yafet returned for a week of leave before going back to the military. I hoped that he would forgive me and this would rub off on my family.

The opposite happened. They all decided to not talk to me. When they saw me coming they turned the other way. I was nothing to them, and it broke me. Just before Yafet was to return, he slipped away in the middle of the night. Zeray learned that he had a route set up and had paid people to get him across the border to Sudan. At that moment I knew it was absolutely true that he had stolen my gold and used it to help buy his way out of Eritrea. There was no other way he would have had enough money.

I had been right all along, but really he'd stolen a lot more than the gold. With it, he stole my family, and Selemon's freedom.

Chapter 72

Yafet had been gone for about a month when the military men arrived. They banged on my father's door. They were looking for Yafet's wife, Weini. I watched from my house in silence. Since Yafet was gone, she would be taken to prison. That is how it worked. If a family member escaped, others either paid 50,000 nafka, or about $3,000 dollars. If they did not have the money, they were thrown in jail. This was how the government made people return.

There was a commotion and then Weini stood in the doorway. The men talked with her and my father and Rosina. I couldn't hear what was being said. Any minute, I expected them to handcuff her and take her away.

Instead, she produced a large envelope. One of the soldiers took it and looked inside. After a little more talking, the soldiers turned and walked away. Their truck sped off and dust kicked up around my house. I looked through the dust in complete disbelief. They had paid the money to keep Weini out of jail.

I limped back into my house, my hip ached and I looked like a skeleton because I'd lost so much weight. I crumpled onto the couch and curled up into a fetal position. Low sobs came up from my chest.

They would not return the money that was stolen from me, but they would pay for Weini after it was her husband who ripped me off and set Selemon up for a life of hell.

John came into the room. "Momma, are you okay?"

"I'm fine little man," I replied.

"I am worried about you. I heard you crying in the middle of the night and you barely eat your food."

"I know, but do not worry. I will be fine. It has just been hard for me right now."

John seemed to accept this and snuggled up next to me. I put my hand on his back and rubbed. I just wanted my family together. I just wanted to be able to protect Selemon and all my other kids. I did not even care about myself.

I thought I would begin to get better. Instead, I got worse. It felt like all that had happened in my life had finally piled up on me and I could not take it anymore. I reached a point of complete despair. I was lucky to sleep one hour a night and I had to force myself to eat a piece of bread.

My hip had also grown more and more painful. Taking just ten steps caused pain to radiate down my leg.

One day I tried to talk to my family. I wanted them to ask for forgiveness. Now they had to know that they had done me wrong, but they still would not talk to me. If any of them would have said they were sorry I would have gladly accepted it even without getting the gold. I just wanted to be a part of my family again.

This never happened, and as 2007 gave way to 2008, I was completely broken. Zeray had been talking about suing Rosina for some time. I could not stomach this idea. He still kept at it though. "They cheated you," he'd say. "It is your gold, our gold, we deserve it. It can still help Selemon."

It was the last argument, about helping Selemon, which planted the seed in my head. Maybe it was our only hope to find his escape from Camp Sawa?

Finally, after 18 months of being dead to my family, Zeray and I sued Rosina. This of course created a whole new firestorm of anger from my family. It hurt me, but not so bad. I was already so hurt, both emotionally and physically. The pain in my hip had remained and even gotten worse. I had been to a doctor and he said I may need surgery. This scared me a great deal.

The court date came and we all left the farm at about the same time, but did not travel together. The courthouse was down the street from the police station and it looked similar, just an old building that looked as if it was begging for the day when it could tumble to the ground.

We all sat down at the tables and the proceedings got started. We explained our side and then Rosina explained hers. "I did not ever receive any gold from Abeba. She is lying about it. She has never liked me."

I could not believe she would say such a thing. Then I remembered that she had testified to something completely different when the gold went missing. I had the police show the report. It clearly stated that she had placed the gold in the closet and right at the bottom was her signature.

With that, she lost the case. She had lied for much of her life, even slept with my husband, and I had still tried to forgive her. Unfortunately, she nor the rest of my family would forgive me even though I was not at fault. The court's decision gave me some kind of validation, and it also gave me hope that we could still help Selemon.

After so long of being in complete despair, I felt I had something to reach for. I just did not know if I would be able to grasp it.

Chapter 73

It took some time for the court to decide exactly how much Rosina should pay us. Then in February of 2009 we got the paper. She owed me 300,000 nafka, or almost $15,000. I could not believe it was this much because it was more than the gold was worth, but I didn't complain. Over the next couple months I started receiving the money. I did not know where it came from, and I did not care.

Zeray quickly got ahold of it and put it in the bank. "We don't want you to lose this like you lost the gold," he said to me.

This was an unfair, but expected, statement. And the money probably was safer in his bank. I immediately began asking Zeray to start looking for a way to get Selemon out. He was now 17 years old and just a few months away from being sent to Camp Sawa. The news from there had continued to be horrible. The kids were beaten and forced into big shipping containers. They lived in tiny spaces and ate food that was absolutely sickening.

Zeray said he would talk to a few people, but he did not seem too focused on it. "You have to use some connections," I said to him. "We have the money now."

"It's not so easy, Abeba. You know there are spies all over the country. They will turn me in without even having a second thought about it, and I will be in prison again."

"Just hurry," I pleaded.

This only seemed to irritate him. Now we had this money and I got the feeling that he was more focused on spending it for himself instead of helping his son. One week after another passed and he had created no possibilities for Selemon.

I had no idea what I was doing, but I started talking to those who might be able to help. Then one day I saw one of his friends in the village. I was there to visit the doctor because my hip hurt every day and all day. I bumped into his friend and we walked down a side street behind a building.

"Zeray has talked to you about a route to Sudan for Selemon," I began. "Have you been able to find one? How long will it take?"

The man blinked and looked at me oddly. "I have not talked to Zeray about this."

I understood. He was being careful. For all he knew, I was a spy. "I see. You have not talked to Zeray, but if you had talked to him would you think that a route would be possible for the right price?"

"No Abeba, you do not see. I really have not talked to Zeray about this at all. I'm sorry. I cannot help you."

He turned and walked away, and I stood there dumbstruck. Could this be true? Zeray had told me he had talked to this man. He told me the man was looking into a route.

I limped home as fast as I could. When I arrived, Zeray was sitting at the kitchen table. Five beer bottles were spread out in a semi-circle. He wore a white tank top and a thin film of sweat had formed on his forehead.

I sat down across from him. "I ran into your friend, Dawit."

I stared at Zeray to see his reaction. He lifted his beer to his lips and took a sip, and then a smirk crept onto his face. "What did he say?"

"You know damn well what he said. You have not talked to him even though you told me you did."

He took another drink. "So what."

"So we are trying to save Selemon!"

"You are trying to save Selemon," he said. "Of course it would be good if he was out of here, but we cannot spend all this money for his escape. He is a strong boy. He will be fine at Sawa."

I stood and smacked one of the bottles with the back of my hand. It flew into another bottle. They spun off the table and crashed into the floor. "You bastard," I yelled. "Give me the money and I will do it on my own.

Zeray just smiled. "You're not getting the money, Abeba. You will only lose it."

I considered grabbing one of the bottles and hitting him in the head. I would bash his skull if I could, but I did not have that violence in me. Instead, I just turned and stormed out of the room.

He had seemed to be there for me in at least some small way. Now I knew it was for nothing but the money. I continued to work on finding a way to get Selemon out. To hell with Zeray.

Selemon's time for Sawa got closer and closer. One evening I sat down with him. "You know

I have been trying to find a way to get you out of Eritrea. I do not know if it will happen, but please promise me that you will not try to escape on your own. Thousands of people are shot at the border. It is too dangerous and I couldn't stand not knowing what happened to you."

Selemon reached out and grabbed my hand. "Don't worry, Momma. I will not escape. I have accepted that I will go to Sawa and I will be fine."

His eyes were so soft and full of kindness. He knew that I wanted what was best for him. He also knew that I could not get it. He was sparing me heartache by saying such a thing, and I loved him so much for it.

Two weeks later, I had a route, but the process of setting it up took too long.

My little Selemon was taken away.

Chapter 74

It was so frustrating to ride the bus right across the border into Sudan. If only I could have done this with Selemon everything would have been okay, but the checkpoints and men with machine guns made me realize that this idea was ludicrous. Zeray and I were old enough to leave the country. Selemon was not. I had thought a lot about Selemon. He was still at Sawa and I had not heard from him. I worried about him every day and prayed that he was alright. Zeray and I were now in Sudan so I could have surgery on my hip.

I'd hobbled around for so long, and now I could barely walk. The doctors were unsure what was wrong and I had begged Zeray to let me go to Germany where I could get proper treatment.

Zeray was not only against this, he didn't even want me to tell Hannah and Sahra and Muse about my pain. He used his previous argument that they would worry about me too much.

Early one morning I tried to get out of bed and my hip popped. The pain was excruciating. I slowly dropped back into the bed. Michael and John ran into the room after hearing my screams. "What is wrong, Momma," Michael asked in a worried voice.

"It's my hip. Something happened to it. Go get your father."

Zeray arrived a moment later and I told him what happened. "Are you sure you are not being dramatic?"

"No, something is very wrong. I have to go to the hospital."

Reluctantly, he agreed. It was a terrible process getting me out of the bed and into the car. Every movement shot pain all the way through my body, but finally we made it.

The doctor in the emergency clinic looked at me and pushed on my hip. It hurt so badly that I almost passed out. "I believe it is broken," he said. "She will need surgery."

This forced Zeray's hand, and while I was still in the hospital getting medications he called Hannah and Sahra. Later, I found out that they asked him to take me to Dubai because they had good medical care there.

Zeray never even mentioned this to me. Instead, he told me we would go to Sudan where there was supposed to be a very good hospital. I also learned that my children in Germany had sent money so I would be in a nice hospital. When we arrived at the dilapidated building I knew that this was a poor government hospital and I doubted that they "specialized in bones" as Zeray had said.

The walls were stained yellow creating a grimy feel to the room. And the equipment looked like it was from the 1970s. There was a smell that hung in the air, a mixture of urine and blood and something else that I couldn't identify. "Zeray, this place is not good for my surgery," I said.

"It's fine. They will treat you well. I'm sure of it."

They did not treat me well. I was wheeled into the room for surgery and they barely told me what was happening. All I knew was that my hip would be removed and I would have a new one put in its place. I did not know the dangers of the surgery or how long it would take me to recover, if I recovered at all.

As the doctor gave me a needle to put me to sleep I thought about Michael and John. They were now nine and seven years old. Thanks to all of the craziness with the gold and Selemon being sent to camp and my sickness, we had missed the opportunity to get them out of the country as well. I could only hope that in seven or eight years we would be living under very different conditions.

The medicine began to work and my vision grew fuzzy. Soon, my eyes were closed and I was asleep. The surgery must have been horrible, because when I awoke the pain found its way through the medication. My hip felt as if it was burning and my left leg was swollen.

I slowly became more alert and a nurse told me that the surgery was a success. I was given some water and fell back asleep despite the pain. A few hours later, I was awakened.

"It is time for you to go," the nurse said.

I thought she meant it was time for me to go to a different room. Instead, I was placed on a long gurney and four men entered the room. They carried me toward the front of the hospital. "Where are we going?" I asked.

"Is that not your husband?" one of them said.

I looked ahead. Zeray stood by the hospital entrance. He opened the door and walked outside with all of us. A cab was waiting. "I cannot go yet. I just had the surgery," I pleaded.

"We are finished. You will recover fine," another of the men said.

They helped me into the cab and I looked down at my hip. "But look, there is blood from my hip!"

"Your husband has your medication."

"Put a towel down first," the cab driver said.

I was situated in an odd position on my right hip with my head against the window. Zeray climbed in the other side. "It's not so bad is it?"

"I'm in horrible pain Zeray. They replaced my hip."

"You will be fine. I will take care of you."

"Why didn't you take me to a good hospital? Why didn't you get me the right treatment? Is money that important to you?"

He leaned over toward where I was resting and put his face close to mine. "How dare you talk to me like this? I just saved your life and don't you ever forget it."

The cab driver pulled away from the hospital and took us to a hotel. It was a rundown building with tiny rooms that only had two small cots and a TV. We stayed there for two weeks. Zeray did give me my medication and gave me some water and food. I slept in a painful haze for much of the two weeks, and often when I'd come out of it Zeray would not be there. Sometimes he came in and smelled like beer. I wasn't surprised.

Finally, we took a very painful flight back to Eritrea. My hip was still swollen, and now I had sores on my legs and backside from being stuck in the bed for so long. At least Michael and John were waiting for me on the other end.

Chapter 75

Germany 2012

The winter in Germany was something I couldn't have imagined when I lived in Ethiopia and Eritrea. The sun barely lifted above the horizon and it always felt cold, dark, and gray. I had a terrible time keeping warm and spent my days lying in bed trying to get strong enough to face the radiation.

I was in the hospital for another week after leaving intensive care. The doctor said that I would need six weeks at least before I was strong enough for my first dose. Sahra did research about radiation and she had told me what I could expect. I also had an appointment scheduled with a doctor in a few weeks.

While I tried to stay warm and waited for my body to get stronger, my children and I started talking about the possibility of getting Selemon and Michael and John out of Sudan. It would be a very difficult task to get all three of them. Often, people thought they had a reliable source and would pay a lot of money only to get a phone call that more money was expected or their loved one would be shot.

It was a crazy thing because we Eritreans saw Sudan as a gateway to a new and better life, a free life, and yet so many of us got stuck in Sudan. Muse had made some calls to people he knew in Sudan. Hannah and Sahra had been working hard to find possible routes. And all of them had been saving money.

As my body became stronger and I got closer to my first radiation treatment, it seemed a plan for an escape from Sudan was coming together. I prayed every night that it would happen soon.

I'd gone to a couple appointments with my doctor and he had explained how the radiation would work. Still, when the day finally came I was terribly nervous.

My hip wasn't as sore and my body was stronger, but not anywhere near how it used to be. I was taken to a room that had almost nothing in it. I still did not know much of the German language and Hannah was there to translate.

I would be in the room by myself for one week after taking two pills. I said my goodbyes to Hannah and the door was shut. I took the pills that were waiting for me on a small table. I knew I was basically swallowing radiation that was designed to kill my cancer.

I settled in and tried to relax, but it was not long before my mouth felt dry and my stomach felt funny. Over the next few days I was miserable and bored. My body swelled and I had almost nothing to do.

As I lay there hour after hour, I again talked a lot to God and I thought about my life. I had been through so many horrible things and I know that others would shake their heads and feel sorry for me, but I do not feel sorry at all.

I am sure that I could have done things differently, but I'm also sure that my life happened as it was supposed to happen, and now I have many wonderful children. I thought about my kids. I prayed that Selemon and Michael and John were well. I knew Hannah and Sahra and Muse were doing well, but I prayed for them too. And then I thought about Fili, my first-born son. It was 14 years earlier when we were ripped away from our lives in Addis Ababa.

I doubted I would ever find out where he was or what happened to him, and that thought made my already dry throat a little dryer.

Chapter 76

Eritrea

When we pulled into the farm I was listless due to the medication. It was the only thing that saved me during the two weeks in the hotel and then the plane ride.

The medication dulled the pain and put me into a state of being awake but feeling like I was dreaming. Zeray helped me out of the car and called for Michael and John. Both boys came running from around the house. Their joy from us being home quickly faded when they saw me. My face was slick with sweat and my hair was a mess. My pants had blood stains on them from the day after the surgery, and I am sure I looked like a zombie.

"Boys," I murmured, "it is so good to see you."

"It's good to see you too," Michael said.

"Go get a chair so we can move your mother," Zeray demanded.

Both boys ran off to get a chair.

Finally, after a lot of work and stabbing pain I was inside the house and on my bed. I looked down at my leg and noticed that it was swollen horribly. I had no idea if this was normal. Maybe it was, maybe it wasn't, but I knew that the way I had just had surgery and then been thrown out of the hospital was not normal.

I continued my regiment of medication and sleeping. When I was awake, I remember Zeray bragging to others about how the surgery was a success and it was a good thing he got me to the hospital. He also bragged about how he took such good care of me at the hotel. I could not believe he was actually acting proud for what he had done, but I did not have the strength to argue.

After four days the swelling in my leg had gone down some. Now though, my back and shoulders ached from lying in the bed for so long. A doctor came out to see me. He told me that I was recovering, but that the surgery was not done well and I had an infection. "You will be in a lot of pain for a while, but it will be important for you to start moving around in the coming weeks," he told me. "The medication should take care of the infection."

I thanked him and then continued to lie in my bed in a drugged state while my hip slowly healed. After another week, the doctor returned and gave me more medication. I was also given crutches and he told me that I needed to start moving around.

I did as I was told even though my hip still hurt pretty badly. I slowly got stronger. I could not move very fast though and walked with a slight limp. Michael and John were so caring. They constantly asked me if they could help around the house. Sometimes I accepted their offers, but more often than not I told them to go play and have fun. I had quickly realized that when they helped, it usually ended up with them ready to fight each other. They were definitely all boy.

Finally, months after my surgery, I felt I was back to being myself. I knew that I would never fully recover, but I was okay with that. I was now almost 50 years old and I had lived a good, full life. I had many wonderful kids and they were doing well. I had not heard from Selemon, so I only hoped he was doing well, but then one day I heard Michael and John screaming with excitement.

I walked to the front door and looked out. Michael and John were running toward their big brother. Selemon was home!

Chapter 77

We sat in chairs in the backyard after eating beef stew with the best brisket I could get. It was something of a treat because good food had become harder and harder to come by, even on our farm. I felt we had reason to celebrate since Selemon was home. He'd be here for just a few weeks before he and two of his cousins would visit relatives in Ad Abeito and then go back to their national service, or national slavery as most Eritreans called it around people they were sure they could trust.

The night wore on and the men drank beer and laughed. It was a good time and I was so glad to have my boy home. I'd felt like I had let him down. Since he left, I had started hiding some money on my own. I had to ensure that I would not be dependent on anybody else if another situation like Selemon's arose.

Later in the night when it was just Zeray, Selemon, Michael, and me, Selemon started telling stories of his time in the camp. "Momma, the stew was so good," he said. "In Sawa we get almost nothing to eat. Even when we were supposed to be trying to finish our school we get fed nothing but black bread. I didn't even know bread could be black," he said with a smile.

I smiled too, and gazed up at the night sky. The stars were dots of brilliant light painted on the dark canvas. I heard once that they were not stars at all, but instead windows into the light of heaven. I liked to think of this at night. It comforted me to imagine that I could see a brilliant place like heaven with my own eyes. It gave me hope.

Michael asked Selemon a question. I did not hear it because I was lost in thought. "Yes, I was scared often. Even during school I had to learn all about weapons, and they are always telling us how dangerous Ethiopia is. I never say to anybody that I was born there."

"What do they do to you at the camp? How do you sleep?"

"We sleep in big metal containers. They pack us into them and we are basically on top of each other. It is terribly uncomfortable. And sometimes people lose it and lash out at the officers. I have felt this way before too, but I would never act on it."

"Why not?" Michael asked.

Selemon leaned forward and talked quieter, as if he'd become concerned that somebody outside of our little circle would hear him. "The ones who lashed out were tortured badly. They would tie their hands behind their back and throw them out in the sun for days."

"But this is at Sawa," I said. "This is not the prisons. I do not understand how they can treat you this way."

"They do what they want, Momma. I think their job is to create such fear in us that we would never rebel against the government. It works. I am scared of doing the wrong thing all the time."

During this conversation Zeray had sat quietly while sipping on his beer. "Do you think of escaping?" he abruptly asked.

Selemon sat up a little straighter. "It hasn't crossed my mind. I know what happens to those who try to escape."

"Do you know what happens to the parents of those who escape?" Zeray asked.

"Yes, they pay or go to jail. Don't worry, Father, I have not even thought of it."

I looked back and forth between my son and my husband. It seemed they were playing some game of testing each other that I could not completely comprehend. I got the sense that Selemon was not being completely truthful to Zeray, and that Zeray was giving Selemon a warning.

A wave of fear splashed over me when I thought that just maybe Zeray would consider turning Selemon in for the talk we'd just had. It would protect him, and that is really all he cared about.

I quickly changed the subject. "There is no need to escape now. You will finish your service and be back here before long." I smiled even though I didn't feel like it. "Tomorrow I'm going into the village. I would like for you to come along so some of our friends can see you. They ask about you all the time."

Selemon relaxed a bit. "Okay, Momma."

"Zeray, would you like another beer?" I started getting up to grab one before he could answer.

My ploy seemed to work. The conversation shifted and I breathed a sigh of relief.

As I got Zeray's beer I looked up at the stars again. I hoped the old saying was true about the stars being windows to heaven, but then I wondered how heaven and hell could be so close together.

Chapter 78

The days passed much too quickly. Soon it was time for Selemon to leave. Zeray had said his goodbyes earlier and had gone to work. I put my hands on Selemon's shoulders. "Be careful out there. Do not try to be a hero."

Selemon would soon be sent to the south not far from the border where the armies were amassed. The idea of him in such a place scared me so badly.

"Do not worry. I will do what I can to stay safe."

I pulled him toward me and gave him a big hug. I did not want to let him go. Finally we pulled apart and he directed his attention to Michael and John. "You two take care of Momma."

"We will," Michael replied in a serious tone.

With that, he walked away toward the bus station where he would meet his cousins for the trip to Ad Abeito to see other relatives. I watched Selemon go until he turned the corner off the farm and faded away behind some trees. My heart felt heavy as I glanced up to the sky. "Take care of him," I whispered.

After the first night when Selemon arrived and Zeray talked to him about escaping, thoughts of escape remained in my head. A few days afterward, Selemon and I were in the fields and I decided to talk more about it. "Have you really thought about running?" I asked.

Selemon looked at me and wiped sweat away from his forehead. "Of course I have thought about it, Momma, but I will not try. I have seen others get shot dead when they have tried to run, and I know what would happen to you."

"I would not blame you for leaving. You could get to Germany with your brother and sisters. We will be okay. I've been saving some money."

"Have you saved enough to pay so you will not go to jail?"

I looked down at a tomato and wiped away a little bit of dirt. "No, I do not have enough yet, but I will go to jail if it means you can get away."

"I couldn't have that," he said emphatically. "I will finish out my time no matter how bad it gets."

Now that conversation was just a memory. Selemon was gone once again. Michael and John and I went back inside the house to get lunch ready. The boys were sad to see their big brother go and they told each other stories about the things they had done with him over the last three weeks. It was funny because both were always there with Selemon and they both knew all the stories.

It was the next day in the evening. We were all sitting around the table when the phone rang. Zeray snatched it up. "Hello," he said in a gruff voice.

He did not talk for a moment and I could tell he was listening.

"Yesterday afternoon," he said.

He waited again.

"Of course I'm sure of it."

Another pause.

"Okay, let us know."

I looked at him expectantly as he hung up the phone.

"Selemon and the others did not make it to Ad Abeito. They don't know where they are."

A million terrible thoughts raced through my head. "What do you think happened?"

"He tried to escape," Zeray said in a matter of fact tone.

"I don't believe it," I said. "I talked with him about it and he assured me that he did not plan on trying to escape."

Zeray looked at me as if I was a child. "Oh that's good. I guess if he told you he would not escape it must be true."

I looked at my food. Now I was not hungry.

"Will he be okay?" Michael asked.

"He'll be fine," I said before Zeray could answer.

I could not sleep that night or the next. My hip had healed, but lately I had noticed a dull ache once again. It was hard to be comfortable at night, and now I worried about Selemon as well. I began to feel more and more like I did when my family disowned me. I was slipping away into a darkness of despair.

After a week I decided to call Hannah and Sahra. If Selemon had truly escaped I thought that he would contact them. I did not tell Zeray about this. He'd just tell me not to worry them because they will get stressed out and have a car wreck on the autobahn.

Sahra answered and I felt her smile through the phone. As I rehashed the events I could tell that she wasn't smiling anymore. "No, we have not heard from him," she said. "If we do we will call you right away."

We talked for a little longer and then Sahra said that Hannah had just come home. "I'm putting you on our speaker phone," she said.

I caught Hannah up on what was happening and then said, "I don't know how much more I can take. I am so sad and worried."

"Momma, you are strong," Hannah said. "You will find Selemon. I know it."

"It will be okay. You can handle this," Sahra added.

Finally, I hung up the phone. My girls had given me a spark of hope, but I still felt dejected. I just knew something else had happened to Selemon. He had not tried to escape.

When Zeray came home I said, "I think we should tell the police."

He took a drag off his cigarette and blew the smoke in the air. "You're mad Abeba."

"We have to see if they will look for him."

He shook his head. "They will not look for him. They will say he escaped and they will come for us. Do you want that?"

"I just want to find Selemon," I said in a resigned tone. I knew that Zeray was right.

"All we can do is wait," he said.

And wait is what we did. One month turned into two and I had fallen into a terrible depression.

With Selemon now gone, so much emotion had been stirred within me. I thought of Fili constantly. The not knowing what happened to him was so hard, and now I was going through it with Selemon. In my mind I watched him walk away from me on that last day a thousand times. I replayed the conversation we had in the field over and over.

My boy was still somewhere in Eritrea. I was sure of this, but I could do nothing to find him. I feared he had been killed. It happened so frequently now thanks to President Afewerki's iron fist. One minute a person was here and fine and the next they had disappeared for some unknown reason. Afewerki had turned Eritreans against Eritreans and we all lived in fear.

How could I have failed my boy?

It was almost exactly two months to the day of his disappearance when we got the phone call about Selemon. We sat in the house and Michael and John and Zeray ate their food. I had picked at a piece of bread earlier, but I did not feel like eating much else.

The phone rang and I hobbled over to it. My hip was once again in constant pain, as if the surgery had fixed nothing. "Hello," I said.

"Is this the Habtu family?" I did not recognize the voice on the other end.

"It is," I replied.

"You are the mother of Selemon Habtu?"

My heart started racing. "Yes, I am Selemon's mother."

"I saw him today."

"You saw my Selemon! Is he alright?"

"He is in a secret prison. I was visiting my cousin and he begged me to contact you so you would know where he was."

"Oh thank you God," I said. "And thank you so much for calling."

He told me where the prison was and we hung up the phone. I turned to Zeray. "We have found Selemon! He is in a prison here in Eritrea."

"Do not be too happy. He is still in prison," Zeray said.

"At least we have found him and he is not dead," I replied.

Chapter 79

I didn't understand why Zeray had not wanted to drive his new car, the one I was sure he paid for with the gold money. His old car had no air conditioning. My back was wet against the seat and I used a cloth to wipe sweat away from my eyes. With Zeray behind the wheel, we rumbled along a dirt road. The windows were rolled down halfway making it hard to hear much more than the wind. The prison was supposed to be just a few kilometers ahead. We'd driven through nothing but desert for the last ten kilometers.

At first it just looked like a big clump of shrubs, but as we got closer I saw that it was a green shack. Zeray slowed as two guards stepped out from it. One raised his arm signaling us to stop. The car clanged and rattled as it came to rest, engine still running.

"Who are you?" one of the guards said tersely.

"I'm Zeray Habtu and this is my wife. We have learned that our son is in the prison."

The guard held a hard look as he sized up Zeray. "What is your son's name?"

"Selemon Habtu."

I wiped my hands on the cloth. I feared that he would not be here. All I got was a phone call from a stranger. He could have been mistaken. The other guard walked back to the shack and looked at something on the wall and then nodded.

"Yes, he's here. Go straight ahead until you see the cars. Park there and then walk to the next guard station."

Zeray nodded and pulled away. With the car stopped it had felt like the heat had doubled. As we picked up speed I stuck my face toward the refreshing air, but maybe it was really just me who felt refreshed. I was one step closer to seeing my son.

The parking lot was nothing more than a cleared patch of dirt. It housed four military vehicles and four old cars. Zeray pulled in next to one of the military vehicles and we lifted our sweaty bodies out of the car. I was in a hurry, but Zeray seemed more measured. "Let's go Zeray, please."

He did not respond. Instead, he scanned the horizon. I followed his line of sight. Some one hundred meters away was the other guard station, and beyond that I could just make out a cluster of small buildings.

We slowly made our way to the guard shack, my hip shooting pain down my leg with every step. A man told us to stop. "Raise your arms," he commanded.

We did as we were told and he gave us a quick search. Satisfied that we were clean, he called another man over to lead us to a room. I saw a group of men in the distance. They were squatting over something. Beyond the men was a larger building. I guessed it was where Selemon was. We came to a silver building that looked like a box car from a train. He directed us to sit down at a small table.

It was there that we waited. I anxiously rubbed one hand with the other and shifted my weight in my seat. Zeray seemed calm until he leaned over to me. "Be smart about this, Abeba. Keep calm no matter what," he whispered.

I looked at him and nodded that I would.

"I mean it," he said.

"Okay, I will remain calm," I said.

I didn't completely understand why Zeray was telling me this, and then the door was pushed open and light filtered in. I turned to the light and saw three figures, two big men stood with a horribly skinny man between them.

One of the big men pushed the little man forward and the other closed the door. With the light shut out I could see that the skinny man was Selemon. The guards guided him to the chair across from us. I started to stand and reach for him, but Zeray put his hand on my shoulder. I returned to my seat and reached across the table. I clasped Selemon's hand in mine. "My baby," I said. "Oh thank God you are here."

"It's so good to see you, Momma."

"Jesus, you look like a damn skeleton," Zeray said.

This brought a smile to Selemon's cracked lips, and as much as I hated to see it, Zeray was right. My boy had wasted away. He had to have lost 15 kilograms. His soiled gray shirt hung on him loosely and his hollowed face had two cheek bones that looked swollen. Then I noticed that the area above his left eye really was swollen, and I felt the cuts and rough spots on his hand. I could not bear to think what my little boy had been through.

"Are you alright?" I asked.

"I am as good as I can be."

"We will get you out of here," I said.

Before Selemon replied, Zeray interjected in a loud voice. "We will not get him out of here. It will be up to the officials to decide."

I understood. "Of course, I mean that we will hope they show mercy and release my baby."

I caught a glimpse from Zeray that showed his approval for my recovery. Then he gave me an almost imperceptible order under his breath. "Distract them."

It took a moment to process his words. Then I leaned back and waved my hand over my face as if I was too hot. "Please sir," I said to the nearest guard. "Do you have any water at all? I am so hot."

He looked at me as if I was crazy. "No water."

"But you don't understand." I leaned forward and stood. I had hip surgery and it is so painful."

"I do not care," the guard said.

But my attention was brought to Zeray as he whispered to Selemon. "Do you want to get out of here?" he said. "You have to fake an asthma attack."

I replied to the guard. "But I am in pain and I'm old."

"Sit down and shut up right now," the guard said.

I slowly lowered myself back into my seat and let out a low groan while listening intently to

Zeray and Selemon. "For asthma? They will most likely let me die," Selemon said.

"I have connections." I almost missed it, but as Zeray shifted he slid something across the table to Selemon. "Take this," he said.

Selemon barely moved and he had the object under his hand. I had no idea what it was and I was completely floored with what was happening. Zeray had mentioned nothing about this to me and now I understood why he kept telling me to be calm. I realized just how dangerous this was and started ringing my hands together once again.

"Fake your attack and pretend to have a seizure after chewing on that. It will work," Zeray said in a barely audible voice.

"Or I will die trying," Selemon said in an equally quiet voice.

Zeray just shrugged.

Moments later, the guards told us our time was up. I again reached out and put my hand over Selemon's. "I love you so much," I said. "I hope we will see you again soon."

His cracked lips turned upward into a smile. "I hope so too, Momma."

A weight of fear settled onto my shoulders as I recognized that an escape plan would really be a do or die proposition. I took my hand off of his knowing that it might be the last time I ever touched my son.

Soon we were in the light and walking back to our car. Neither Zeray nor I said a word about what happened until we were driving away. I couldn't decide if I should be mad or scared or elated, but I fully understood that it was out of my hands. Now I would just have to wait to learn of Selemon's fate.

Chapter 80

The hot car ride, the emotions from seeing Selemon, and then being thrown into an escape plan had totally drained me. As soon as we got home I gave Michael and John a hug.

"How is he?" Michael asked.

"When will he be home?" John chimed in.

"He looks great and he is in good spirits. I don't know when he will be home, but I hope it will be soon."

There was no way I could tell them the truth. They would be crushed to learn that their big brother was nothing more than a ravaged skeleton and hopes of escape rested on a crazy plan of chewing on a matchstick and faking an attack. And then what? I wasn't sure what would happen if the plan worked. Where would they send him? Would he come home? Would he go back to Sawa?

There was no real way to answer these questions because there was no uniformity to how somebody was punished or spared in Eritrea. We just had to wait to see what happened.

The trip had taken its toll on my hip as well. It now hurt every moment of the day and I could not find a position that gave it relief. It was two days after seeing Selemon when I decided to dig through a box to see if I had any pain medication left over from after the surgery.

Deep in the corner of the box I found a plastic container with five pills in it. They had to be over a year old and I didn't know if they expired or not, but I didn't care. I popped three of them in my mouth and washed them down with water. I remembered that I was supposed to take two, but now my hip throbbed and I just needed a break from it.

In a matter of minutes my head felt a little funny and my body relaxed. The pain in my hip began to fade as well. I sat down in a chair and enjoyed the moment of relief. The house was quiet, Michael and John were at school and Zeray was gone, where I did not know.

I sat in the silence and let my brain wander. I thought of the pictures I had received from Muse and Hannah and Sahra. They were grown up now and the German countryside was so green and plush. I thought of being there with them. Then I drifted over to my little boys, Michael and John. They did not really comprehend it, but their lives could be so much better.

I took a sip of my water and relished my slightly groggy pain-reduced state. It had been a long time since I was able to just stop. Then my thoughts fell on Fili and Selemon. I remembered that last morning so long ago when Fili went to work. "Be careful," I'd said.

"Of course," he replied.

There had been some unrest in Addis Ababa at the time and we had heard some rumors, but none of us could have expected that they would come banging on our door that day and send us away. There is so much I would have liked to say to Fili. If only I would have hugged him tightly and told him just how much I loved him that morning, but I didn't.

Now it was Selemon who had been taken away. I knew there was hope that he would return, but I also knew that he would be different than he was before. I could see it in his eyes. The prison had changed him. My kind and loving boy was still in there, but a layer of hardness and despair had been caked over it.

I could only pray that I would hold him again and help wipe away that layer. I took another drink of water and felt my body relax a little more. I decided that I should take a nap. I started to lift myself up from the chair and noticed that I felt lightheaded. I relaxed again and took a long drink of water. As I sat the glass down the ringing phone startled me.

It was only across the room, but I looked at it as if it was a kilometer away. I will let it ring, I thought, and then my mind cleared a bit and it hit me that it could be a call about Selemon. I stood quickly and took a few unsteady steps to the phone.

"Hello," I noticed that my tongue felt thick.

A man on the other end started talking. I listened and said, "Okay."

He hung up and I stood there with the phone in my hand as my thoughts swirled through my jelly-filled brain. Finally, I placed the phone back on the hook and walked toward my bed.

I plopped down and fell onto my back. Did I just dream that call? If not, what did it mean? I stared at the ceiling and tried to focus. It was a real phone call. I was sure of it. The man had said that my son, Selemon Habtu, had experienced some sort of asthma attack and seizure while in prison. The doctor said he would recover.

This part played out in my head and it seemed that Zeray's plan and Selemon's execution of it had been flawless. It was the next part of the conversation that worried and confused me. They were sending Selemon to an insane hospital? Later, he would finish his training and his national service.

My vision grew fuzzy and I could tell I was about to fall into a deep and dreamless sleep, and I was okay with that.

It wouldn't be until weeks later when we learned that Selemon spent time in a horrible hospital for the insane and mentally retarded, and then was sent back to Sawa. At least he was no longer in prison.

Chapter 81

After taking the three pills and sleeping for a long time, I told Zeray about the call. He just shrugged. "I told you it would work."

"How could you have been so sure?"

"I am very smart Abeba, and remember, I have connections." He smirked.

"Well I am glad it worked," I said, and left it at that.

A day later the pain in my hip returned with a fury. I took the final two pills and drifted through the day with relatively little pain, but I knew that it would not last. I asked Zeray for money to see the doctor. "My hip is much worse," I said. "I need to have it checked and get more pills."

"That is ridiculous," he replied. "Your hip is just not strong after the surgery. There is nothing wrong with it."

"That is not true. It is swollen and it hurts. I need to go to the doctor."

"Why do you think I have money for that?" Zeray said.

"I know you have money from the gold."

A coldness slid over Zeray's eyes. "How dare you question me? That money is all but gone. Do you have any idea how hard it is to live here? Everything is too expensive. And you asked about how I knew my escape plan would work. I paid off some people. That is how I really knew."

I could not believe these words. Zeray would not pay to get Selemon out of the country, so why would he pay to help him escape the prison. He did not grow a conscience and become a decent man.

"So you are telling me that you do not have any money for me to see the doctor?"

"That is exactly what I'm telling you. You have cost me a lot of money lately."

I stood taller. "And our children have sent you a lot of money."

The coldness in his eyes seemed to turn hot in an instant. "If you do not stop questioning me, I will give you a reason to see the doctor."

I kept my eyes on my husband. He was now older and his shoulders stooped a bit. His hair was gray and his cheeks sagged as if they were heavy, but he still had that temper swimming just below the surface.

"Fine," I said, and limped away.

Since he would not pay for a trip to the doctor, I would have to do it myself. When Zeray left I went out to my father's barn and pulled the tiny box from the shelf. It was hidden behind an old picture and some cans. I opened the box and pulled out some money. There was not a lot in it, maybe 10,000 nafka, but it was what I had saved through the years.

With the money in hand, I went to the doctor.

It was the same doctor's office I had been to before, but a different doctor. The one who had been taken away years earlier had never returned. The new doctor was younger and very serious. He looked at my hip and moved it around. "You had surgery in Sudan?" he asked.

"Yes, it's been about two years now."

He looked at the scar that ran along my hip and pushed in different places. "They did a terrible job. You will need an x-ray at the hospital, but I think you will need to have another surgery."

"Another surgery? The first one was so terrible."

"I would suggest going to a good hospital this time."

Worry swelled in my chest. If I really needed another surgery I would not have enough money. I would have to call Hannah and Sahra without letting Zeray know about it. I was sure they would not worry. Instead they would be able to help.

The doctor gave me more pills, and I went home and debated about whether or not to call Hannah and Sahra.

Finally, after a couple weeks of going back and forth about if I should call or not, I dialed my daughters' phone number. Thankfully, Zeray was not home and I had no way of knowing when he would return. Hannah answered on the fifth ring. As always, she was glad to hear from me, but my phone calls worried her. She feared I was calling because something was wrong. This time she was right, and I laid it all out to her.

I told her of the gold and how it was stolen. I told her about my family and how I was now an outcast. I explained that I'd had terrible complications from the bad surgery. I gave her details of everything that had happened with

Selemon. I talked about the horrors that were going on in the country. I just spilled it all. Once I started, it all tumbled off my tongue. I couldn't stop it.

Hannah listened and asked questions or provided me with consoling words from time to time. Finally, I talked about the doctor's visit and how the money from the gold was apparently gone. And then I was finished. I slumped in my chair and sighed deeply. "That is it Hannah. That is everything that has happened that you have not known about."

"Momma, you will not live like this much longer." There was firmness in her voice that I'd never heard. "Muse and Sahra and I are going to get you and Michael and John out of that hell."

"You can't. There is no way," I replied.

"There is a way. There is always a way. We will start making calls to people we know. We are getting you out of Eritrea and away from your terrible husband."

"What about Selemon? I cannot leave him."

"He is already doing his service. We will have to wait until we have the rest of you first. Then we will figure out how to get him."

"I do not know what to say."

"You don't have to say anything. We are going to send you money as soon as we can so your hip can be fixed."

"Thank you, Hannah. Zeray always said that all of this would worry you too much."

"It doesn't worry me. It makes me angry. We will get you out, Momma. Expect the money soon."

We talked a little longer before hanging up the phone. I felt both exhilarated and scared. I knew that the first order of business was the money for my hip, and then I'd hope the rest would fall into place. Unfortunately, the money would not arrive in time.

Chapter 82

There were puffy white clouds painted on the blue sky and a warm breeze rustled through the fields. I finished picking the last of the vegetables and walked with my basket toward the house.

I saw Michael and John coming up the road. They'd been at school. I thought about what Hannah had said. The idea of taking them away from here made me smile.

We arrived at the house at about the same time. "How was your day at school?" I asked.

They both gave me the normal response, "Fine."

"Did you learn anything?"

"Not much," again the normal response.

"Will you help with these vegetables?"

They put their stuff down and started helping me clean and chop the vegetables. I had a strange feeling of contentedness drift over me as I sat in the sun and worked. Maybe it was from the pills that took away my hip pain and made my head a little foggy, but more likely it was because I thought I'd made the absolute right decision by calling Hannah. Now it seemed there was hope for a different and better future.

For so long I had just been surviving. My energy had been totally drained ever since the fallout with my family. I'd stumbled through each day in a daze without any real hope. Now though, there was a spark in my heart.

"What are you doing?" Zeray's voice startled away these thoughts.

"Just cutting some vegetables," I replied.

"Really, because it looked like you were staring off into space?"

"I was just thinking."

"You should not do that too much." He chuckled and walked away.

I quickly got back to cutting the vegetables.

Michael and John lost interest and headed to the fields to play. I didn't know where Zeray went, but I guessed he was inside with his beer. After the vegetables, I started pulling clothing off the line. They were dry and fluttering in the wind.

I was amazed at how much better my hip felt with the medication. Now I could do these chores without the agonizing pain. As I pulled a shirt off the line I heard some commotion to the front of the house. I saw Michael and John running that way. I put the shirt down in the basket and walked around the house.

As I turned the corner, I stopped dead in my tracks. There in the street sat two military cars and a truck with a covered back. Four military men stood outside of the cars talking with one of the men who rented a room from my papa. The man pointed toward our house as Zeray came out of the front door.

Michael and John were in the street close to the trucks. They were bold and unsure at the same time. I was just unsure, and my feet would not move from the spot on which I stood.

The men had guns slung over their shoulders and they strode right toward Zeray. He had a beer bottle in one hand and a cigarette in the other. He took a long swig. "What is this?" he yelled.

"Are you Zeray Habtu, father of Selemon Habtu?"

When I heard Selemon's name my feet started moving. A moment later, I was right next to Zeray. "Yes, Selemon is my son."

"Is he alright?" I asked.

"No he is not alright," the man who seemed to be the leader said.

"Is he hurt?"

"He has escaped," the man replied gruffly.

"Escaped? From where?" Zeray asked.

"Sawa, just before deployment. Is he here?"

"No, we have not seen him."

I felt a hand reach for mine and I looked down. It was John. Michael stood right next to his brother. They both looked scared.

"Then we have no choice. By order of President Afewerki you must pay 50,000 nafka for your son's escape. Do you have the money?"

I looked at Zeray and he reminded me of a trapped animal. His usual cockiness was not there. "No, I don't have the money now, but I can get it in a few days."

The man scoffed. "I'm sure you can. And are you Abeba Habtu, mother of Selemon?"

John's grip tightened. I felt his body against my leg. "Yes, I am Abeba."

"By the order of President Afewerki you must pay 50,000 nafka for your son's escape. Do you have the money?"

Now I felt like the trapped animal. "I can pay you ten thousand," I said.

This drew a scornful look from Zeray, but at the moment I didn't care.

"We don't give discounts." The man laughed.

In an instant the men sprang into action. Guns were drawn and we were pinned against the wall of our own house.

"No, no, no," I heard Michael yelling as John continued to hang onto my leg.

"Get the hell away," one of the men said.

They did not listen to him.

"Your parents are going to prison. Remember this," another man said, "don't ever cross the Eritrean government."

Adrenaline and fear raced through my veins. My hands were cuffed with a plastic tie and I did not resist. I turned to my babies as they cried and yelled. "It will be okay. I promise," I said.

The rough hands dragged us toward the truck. I looked at Zeray and he looked at me. "This is your damn fault," he yelled. "You brought this on us you bitch."

I let the words bounce off of me and turned to Michael and John. "I love you, I love you, I love you," I said. "You have to call your sisters. They will help."

My boys had tears streaking down their faces as they followed us. I watched as Zeray was thrown in the back of the truck. I was marched to one of the cars and pushed into the backseat. The door was slammed shut and I pressed my forehead against the window.

Michael and John pressed their hands against the other side. "Momma, Momma," I heard my little eight-year-old John yell through the window.

I fought back the tears and yelled back. "Be strong Michael. Be strong John. It will be okay. I love you."

The car pulled away, and Michael and John ran alongside it. As we sped up, they fell behind. I turned my head and watched as they faded away.

Chapter 83

Germany 2012

The hospital room was much different than the one where I went to take my radiation and then sit for a week. I'd done that type of internal radiation four times over the course of many months. Each time was terrible because my body swelled and I lost my appetite for weeks.

After each radiation treatment the doctors had run their tests and looked at me with concern. My cancer was not responding to the treatment as they had hoped. Maybe the radiation had worked a little bit in that it had slowed the spread of the cancer, but it had not done anything to make it go away.

Now I was doing a different type of radiation. "This one combined with the other will start to work," Sahra had said. She and her sister were so much alike. They were both positive and courageous no matter how long the odds.

Both my girls helped the nurse as they maneuvered me onto the bed where I would get my treatment. There was a large circular machine above me. The nurse exposed my hip and lower stomach showing the markings that were made by the doctor earlier. She then moved the circular machine over my hip and put it into place. She also placed a shield above my stomach.

My kids had to leave and I took a deep breath and reminded myself that this wouldn't hurt. It would help blast away my cancer so I could see my dream of having all my children together become a reality.

The nurse left the room and I was all alone. Hannah had told me that the treatment would last about half an hour, so I tried to relax as the machine started up. A hollow voice spoke to me. It was the nurse. "Ready," she said in German.

"Yah," I replied.

The machine clicked and whirred and sometimes it sounded like it was sucking the air like a vacuum. I let my thoughts drift as the machine did its work and I found myself thinking of Zeray. I remembered him yelling at me and accusing me of causing our arrest as he was thrown into the back of that truck almost two years earlier in Eritrea.

I had no idea where he was now, and I knew that I should have cared, but I did not. I remembered the long walk I had taken to his village when I was just a kid. Back then we had the curfew and I had to make it by six in the evening or there was a very real chance I would be shot. I thought of the horrible house in Addis Ababa where the drunken man peed all over the floor, and I remembered those times when Zeray closed his fists and beat me with them.

I guessed that Zeray was still in prison, and that was where he deserved to be.

The machine made a strange sound and the nurse's voice came over the speaker. "That is all," she said.

Now we would have to wait to see if this treatment was more effective than the last.

Chapter 84

Eritrea

It was turning dark when we arrived at what I assumed was the prison. We were in the middle of the desert and surrounded by big rocks and dirt. In the middle of the rocks were a dozen shipping containers. They were painted the color of the dirt and each had a number on it. The first started at number 84 and the last was number 96.

I was pulled out of the car and my hip screamed. "My hip is very bad," I said.

Nobody replied.

I was dragged to a container with the number 95 on it. The guard turned a lever and lifted. The big door at the end of the container swung open. The day's waning light crept into the darkness and I looked inside. What I saw made my knees weak. Staring back at me were about 20 sets of scared and empty eyes of girls and women.

The guard pushed me and I stumbled into the container. It wasn't much more than three meters wide and ten meters long. I tripped over a young girl's leg and fell to my hands and knees. I looked up about the time I heard metal on metal as the doors were pushed shut behind me. I saw those desperate faces until the doors were latched, and then there was nothing but darkness.

Despite my hip shooting pain throughout my entire left side, I crawled forward and felt my way through the crowd. "There is a place over here," a voice said through the darkness.

"Thank you," I replied and started to crawl toward the voice.

"Don't worry. Your eyes will adjust some."

I found the voice and put my back against the cold steel.

"Where are we?" I asked.

"Not sure where exactly, but hell can't be much worse than this prison."

I couldn't believe it. I was in a secret prison. Even though this was always a looming consequence of all Eritreans I didn't really think it would ever happen to me. I was now an old woman of 50 years of age. How could I be in prison?

I knew the answer, and despite my terrible situation it made me a little bit happy. Selemon had escaped. That had to be the case. He had to have gotten to Sudan, or maybe even Djibouti. He was free of President Afewerki and the terrible prison of a country he had created. I just knew it was true, and now Zeray and I would pay the penalty.

My thoughts fell to Michael and John. My family had basically disowned me, but we still lived close together. I had to hope that they would help out my little boys. I was sure that they would, but still I could not believe that I was separated from them.

My entire life had revolved around keeping my family together and safe, and yet I had lost every one of my seven children in one way or another. Fili had been gone for over a decade. Muse and Hannah and Sahra were in Germany, Selemon was somewhere. Michael and John were in their own home but I was far from them in a frigid shipping container in the desert.

A scream from one of the other containers made me jump. The girl who had talked to me earlier touched my shoulder. I looked her way and could see the outline of her face. She was right, my eyes were adjusting. As if she could read my mind she said, "They are torturing somebody. Your eyes will get used to the dark, but it is much harder to get used to the screams."

I felt a chill slide down my spine that made my body do an involuntary shudder. This really was hell.

The screams went on for about an hour. Sometimes they were consistent, other times they cut through the silent night in hideous bursts. I tried to draw my knees up to my body, but my hip wouldn't let me. I shifted to my right and closed my eyes. With the smell of our dirty bodies mixed with the awful screams echoing in my head, sleep was almost impossible.

Chapter 85

I heard a distant clanging. It was on the edges of my consciousness. I slowly opened my eyes and remembered where I was. A thin light probed the darkness through the small crack at the top of the container's door. I could barely move. My neck and my back felt as if they had rocks in them, but those pains were nothing compared to my hip. It felt like it did when it was broken.

I looked around the container at the other faces. There were young girls no older than 18 years old with far-off looks in their eyes, and some older women in their 30s I guessed. They too carried a hopelessness that made their bodies appear to be both alive and dead. I didn't think I had any way of knowing how long each had been locked up in this container, but then I realized that the skinnier ones had probably been here longer.

The door was yanked open and a wave of harsh sunlight rolled into the room. I squinted against it and saw three silhouettes of big men standing in the doorway. "Everybody out," one yelled.

The women struggled to their feet and helped each other up. I tried to push myself off the floor, but my hip would not allow it. The woman who was next to me was already on her feet. I looked up at her. "My hip," I said. "I can't move it."

"Shhh," she mouthed, and then grabbed my arm and pulled.

I rose to my feet and let out an involuntary yelp at the stabbing pain. She looked at me with sad eyes and then moved toward the door. I tried to follow, but I had to drag my leg behind me. I was the last one to cross the threshold into the light.

"What is wrong with you?" one of the guards asked.

"It's my hip. I had surgery on it."

He pushed me forward. "Get over it," he demanded.

We were led around the rocks to a small clearing. The sand was darkened in the area and the guards lined us up. I understood that this was where we were to go to the toilet. I had not realized it before, but I did need to relieve myself.

The women squatted to do their business and the guards let their eyes fall over them. They had no shame. Of course watching us urinate was a small intrusion compared to some of the other things they did. I had noticed last night that some of the noises were from the guards and they were produced from a different kind of torture. Their pleasure was our pain.

I tried to squat to relieve myself, but my hip hurt so badly. I eventually settled into an odd position and was able to go. It was so humiliating and the guards knew this. They smirked in a way that made me want to cry.

We were led to a different area where there were a handful of sparse trees and some more rocks.

We were given two pieces of bread and a cup of dirty water. I glanced around the group. Everyone ate in silence. I put my head down and did the same. The bread was hard and stale and difficult to swallow, but I ate every bit of it while washing it down with the warm water.

After about half an hour they rounded us up and walked us back to our container. We were forced inside where we returned to the floor. The door slammed and our world was pitched into relative darkness. It could not have been past nine in the morning and it seemed our day in the sun was over.

As the hours passed, the container began to heat up. Soon I leaned forward because the metal began to get hot. My back was soaked and sweat dripped off my face. "How do you make it?" I said to the girl next to me.

"I don't know," she replied. "You just do or you don't."

I understood exactly what she meant.

The container turned into a gigantic oven and soon the walls were slick with condensation. It was like thin waterfalls of sweat sliding down the wall to the metal floor. There was nothing to do as we sat there in the dark with our sliver of light.

I knew that it would not be long before I'd go crazy, so I fought it by talking to God and thinking about my children. I held on to what Hannah had said about getting Michael and John and me out of Eritrea. It looked like that would never happen for me, but just maybe they could free Michael and John.

I rode that thought through the burning day and drifted in and out of fitful sleep due to mental and physical exhaustion. After many hours, the door was pulled open and once again we were hauled out.

This time when we took our toilet break almost nobody had to relieve themselves. Then we were given a cup of water, no food.

I sucked down my water greedily. After sweating all day I knew that I was dangerously dehydrated. I didn't think the water would be enough for me, but it wasn't like I could ask for seconds. We were given another half an hour on the outside and then with the sun sinking to the west we were pushed back into our cell.

It was still scorching hot, and I began to sweat again, but as the sliver of light faded I began to get chilled. Because of my arrival time the previous night I was not forced to endure the day's heat. Now it was agonizing as our giant oven turned into a refrigerator. I shivered as my sweat dried and I lay awkwardly against the wall. I prayed to God to give me a miracle because that was the only way I would survive.

Chapter 86

The routine from the first day became the routine every day. For 23 hours I sat in the cramped container that got blistering hot in the afternoon and frigid at night. The one hour of freedom from the darkness was filled with two toilet breaks, two pieces of bread, and two cups of water.

Despite not talking much I was able to learn why some of the women were in here. The reasons for being thrown in such a hell were horribly minimal. One girl had reportedly "talked bad about the government" and another was in because she was with her brother when he spoke badly of the government. Then there was the girl who was accused of planning to escape and the two mothers who were much younger than me. Their sons had escaped and they could not pay.

Finally, there was the pregnant woman. Her name was Sophia and she was very close to giving birth. Since I had given birth seven times I had gravitated toward her. She'd been in the prison for at least two months because she was accused of practicing the wrong type of Christianity. Afewerki had banned many religions years earlier and people were in prison because of it.

She too had been forced to leave her other children behind when she was taken away. She was due very soon and I couldn't imagine that they would expect her to give birth in this cell.

I tried to keep track of the days, but after just two or three weeks they began to run together. My hip had grown more and more painful. Without medication every minute was agonizing. I'd also noticed that in the last few days it had become much tighter, like it was swelling from the inside. I tried hard to not let this pain show, but every time we were expected to get up I moved slower.

My companion, because she was moving just as slowly as me, was Sophia. One morning the guards opened the door and yelled at us to get up. Sophia struggled to her feet. I tried to do the same, but I felt hot and weak. Despite being so pregnant her water could break at any minute, she reached down and helped me to my feet.

Sweat coursed down my face as Sophia and I hobbled toward the light at the end of the container.

"Hurry up," one of the guards yelled.

"Sorry, she is about to have her baby and I'm sick," I replied.

It was a risk to say anything back to them. The guard might decide to beat me, but I was too weak to care. Instead, he just looked at Sophia and me with disgust.

I was unable to go to the toilet or eat my bread. I gave it to Sophia and then drank my water. Soon we were back in the darkness of our container. The day heated up and the sweat rolled off the walls. Sophia and I sat next to each other trying to move as little as possible.

After many hours, she let out a low moan.

"Are you alright?" I asked.

"I think the baby is coming soon."

I sat up straighter. "Are you sure?"

She let out another low moan. "I keep having cramps."

I looked at the sliver of light. I had become able to look at it and have an idea of when the guards would come for our afternoon toilet and water. "You don't have much longer until the guards come. I will tell them you are having the baby."

Sophia did not reply. Instead, she put her head back and groaned.

News spread through the container that she was having her baby soon and there was a ripple of energy. We were all in this together, and the idea of having a baby in this hell was hard to comprehend. Finally, we heard the latch on the door and then the light flooded in.

The guards told us to leave, and as the other women filed out they told them about the baby. I used the slick wall and every bit of strength I had and pulled myself to my feet. The guards peered in at the darkness. "Come on," one of them yelled.

"I'm helping her," I replied. "She is about to have a baby."

The guard entered the darkness and stood over us. "Get her up."

"I can barely move myself," I said. "My hip is very bad and I have a fever."

I didn't know if I had a fever or not, but as the day had worn on I'd thought about Selemon and his escape from prison. I decided that this moment would be my best and maybe my only opportunity to leave this place.

"I don't care. Get her to her damn feet," the guard yelled.

I put all my weight on my right leg and put my right hand firmly against the wall. Then with my left hand I gripped Sophia's hand and pulled. As she rose to her feet she let out an audible gasp. "My water just broke."

The guard stepped backwards. "What the hell!" he exclaimed.

"She's having the baby!" I said.

"Let's go," the guard demanded.

We hobbled toward the light, but once outside of the container we stopped. Sophia clutched her stomach and groaned as I leaned forward struggling to hold her weight.

Another guard walked over to us. "What the hell is going on?"

"She is having a baby." He pointed at Sophia. "And she is sick." He pointed at me.

"Sounds like an escape plan to me."

"You think she is faking having a baby?"

The guard looked at Sophia and then back at the other guard. "No, I guess not."

"Get the commander."

The guard hurried away and Sophia and I stood there in an awkward position. The guard that stayed behind scooted back a few feet. He wanted no part of this. I leaned in toward Sophia. "Are you having contractions?"

"Yes, but light," she replied.

"When the commander comes, have a big one," I said.

She understood.

A moment later, the commander and the guard approached. Sophia clutched her protruding belly and let out a blood-curdling moan that made the men stop.

"Is she really having a baby?" It was the commander.

"Yes, she will have it very soon," I replied.

He thought for a moment. "Put her in a truck and get her to the doctor."

"I should go too," I said.

"No, you should shut your mouth."

I looked down and decided that it was now or never, so at the risk of being beaten severely I did not shut up. "I've had seven babies. I can help deliver the baby if she has it in the truck. Besides, my hip is very bad. I need to see a doctor." I pulled my pants to the side revealing my hip. It was swollen and discolored.

The guard thought for a long moment until Sophia let out another growling moan.

"Fine, but you will return after seeing the doctor."

We waddled over to the truck and the guards helped us in the back. Soon, we were driving. It hit me that I was pulling away from the prison.

I vowed to never return.

Chapter 87

We arrived at the hospital after about 45 minutes of bouncing along the road. For a while I feared I might actually have to deliver Sophia's baby, but thankfully we made it before the baby came. We were in a covered truck so I didn't even know which town we were in, but the hospital was small and dirty.

Sophia was rushed into a room and I was placed in a wheelchair and directed to another room. I sat in there and waited for a long time. All the while I tried to figure out how I could get well and then slip away.

A doctor finally entered the room. "How is Sophia?" I asked.

"The girl from the prison?"

"You know she's only there because she was following the wrong religion."

The doctor quickly looked down at his notes. "She had her baby, a boy. She's fine. And you're from the prison as well?"

"Yes, my son escaped so I was locked up."

Again the doctor returned to his notes and then started checking my hip. A nurse came in and drew blood, and then I was given an IV that dripped antibiotics directly into my arm.

"You have a bad infection in your hip and I think it might be more than that. Your previous surgery was done terribly," the doctor told me.

"I'm well aware of that. I've been living with this pain for a long time now."

"The antibiotics will help, and then we will figure out what to do next. We're going to put you in a room."

"Thank you," I said, and noticed that it seemed the man had a soft spot for me. There was a very good chance that he too had been dealt a rotten hand by our government.

The bed felt so soft and comfortable. I could not believe how relaxed it made me. The antibiotics and the new pain medication made me relax even further and I fell into a deep sleep. I dreamed of Michael and John being sent off to national service even though they were just little boys. And then I dreamed of seeing Selemon in Sudan. I was awoken by a nurse who was working on the beeping machines.

"How long did I sleep?" I asked groggily.

"All through the night and most of the morning. How do you feel?"

"Amazingly well," I said. "How is Sophia, the one who had the baby?"

"She is fine and in the room just down the hall. Her brother is here and he wants to see you when you feel up to it."

I slid myself up a little bit and my hip didn't hurt at all. I understood that the pain medication had something to do with that. "That would be great. I am ready to see him," I said.

About ten minutes later a tall man with a balding head and a kind smile tentatively entered my room. "Hello, I'm Sophia's brother, Osman. She told me about you. Thank you for all your help."

"It was nothing. She helped me too."

"Well if you need anything I will be glad to help."

I thought for a moment and then motioned for him to come closer. He stepped forward and I spoke in a low voice. "Is there a guard out there?"

"Yes, only one, and he is just sitting in the waiting room. Why do you ask?"

"I cannot go back. Can you call my children in Germany and then help me escape."

Osman looked over his shoulder and nervously rubbed his hands on his pants. "I will call them," he said. "Write down the number."

I quickly grabbed a pen and jotted down the number. "Tell them I will return to my house soon and I will get my children. We'll need help to get to Sudan."

Osman looked over his shoulder once again and then took the number and shoved it into his pocket. When he pulled his hand out, he had a wad of money. "Here, take this," he said.

I palmed the money and shoved it under the sheets. "Thank you so much. Please tell Sophia that I will always think of her."

"I will," he said. "And I will call as soon as I get a chance. I wish I could do more."

"You have done more than enough."

Osman left the room a moment before the nurse returned with food. I ate hungrily and then fell asleep once again. When I awoke it was late. I didn't know if I'd had enough antibiotics to stop the infection, but it didn't matter. I needed to go. I pulled the needle from my arm and slid out of the bed.

I checked the hall. It was empty at this time of night. I felt a dull pain in my hip, but I could move so much better than before. I turned back to the room and saw that there was a shirt and pants on a hook on the wall. I hobbled toward them.

Just as I was about to take off my hospital gown I heard a noise behind me. Somebody had just come into my room.

Chapter 88

The door shut softly behind me. I squeezed my eyes closed for a split second. Surely the guard had come to check on me. I was caught.

"What are you doing?" It was a man's voice.

I turned as my mind groped for a reason why I would be out of my bed and standing in front of these clothes.

"You should still be in bed," the man said.

I faced the man and the air rushed from my lungs. It was the doctor, not the guard.

"I just felt like I needed to get up," I said weakly.

He walked toward me with concern on his face. "Just needed to get up?"

It was obvious he did not believe me. "Please, don't tell on me," I said. "I have to get back to my children. The prison is terrible. I can't go back."

"You are in no condition to go anywhere," he said.

"Please help me," I begged.

He started to respond, but the door opened. "What is going on?" the guard said in an accusatory tone.

He looked back and forth between the doctor and me. It seemed that time ground to a halt as the guard's penetrating eyes bore into me.

"She had to go to the toilet," the doctor finally said.

"Why does she not have her needle in her arm?"

"She woke up groggy and accidentally pulled it out. See, there is blood on her arm from it. It's a good thing I happened to check on her."

The guard continued to stare at us as he tried to process the information he'd just received. "Fine," he finally said, "go back to bed. I'm right outside."

I couldn't believe the doctor had just covered for me. In doing so he put himself in danger as well.

The doctor lightly gripped my arm and led me back to the bed as the guard left the room. He helped me into the bed and then prepared to insert my IV once again.

"Thank you so much," I said. "I really do have to get out of here and back to my children."

He nodded in a way that showed he sympathized with me. Then he spoke in a very low voice. "Tomorrow, I will recommend that you return home for two weeks of bed rest. I'll tell them that we cannot keep you here for that long and that you aren't ready to return to the prison."

These words reached into my chest and warmed my soul. "I don't know what to say. I can never thank you enough."

A thin smile formed on his face. "I'm your doctor. It is what I think is best. I need you to rest tonight. I expect you'll have a busy two weeks."

He gave me two pills and a glass of water. I took them and thanked him once again. Moments later, he was gone and I was drifting off to a peaceful sleep. Before sleep found me I thought of how there was so much cruelty in the world, but it was matched and exceeded by kindness.

Chapter 89

After a short walk down the hallway, I turned to the left and saw the door to the outside. The guard leaned against the wall with his arms crossed over his chest. He saw me approach and pushed himself off the wall.

"You must remain at your home," he said. "You will be picked up in seven days."

"I understand."

"If you try to escape you'll be very sorry. We will check on you."

I nodded. "May I go now?"

"Yes," he replied.

The doctor had recommended two weeks, but I was given just one. This would make it that much harder to set everything up.

The night air was warm and I looked up at the stars. It was the first time I'd seen them in a long time.

I hoped that they were windows to heaven and I hoped that God was watching me and ready to guide me home. I reached into my pocket and grabbed the money that Osman had given me. It turned out to be 180 nafka. I figured it would probably be enough depending on where I was.

The streets were nearly empty and I looked up at the signs. Finally I saw one for the bus station. I turned and walked that way.

It hit me that I was a free woman. Now it was time to get my children and become free for good.

I arrived at the station and bought a ticket for the first available bus. It wasn't leaving for twenty minutes so I stood in a corner and kept my eyes glued to the street that I had just walked down. I had just been given the pass to leave, but I feared that it would be taken away from me before I left.

After what seemed like an eternity the bus pulled away from the station. It took me to a town called Nefasit, east of Asmara. From there, I found a bus home.

I was now on the final leg of the journey, a short bus ride to my village. It was just after noon and as I approached my village a thousand thoughts ran through my head. I wondered if they really could take away my week of rest. Then I thought of Michael and John. They would still be in school and I was unsure if I should get them from there or not.

I worked on formulating a plan and tried hard to consider every possibility for our escape, but there was no way to be sure about anything until it happened. The bus came to a stop with a hiss. I exited and started walking toward the farm.

Upon reaching the farm I cut through a field instead of using the main entrance. I decided to go in from the back because I was unready to see my family. I walked as quickly as my hip would allow. Luckily, it felt much better.

I stopped next to the small barn some one hundred meters from the back of my house. In the distance I saw men working in the field. I looked at the cars parked next to the houses and on the street. I recognized all of them.

Slowly, I headed to my back door. As I walked I surveyed the farm. It had been my home for much of my life now, and I knew that very soon I would be walking away from it, and all of my family that lived on it, forever.

I got to the back door without anyone seeing me. I put my ear to it and listened to determine if anybody was in my house. After a minute I was satisfied that it was empty. I twisted the handle and pushed the door open just wide enough for me to slip through.

Once inside, I closed the door quietly and stood with my back against it. I took a few deep breaths and closed my eyes for a moment. "Thank you, Father, for giving me this chance," I said.

I grabbed a glass of water and popped two of the pills that the doctor had given me. My hip had started aching again and I wanted just a little bit of relief.

I was exhausted and in desperate need of a nap, but I needed to call Hannah and Sahra first. There was still much work to do if there was any hope of escape to Sudan.

Chapter 90

The phone rang once. "Momma?" It was Hannah.

"Yes Baby, It's me."

"My God! We got a call from a man named Osman. Have you escaped? Are you okay?"

"I'm fine. I'm at the house. The doctor gave me one week at home to recover so we don't have long. I need to know if you have talked to anybody."

"Yes," Hannah replied quickly. "Sahra and I talked with Dawit. Do you know him?"

Dawit was the man I talked to when trying to get Selemon out of Eritrea. I was surprised he had not been swept up by Afewerki's men. "Yes, I know him. Can he help?"

"He says that he can. He needs a few days and it will be dangerous, but Muse is already in the process of sending him money. He will contact you within the week."

"Okay, thank you and I love you guys." I said.

Hannah took a deep and nervous breath. "Momma, Selemon went to one of the refugee camps along the border. He was there for two months. We were able to get him some money for papers so he could get out of the camp. Whatever you do, don't go to the camps. I know that you know this, but they are more terrible than you can imagine, not much better than Eritrea. Selemon told me some horrible stories of starving and kidnapping and even organ harvesting."

"Where should we go?" I asked.

"Find a phone and call these numbers," Hannah said, and then she read off the numbers. "It's very hard for Eritreans in Sudan."

I of course knew this. Eritreans had been fleeing to Sudan for 40 years and it was a tiny step up from our own country, but I realized Hannah needed to warn me for her own peace of mind. "I'll stay away from the camps," I replied.

"Momma, please be safe."

"I will. I promise. I love you all."

"We love you too and we'll see you soon."

"I'll call in a few days if I have not heard from Dawit."

I hung up the phone and a wave of fatigue rolled over me. Michael and John would be home soon, but I was unsure if they would even come to the house. I decided to meet them by the school.

I didn't know how the boys would react. The last time they saw me I was being hauled away in a police car. That was over a month ago.

Now, I stood between a tree and building and watched as the students started flowing out of the school door. I felt myself moving toward it.

I stopped and remained where I was. The boys would come this way and I didn't want a lot of people to see me. Finally, Michael with John following close behind exited the old building. They were almost at a jog and heading right toward me, but they had not seen me yet.

I moved away from the tree and the building. I stood at the edge of the street and watched my boys approach. They were only a stone's throw away when John spotted me. His face seemed to drop with shock and his bag fell to the ground. He broke into a run, and then Michael saw me as well. He raced after his brother.

I bent down to greet my boys. "Momma, Momma," John yelled. "You are here!"

"Yes, I'm here, John. I missed you both so much."

"But how, Momma?" Michael asked.

I knelt down despite the pain in my hip. "I left the prison to help a lady have her baby, and then the doctor gave me medicine and a pass so my hip can get better."

"You escaped?" John asked.

"I know you'd like to think that." I smiled and rubbed my hand over his hair. "Really though, I was let go."

I'd thought a lot about what to tell them, and decided that it would be best if they only knew a little bit until right before we made our run for Sudan.

Chapter 91

I spent the next few days in my house. I'd seen some of my family in passing, but for the most part I took my pills and slept. I knew I'd need as much strength as possible for what was to come. Finally, on the fourth day I got a call from Hannah.

"Muse spoke with Dawit. He is working on a way out, but it is difficult. He hopes to have it ready in two days."

"I only have three days until they come get me," I replied.

"I know, Momma, and Dawit knows this as well. He is working hard."

"Thank you, Hannah," I said. "I know it will work out.

As soon as I hung up the phone there was a knock at the door. I pulled it open to see two policemen. "Are you Abeba Habtu?" one of them asked.

"Yes," I replied worriedly.

"We are here to check on you to make sure you do not leave."

"I will not leave." I rubbed my hip. "I am too old and my hip hurts too badly."

The men asked a few more questions before leaving. Their visit coupled with the phone call about Dawit made me realize that there was a very real chance that this would not work. I did not know what I would do if just days from now I was hauled away to prison once again. I didn't think I would be able to survive it physically or emotionally.

It wasn't until the evening of the sixth day when the phone rang. It was time to go.

I grabbed a bag from the front room and started putting items in it. I got some clothes for Michael and John and found their favorite toys, and then I stuck some clothes for myself on top. Finally, I went to a drawer that had some old photos in it. There was one with Fili and me when he was just a baby in Addis Ababa, and another with Fili and Muse playing at a swimming pool, and then I found one of all of us just before Muse and Hannah were sent off to Germany. I remembered clearly the day our neighbor took it. I stood next to Zeray, and Fili, who was almost as tall as him, stood on the other side. Hannah and Sahra and Muse stood just in front of us and then Selemon, who was just a few years old, stood in front of Sahra.

I looked at that photo and had a pang of regret. We looked happy in it, especially me. My family was together and that moment was captured in the photo. I tucked the photos into a pocket on the old gray bag and then slung it over my shoulder.

I slipped out the back door and looked around the corner. There were still men hard at work in the fields despite it being evening time. Everything seemed normal on the farm. I put my head down and walked toward the barn as fast as my hips would allow.

I reached it without running into anybody, and slipped inside. It was empty, and I hustled over to the shelf where my money was hidden. I moved the cans and found the box. As I started to open it I had an overpowering thought that it would be gone, but when I lifted the lid it was there. I shoved it in the bag and headed for the door.

As I pushed through the door I almost ran smack into somebody. I looked at him with shock. He returned the same expression. We both stood there frozen as my mind tripped over itself while struggling for words.

Chapter 92

It had been a long time since I'd been face to face with my father. He looked old and worn, but his face still held its jagged features and his eyes were still alert. As we stared at each other it seemed time had stopped and the world had shrunk to this moment.

"I'm sorry I have not come by," he finally said.

"I'm leaving," I said. "I'm taking the kids."

"You are escaping? Abeba, this is not the way."

"It's the only way."

He wiped sweat from his neck.

"I don't have a choice, Papa. Please don't turn me in."

A look of hurt crossed his face. "I won't, but you need to leave now. I will have to tell the police the truth when they come."

His words bothered me, but it wasn't as if I had a choice. I had to escape and I knew I would never see him again so I just looked at him and said, "Thank you."

He stepped to the side. "Be careful."

I wanted to hug him. I had forgiven him and the rest of my family because they meant everything to me and I wanted him to be my papa again.

Instead, I put my head down to hide my glistening eyes, and started to walk. "I will," I replied.

After a few steps I heard him say in a halting voice. "I'm sorry."

I turned. "Me too," I said.

I walked away from my father with tears hanging in the corners of my eyes.

I called for Michael and John. They ran in from the fields.

"What is it, Momma," Michael asked.

"We have to leave. We are going to Sudan so I don't have to go back to jail."

"I don't understand," John replied.

"We really have to go?" Michael asked.

"Yes, we have to leave. I'm really sorry, but we have to go right now before they come back to get me."

Michael's voice had changed a bit as if something was stuck in his throat. "We are ready to go with you right now," he said.

John immediately agreed with his big brother. It was such a big thing for Michael to say. He could have easily complained because he was about to leave his life behind. Instead, he was ready to go with me in spite of the danger.

Moments later, they each had a small bag and we all walked quickly away from our farm toward the heart of the village. I kept my head down and told the kids to do the same. After just ten minutes we arrived at the store next to the doctor's office. It was here where Hannah said we would meet Dawit. I was unsure if I should go in or wait outside. After a moment of hesitation I walked inside. It was something like a general store with small things for the farmers and other knickknacks.

I gave a little bit of money to Michael and John and told them to quickly buy a snack and some water. They went to the snack aisle and I pretended to be busy looking at magazines while waiting for Dawit.

Suddenly, he was right behind me. "Listen carefully. I will walk out in a moment and turn left. Wait for a few seconds and then walk out after me. Stay far behind me and I will lead you to a car. It will take you to a truck that will take you across the border and drop you off just to the south of Kassala along the river. From there you will be on your own."

"Thank you. I know this is very dangerous."

He shrugged as if to dismiss my comment. "Do you have the money?"

I pulled out the 5,000 nafka I had moved to my pocket and slipped it to him. "It is not a lot," I said.

"Your son is sending the rest and I trust him," Dawit replied.

Michael and John came up to me with their snacks and water. "Are you ready?" I asked.

They both looked at Dawit and then at me and nodded that they were. Dawit did not say another word. He just turned and walked out the door.

I waited just as he had told me, and then I gripped John's hand and the three of us followed. After a five minute walk we were behind a building where a car waited. Dawit pointed as he walked by and he never looked back. We slipped in the back without saying a word, and the man behind the steering wheel stepped on the gas.

We drove for half an hour to the northeast and came to a village I had been to a few times before. There, the driver stopped by a building with a handful of covered trucks parked along its side. Go get in the back of the third truck.

We crammed in the back with a bunch of crates. It reminded me of my plane ride when I first left Zeray so long ago. Back then I had returned for Fili and Muse. Now I was fleeing with Michael and John in hopes of being reunited with all of my children.

We settled in and the truck started. I was prepared for this. I knew that I was. And really I didn't have a choice anyway. I waited for the truck to move, but it idled for what seemed like a long time. I considered looking out of the tarp, but before I got a chance I smelled cigarette smoke, and then the tarp was pulled apart.

Chapter 93

Looking out from the darkness of the truck into the light made it impossible to make out the figures. There were two men, and one of them took a long drag off his cigarette. In an instant I knew that it must be Zeray. How could he be here? He was surely still in prison. Could he have escaped? What kind of connections did he have? Was I set up by Dawit?

All these crazy thoughts blistered my brain and I felt my body stiffen. The man without the cigarette spoke. "Three of them?"

"Yes," the smoker said, and as soon as I heard his voice I knew it was not Zeray.

"They understand the deal?"

"Yes, Dawit told them."

"Is everything alright?" I asked.

"You need to slide back behind that crate," the man with the cigarette said. "You will find a small space that you should crawl into." I looked at him questioningly. "We shouldn't get stopped, but if we do we want you hidden," he explained.

Michael and John went first, and I followed them behind the crate. The man pulled the cover tight and soon I felt us start to move. We drove for a few minutes and I tried to pay attention to the directions we turned. Were we going towards the west or the south? I was not sure and it really did not matter. I had to trust the cigarette-smoking man even though I knew nothing about him.

"Momma, I'm scared," John said over the sound of the grinding engine.

"I understand, but don't worry. Everything is going to be alright." I said the words with much more confidence than I felt.

"It will be okay, John," Michael said. "We are going to be fine. I bet we will see Selemon soon."

"I bet Michael is right," I said. "Why don't you two try to get some sleep? It will be a long drive."

In truth, I didn't know how long the drive would take. I guessed maybe two or three hours, but there was no way to know for sure. Michael and John settled in and talked to each other quietly, and I decided that it would be a good time to pray to God for safe passage.

I talked to Him for some time until I felt myself drifting to sleep. It had been an intense day and my hip was much better, but it still hurt. The constant pain was draining.

I was jolted awake because the truck came to a stop. It idled, and I prayed once again. "Momma?" John said questioningly.

"Stay quiet Baby. I'm sure it's fine."

The driver's door opened with a squeak and then slammed shut. I listened with everything I had, but heard nobody else. After a minute or two I heard footsteps to the side of the truck, and then the door opened and we were driving again. I let out a long breath and my body relaxed.

"What happened?" Michael asked.

"I'm not sure."

"I think the driver had to pee," John said.

This made Michael laugh and I couldn't help but smile. Maybe John was right.

After another hour of rumbling along, the truck came to a stop once again. This time the driver opened the back of the tarp. "Come out," he yelled.

I shimmied out of the tunnel as my hip screamed at me in protest. Michael and John scooted out much easier. "We're here," the man said.

"We are?"

"Yes, the Mareb is over there, it's dry right now, and Kassala is that way." The man pointed to the north.

"Good luck." He walked back to the cabin of the truck.

A moment later the truck had turned around and disappeared, leaving a trail of dust hanging in the air. It was dark and the insects played a chorus of music over the silence of the country.

I could not believe it happened this way. Escaping the country was nearly impossible for so many and this seemed so quick and easy, but as I looked to the north and saw the outskirts of Kassala, the same place where I'd had my hip surgery, I knew it was true. I looked at my boys and smiled. "We are free."

Chapter 94

Germany 2012

Hannah and Sahra and I sat in the waiting room of the now very familiar doctor's office. I'd spent the better part of a year doing different types of radiation. After my first time of having the radiation put directly on my hip I went back each day for two weeks. It did not hurt or make me sick like the internal radiation when I had to stay in the room by myself.

I glanced around the waiting room. There was an older couple. The man had a frail face underneath wisps of white hair. His wife sat next to him and she had broader shoulders and a rounder face. She sat stoically with her hands in her lap while she stared straight ahead.

A few chairs away from the couple sat a younger woman and her daughter. The daughter had a bald head and was very skinny. The mother smiled and talked to her in a loving voice.

I sat back in my own chair and said a quick prayer for those people I didn't know. I knew what it was like to go through difficult times. We all have our own private struggles that nobody else knows about. Some just have harder struggles than others. I expected that the old man and the young girl and their loved ones were going through a terrible time. I asked God to guide them.

A woman came out of the door. "Abeba Habtu," she said.

Hannah and Sahra and I stood and walked toward the door. In a moment I would find out if the latest round of treatments had helped at all. I hoped so, but recently my focus had shifted to Selemon and Michael and John. It had now been almost exactly a year since I'd seen them and we were close to getting them out of Sudan.

The doctor's office had a dark wooden desk with a shiny top in the center of it. Behind the desk was a bookshelf filled with medical books. The doctor stood from behind the desk and greeted us. "Guten Tag," he said, with a thin smile.

We returned the greeting. He indicated that we should sit in the chairs next to his desk. We knew these chairs well. I sat down and looked at the doctor expectantly. His thick blond hair swooped over his head like a wave and then fell over his ears. His eyes were a deep blue and he had a dimple on his thick chin. He looked more like an aging tennis player than a doctor.

He said something in German to Hannah and Sahra. They nodded in agreement. Sahra turned to me. "He's going to speak in German and then we will translate to you."

I sat up a little straighter and prepared myself for whatever news I was to receive. This was the moment. Hannah and Sahra's constant positivity had rubbed off on me and I was ready to find out that the cancer was on the retreat. I was healing and beating this disease.

As I watched the doctor speak to my daughters and then watched their faces, I feared this was not the case. Sahra turned to me. "The cancer is still there." She tried to hide her sadness, but I could see it in her eyes.

The doctor spoke some more.

"It is not growing, but it is not shrinking either," Sahra said to me in Tigrinya. "He would like to do another round of the radiation on your hip."

"Does he think it will help?"

Sahra turned to the doctor and spoke in German. He replied with a shrug.

"He hopes so, but there is no way to tell."

I had to accept that. There was nothing else I could do.

We walked out of the doctor's office with an appointment for another round of radiation. I could get through this. I would be strong because I was so close to achieving my dream of having my kids together.

Chapter 95

I saw the hotel in the distance. I squeezed John's hand a little tighter. "Look, there it is," I said.

"We're almost there," Michael replied excitedly.

It had been two days since we'd arrived in Sudan. The first night we slept underneath a big tree. Then, after walking for much of the day I paid way too much money for a ride with a stranger. He took us to a small town about 50 kilometers south of Khartoum. I found a tiny room for us to stay in and once again had to pay a lot of money. Finally, we managed to get on a boat that took us up the Nile to the southern edge of Khartoum.

After walking some 15 kilometers, we could now see our destination, a small coffee shop next to the hotel. My feet ached and my hip felt like it was being jabbed with a needle with every step I took, but I was in good spirits. We were about to be reunited with Selemon.

I thought about the talk we had when he was on leave on the farm. Back then, I told him I understood if he escaped. I never expected that Michael and John and I would have to escape as well, but here we were.

The coffee shop had three tables with chairs out front. Nobody sat at them. Michael and John hurried ahead of me and pulled on the glass door. Michael held it open for me and I heard John. "Selemon!" he yelled.

My heart felt as if it was swelling, and for a brief moment I had no pain in my hip. I hustled through the door to find a small shop with six tables and a counter. There was a strong smell of coffee and two women sat along the side wall, but I didn't pay attention to any of that. There in the middle of the shop was my boy Selemon. He was bent over and hugging Michael and John as they talked excitedly about all they had been through over the last few days.

Selemon looked up at me and smiled. He was always such a quiet and caring boy, these characteristics shown through in his smile. "Momma!" he said.

We walked toward each other and hugged tightly for a long moment. He was not as skinny as he was when he was in the prison. I also noticed that his hands were not so rough and swollen. "Selemon, it is so good to see you." I squeezed him with every bit of my strength.

"You too, Momma, I'm so glad you have made it."

Finally, we pulled apart and sat down. Over coffee and snacks Selemon told us about his life since arriving in Khartoum. I quickly realized that it would not be easy, but it did not matter because now we were together.

At the time I couldn't have known just how short my stay would be.

Chapter 96

Selemon led us to his tiny apartment. It was some three blocks away in the back of an old building. The room reminded me of some of the places where Zeray and I had stayed in Asmara so many years ago.

Selemon introduced me to his neighbors from down the hall. They were an older Eritrean couple of about my age. The man was Yonas. He was tall with kind eyes and he walked with a slight limp from his days in the Eritrean army. He was high ranking and fled when things turned bad some ten years earlier. His wife was Helen. She was thin and had short hair. She had been a teacher.

Fortunately, Selemon met them not long after arriving in Khartoum. It's very hard for Eritreans to find work in Sudan and we are treated as second-class citizens. Yonas had helped Selemon a great deal.

We all sat around Selemon's small room and talked of our lives and how terrible things were in Eritrea. Yonas and Helen were very interested in Eritrea because they had been gone for almost a decade.

As we talked, I tried to ignore the pain in my hip, but it had gone from a dull throb to a pulsing pain that felt like I was being hit with a hammer. I stood slowly. "If you'll excuse me I have to take some medicine."

Helen looked at me with concern. "What is wrong?"

"It's my hip. I've had surgery and it was not done well. My hip got a terrible infection when I was in prison and it hurts often. But don't worry, I am okay."

Helen nodded slightly, accepting my explanation. However I could see she was concerned.

That first night Michael and John and I slept hard on Selemon's bed. He insisted that he would sleep on the floor. The rush of making it to Selemon after the difficult trip had wiped us out. When we awoke there was bread on the table and a note from Selemon. He'd gone to work.

The boys and I lounged around the house that afternoon, still recovering from the trip. Helen stopped by with some books for Michael and John and they sat and read them. "How bad is your hip?" She asked me.

"I'm not sure. It hurts terribly and the last doctor worried that it might be more than just an infection."

"I notice how you limp on it. It looks like you are in pain. I have a friend who knows a doctor. Would you like to see him tomorrow?"

I thought about it. I would like to, but I also had a very small amount of money left. "How much will it cost?"

"It won't be much. The doctor is Eritrean. He fled two years ago."

"Yes, let's see him tomorrow," I said as I rubbed my hip.

The next morning I took two of my remaining eight pills and walked with Helen for about a kilometer to the east. We passed through a nice area and then the buildings slowly became more and more run down until we were on a dirt road in the middle of Earth-colored tiny homes.

"Here it is," Helen said.

"Here?"

"Yes, there are many Eritreans in this area and that is who the doctor treats."

We passed through a narrow alley and came to an unmarked blue metal door. Helen knocked and then pulled it open. Soon, I was in a back room looking at a man with thin gray hair and a large ugly scar on his cheek. It was obvious that just like the rest of us he too had a reason to flee his homeland.

I explained to him what was wrong and he checked me out. Then he drew some blood. "It will take a while to get the results, but I am concerned about your hip. Come back in a week and I should be able to tell you what is wrong."

"Thank you. Can you give me more pain medication?"

"I can, but it is not as strong as what you have."

"I will be happy with anything," I replied.

Over the course of the next week I spent as much time as I could with Selemon. We walked through the city and talked about making it to Germany and all the possibilities there. We talked about Muse and Hannah and Sahra. They had been a huge help by getting him papers so he could leave the refugee camp in Kassala, and of course they had come through to help the boys and me make a hasty escape from Eritrea.

They had also told us that they were working hard to save money and make the right contacts to get us out of Sudan.

Finally, it was time to see the doctor again. As soon as I looked at him I knew it was not good. "Your hip is still infected and there is something wrong with your blood. You need proper medical treatment."

"Can I get that here?"

He shook his head sadly. "I'm afraid not. Is there anywhere else you can go?"

That question hung over my head for a moment and I knew the only answer, Germany.

Chapter 97

Muse and Hannah and Sahra had come through for me once again. They found somebody who could get me on a plane to Germany with the correct papers and all, but I told them that there was no way I could go. I couldn't leave Selemon and Michael and John behind.

It had been three weeks since the doctor had told me just how bad my hip was. I had used almost all the medication, but it barely masked the pain. "Momma, you have to go," Selemon said. "We will be fine here. I will continue to work and Helen can tutor Michael and John."

"I know you will be fine, but how can I leave you behind? We have to go together."

"That can't happen right now," Selemon replied. "You go and get better. We will be there before long."

"He is right," Helen said. "You have to get treatment. We will make sure to take care of Michael and John."

"I already talked to Hannah," Selemon said. "She will send some money to Helen each month for the tutoring."

In my head I knew that this was what needed to happen, but my heart screamed at me that I could not go. Why did it always have to be this way? Why was I always saying goodbye to some of my children? I'd lost Muse and Hannah when Zeray forced them to move to Germany, and then I lost Sahra to Germany as well. Then there is my Fili. Just a normal day of going to work turned into the last time I ever saw him. I still played that day over and over in my head all the time.

Now I had come so far with Selemon and Michael and John and my illness was forcing me to leave them behind. I knew that I should follow my own advice that I had given my children through the years. I should be courageous, but as I sat in Selemon's living room I just felt so tired.

"I'm sure there is treatment available here in Khartoum," I said.

Selemon shook his head. "Not like Germany, and besides, they would not treat you right because you are Eritrean."

I leaned back in my chair and looked at the ceiling. I wondered if my dream of being together with all of my children would ever come true. I felt like the world was crumbling in on top of me and despair sat on my chest.

"Momma, we will be okay. We can do it," a little voice said.

I looked over to see John. He sat on the floor with a book in his lap and stared at me with his big brown eyes. He was just nine years old, but in those eyes I saw a much older soul. "It's true. We will be fine. You have to get better."

"Come here," I said.

John stood and came to my side. I gave him a hug as tears formed in my eyes.

"You are right John. I will go and get well and you will be strong. Before long, you will be with me in Germany as well."

There was no way I could know if those words were true. It was expensive and difficult to get out of Sudan. Many Eritreans just tried to walk away to a better life in Egypt and ended up dying in the desert or getting turned away at the border. I could not let a fate like that fall onto my children. However, I realized that once I left Sudan I would not have any control over what happened to them.

I did not sleep that night. Instead, I sat awake and watched Michael and John as they breathed softly and dreamed. I knew that it might be the last night I ever saw them.

Chapter 98

We rode on the hot bus down Africa Street. Michael sat on my left and John sat on my right. We'd been on the bus for an hour through thick traffic, and now we were close to Khartoum International Airport.

I felt so numb, like my arms and legs were heavy. Selemon sat just in front of me. He kept glancing back at us and smiling. I could tell he was trying to mask the sadness.

The bus turned to the left and I could see the airport up ahead. We pulled to the side of the road and came to a stop. We got off and I felt the heat of the city on my already hot face. Selemon held my bag and looked left and then right. I squeezed Michael and John's hands and didn't say a word. My throat felt tight and I didn't trust how my voice would sound.

"That way." Selemon pointed down the street to a small lot. "That is where we meet."

As we approached the lot I saw an old brown car with two men sitting inside. They opened the doors. "Abeba Habtu?" the driver asked.

"Yes," Selemon replied.

"Do you have the money?"

"Do you have the papers?"

The man nodded.

"Yes, we have the money," Selemon replied.

They exchanged envelopes. The one Selemon gave the man held twelve thousand euro. It was not easy at all to get it and the thought of handing it over was painful. But in exchange we received all the papers I needed to leave and a plane ticket to Berlin.

The men got in the car and drove away. We stood in the hot dust unsure of what to do or say. Selemon pulled out the ticket and read it. "Your flight leaves in two hours, Momma. We'd better get to the airport."

I nodded in agreement even though I wanted to turn and go in the opposite direction.

We arrived at the airport and it all happened too fast. The line for check-in was short and soon I stood just outside of the security area. Tears had formed in Michael's eyes, but he held them there. He was determined to be brave. John cried, but he didn't make a sound and quickly wiped the tears away.

"Here, Momma." Selemon handed me my bag.

I took it and then wrapped my arms around him. "I'm so proud of you."

Next, I hugged Michael and then John. I breathed deep and tried to take in every little detail about them. I did not want to let them go, but soon I had to.

I stood. "Take care of each other. I know you will be fine and I love you."

"We love you too, Momma," John said.

"Go get well," Selemon added.

I turned and made my way through security. It seemed like I was stumbling through a bad dream.

My vision felt foggy and my throat and ears felt tight. Once through security, I turned and looked back. Michael and John stood next to a rope and Selemon stood behind them with a hand on each of their shoulders.

They looked so sad and determined. I waved. They waved back. Then I turned and walked away before they could see the tears fall down my cheeks.

Chapter 99

The plane hit turbulence somewhere over the Alps and I was startled awake. For a split second I wondered where I was, and then it all flooded back. Right now, I was in between my children as I had left my three youngest in Africa to go to three of my oldest in Germany.

We were served a light dinner and I had a hard time eating because my hip hurt so bad that it made my stomach ache. After dinner I dozed despite the pain and wasn't jarred awake until the plane's wheels touched down.

I became an excited and nervous wreck. I'd actually done it. I'd gotten out of Eritrea and then out of Sudan. I'd left Zeray behind, and still in prison I presumed. And now I was just minutes away from seeing my children who I had not seen in so long. I even had to remind myself that they were now adults.

I did not know where to go once I left the plane so I just followed the crowd. We came to a row of counters and a man in a uniform asked for my papers. I gave him everything I had. He sifted through it and stamped in a few different places.

He slid everything back to me and then nodded. I understood that I was free to move on. I made my way through another area where the belts spit out the luggage. The only bag I had was the gray one that I'd grabbed at my house in Eritrea before fleeing to Sudan, and it was already on my shoulder.

The doors ahead slid open when people approached. Each time they opened I saw people gathered around some ropes, waiting expectantly. I forgot about my hip pain and sped up a bit. I was about to see Muse and Hannah and Sahra.

The doors opened for me and I quickly started scanning the crowd. There were openings to the left and the right. I went to the right as I continued to search for my children. Then I heard a voice to my left. "Momma, Momma, over here!"

I looked that way and found it came from a beautiful woman. It was Hannah, and right next to her was Sahra and Muse. I turned toward them and they shuffled through the crowd. We met, and I dropped my bag and hugged each one of them so tightly.

So many times I'd had to say goodbye to my children, and now I was getting to say hello. Tears of joy coursed down my cheeks and I couldn't get the smile off of my face.

I'd made it. I had not reached my goal of having all of my family together, but I had made it to Germany. I was with my older children and now I would get the treatment I needed. As we walked out of the terminal I felt so happy, and I thought about how much happier I'd feel to see Selemon and Michael and John come through the doors I'd just come through.

Chapter 100

Germany 2012

As we walked out of the doctor's office I had such mixed feelings. It had been just over a year since I'd landed in Germany and been reunited with Muse and Hannah and Sahra. Even though I learned I had cancer and I'd spent much of the year being sick, I still felt I was lucky. I was getting treatment and spending time with my children.

Then again, it was now clear that the cancer was not going away, and despite our efforts we had been unable to bring Selemon and Michael and John to Germany. Six months ago my children paid men in Sudan a lot of money to get them out. Everything seemed perfect and I prayed so hard that it would work. Unfortunately, the men ended up taking the money and running, leaving my boys stuck in the desert just north of Khartoum. They had to walk back and barely made it, but at least they were not killed like so many others.

Now, I just felt stuck. My children were working hard on another possibility to get them out, but much like the doctor's efforts to destroy the cancer, it was slow moving.

We arrived back home and I sat in my room and read books and tried to remain positive. Hannah spent two days on a trip to Paris to get a fruit for me to take that is supposed to fight cancer, and then Muse and Sahra spent two days in Denmark to find some special Chinese plant that would help as well.

I was amazed at the spirit of my children. They continued to press forward despite the odds. I thought about how they had grown up in a small house in Addis Ababa, Ethiopia, and now they traveled through Europe without a second thought in order to help me.

I was truly blessed to have them.

My next round of treatment came and went, but the results were not much different. The doctor said we should continue the treatment. I was fine with that. The radiation is almost an extension of my life and I can get through it okay. However, I wondered if there will be a point when the radiation will no longer be an option.

One evening, as we sat around the dinner table and I prepared for yet another round of radiation the following day, I expressed my concerns to Hannah and Sahra. "How long do we keep doing this?"

"We will keep doing this for as long as it takes to get you better," Sahra said.

"But it is not fair to you. You both already have so much on your plate with your business and your struggle to get the boys over here. You should not have to keep going through this too."

"Momma, we would not think of doing it any other way," Hannah said.

I put my head down. "My life has been a constant struggle. So often I have just had to endure. I've had good things happen and bad things happen and I don't want your lives to be like that. I have been blessed with wonderful children. Bringing the boys over so we can be together should be our only priority now. We shouldn't worry about my treatment."

Hannah and Sahra exchanged a glance. "Momma," Sahra began reluctantly, "we were going to tell you this after your treatment tomorrow, but we think now is a good time."

"What is it?" I asked with concern.

Hannah pulled out a letter from her bag that was hanging on the back of the chair. She slid it across the table. I unfolded it and read the first paragraph and my hands started shaking. "This can't be," I said.

Chapter 101

The letter was from Yonas and Helen. It told me that my boys received their papers and were scheduled to be driven to Egypt. From there they would take a boat to Malta and then fly to Frankfurt where they would take a train to us.

"How is this possible?" I looked at my girls.

"We finally had the money and found the right people," Hannah said. "We didn't want to say anything until we were sure they were out of Sudan. We just learned yesterday that they are scheduled to arrive in Malta tomorrow. They will arrive in Frankfurt in two days. We will meet them at the Berlin Central Station."

"We will be together, Momma," Sahra added.

"I do not know what to say. This letter is my dream. I cannot imagine this."

Hannah smiled. "It's true, Momma."

I didn't sleep much because I was too excited, and the radiation the following day was nothing more than something to pass the time. I of course hoped it would help destroy the cancer, but right now that was just an afterthought.

I didn't sleep much the following night either. As I lay in bed I thought about all the places I had rested my head. I thought about that first night away from the farm house after being forced to marry Zeray, and that first apartment in Asmara with Zeray's relative. I remembered the drunken man who urinated all over the floor and the tiny house where I lived with Zeray's children, Winta and Kibrom. The nights in Addis Ababa drifted in and out of my thoughts as well, and then there was the horrible day when I lost Fili. I still held out a sliver of hope that one day a miracle would happen and we would be reunited.

All of these thoughts mixed together with the thoughts of my boys. I could picture them at the airport in Malta eagerly waiting to board the plane. I saw them on the train from Frankfurt and I saw them at the Berlin station.

And then I shifted back to the desperation I felt in that horrible prison. I wondered about my friend, Sophia. I hoped she was able to go with her brother and her baby instead of back to that horrible prison.

I remembered my momma and how she used to hide us so our father would not hit us, and I remembered my little brother, Aman, and how he loved to hold Fili on his lap and stare at him. Aman left us too soon when the wall fell on him and I prayed that he was with Momma now.

I don't know why all these memories flooded my brain as I lay awake waiting for the sun to rise, but they did. Maybe it was because tomorrow I would be reunited with all my children except for Fili and my life would be so close to complete?

It was with this thought that I finally found sleep, but I was up early and I had to wait all day. The boys were due to arrive late in the afternoon. Hannah and Sahra had a plan to pass the time. We went shopping for some new clothes and got our nails done. It was the perfect distraction.

Finally, it was time, and I found myself staring at the massive Berlin train station. Its rounded and glassed roof seemed to jut out in all directions. I wondered how we would ever find Selemon and Michael and John in the swarm of people moving hastily about.

"This way," Sahra said.

I noticed that my girls were just as excited as me. Each one of them looped their arm around mine. We walked side by side toward the platform on which the boys would be arriving.

We stood there amongst the throng of activity, and yet I felt as if we were the only people there. A train pulled in and I felt knots form in the pit of my stomach. I had prayed for a moment like this for so long.

"This is the train," Hannah said excitedly.

I found it hard to breathe as people began to exit. We watched every one of them as they walked past us. The crowd thinned and I had still not seen my boys. "Are you sure this is the train?" I asked worriedly.

"This is it," Sahra said, and I noted that her voice had a hint of worry as well.

More people came and went, and then they were there. I saw Selemon first, and then Michael and John. They all carried small bags and scanned the crowd for us.

"There!" I said to Hannah and Sahra.

Sahra let out a little squeal of excitement and we all started toward them.

The boys saw us, and Michael and John broke into a run. Selemon's face broadened into a smile and he began to run as well.

We met at the edge of the platform and I hugged my boys with everything I had. I wiped tears of joy away from my eyes and noticed that Hannah and Sahra shared those same tears. We had done it. We had struggled. We had endured. We had felt sad and lost and alone, but none of that mattered.

Now we were together. I knew at that moment that I was truly blessed, and that wherever Fili was he would be smiling with happiness at our reunion.

Epilogue

Since reuniting with my children we have begun to carve out a life in Berlin. Michael and John already know more of the German language than me and they are enrolled in an excellent school. Hannah and Sahra's business is doing well and Muse helped Selemon get a good job.

We often eat meals together and talk about our lives. Despite our struggles, we mostly have fond memories.

I am still battling the cancer. I will continue to do so because I want as much time as possible with my children. And despite the odds, I still hold out hope that one day I will see Fili again.

We have not heard from Zeray since he was taken to prison. I do not know if he is still there or not. Maybe he is somewhere in Eritrea trying to make a new life. My home country is still under the control of President Afewerki. It still ranks last on the Press Freedom Index and there are still horror stories of secret prisons and poor living conditions.

I can only hope that one day soon that will all change. We Eritreans are a strong people. Very few people know about our country, but we have managed to persevere despite wars and being forced to live in the harshest of circumstances.

I don't know if my story is inspiring. I don't know if it will help others gain courage. I can only hope that it will. If just one other person can face their struggles and find courage through these words, then I am glad I have told my story.

Please remember, no matter how hard it seems and no matter how badly you feel you can always become courageous.

Thank you so much for taking the time to read my story. While it is fresh in your mind please consider going to the Amazon page and doing a short review so others can decide if they would like to read it or not. Please tell your friends about it. You are the key to helping me get my story to as many people as possible.

Hannah and Selemon each have a short e-book available on Amazon. Hannah's story is about her time in the orphanage in Germany. Selemon's story is about the time when he was arrested without cause and thrown into prison. You can find them on Amazon.

GOODBYE AFRICA: A TEN-YEAR-OLD ORPHAN GIRL'S STORY

HELL ON EARTH: TORTURED AND THROWN INTO A SECRET PRISON

Made in the USA
Charleston, SC
06 December 2016